A Sky
So Close to Us

By Shahla Ujayli

Translated by Michelle Hartman

Interlink Books

An imprint of Interlink Publishing Group, Inc.
Northampton, Massachusetts

First published 2019 by

Interlink Books
An imprint of Interlink Publishing Group, Inc.
46 Crosby Street, Northampton, MA 01060
www.interlinkbooks.com

Library of Congress Cataloging-in-Publication Data
Names: °Ujaylåi, Shahlåa, author. | Hartman, Michelle, translator.
Title: A sky so close to us / by Shahla Ujayli ; translated by Michelle
    Hartman.
Other titles: Samåa qaråibah min baytinåa. English
Description: First American edition. | Northampton MA : Interlink
    Books, 2018.
Identifiers: LCCN 2018027807 | ISBN 9781623719838
Classification: LCC PJ7966.J39 S3613 2018 | DDC 892.7/37--dc23
LC record available at https://lccn.loc.gov/2018027807

Printed in the United States of America

For Baba, for Eyad and Dima,
and for Muslih, always

Lively Evenings in Aleppo

April 28, 1947, was a Monday. A radiant spring day in Aleppo, some warmth from the sun had managed to filter through motionless, white clouds. The warm day bade many people to leave behind their concerns at noontime and take a stroll along the river—through what, years later, would become one of the region's most famous public parks, modeled after beautiful palace gardens in France.

This park was located in the Azizieh quarter, right in the center of the city. On the garden's northern side, the balcony of an elegant villa—made of rose-colored Aleppo stone—overlooked the train station. This villa was owned by the lawyer Bahjat Haffar.

The April sun accompanied the people on their strolls for two full hours, but not one minute more. Suddenly, there was thunder and lightning, and all of Aleppo's alleys were flooded with rain. Bahjat Bey's telephone started ringing off the hook. His wife, Madiha Khanum, came into the room bearing two demitasses filled with coffee, a glass of water, and a small vase with sprigs of pure white jasmine on a tray. Her husband hung up the phone, his face drained of any possible signs of calm. He waited for her to place his cup of coffee on the table and sit down beside him. He took a sip. She did the same. He then said soberly, "Get yourself and the children ready. We're leaving for Damascus."

This news made Madiha Khanum feel a little shaky, but she stayed steady. She'd been preparing herself to receive this kind of news for days. In fact, she'd been ready for emergencies ever since her husband had decided to venture into politics.

It had been a tumultuous year for Syrians, and no respite came in the years that followed. The National Bloc fractured into splinter groups; a number of its members formed the People's Party and the rest remained in a party that retained its previous name, the National Bloc. The backbone of the People's Party consisted of men of the bourgeoisie who wanted to declare economic unity with Iraq. They were led by Nazim al-Qudsi and Rushdi Kikhya. Bahjat Haffar strongly opposed this economic unity, but he knew that the Aleppo-based party leadership might sideline him if he maintained this position. He thought that he could perhaps avoid his dismissal, a boycott, or even more violent reactions against him by maintaining a low profile. So he decided to pack up his family and leave Aleppo for Damascus until party life in Syria had re-stabilized.

Bahjat Bey's friends from Aleppo started frequenting his house the moment he arrived in Damascus. These friends were well-placed government employees, politicians, and university professors. They were searching for vestiges of their Aleppo and found them vibrant and fresh at his house. The conversation was always largely dominated by politics, but also involved sharing all kinds of details about Aleppo. Politics unfailingly would somehow manage to lead the conversations back toward food, because like people everywhere, Aleppans believed their cuisine was without equal. They were unanimous in thinking that their city's cuisine was unrivaled in taste and variety, and that the skills needed to prepare it could be found nowhere else in the world.

Bahjat Bey had anticipated this before moving to Damascus and thus had bought a large, detached house. It was located on a newly constructed street that joined together two ancient and storied Damascus neighborhoods, Muhajireen and al-Salihiyah. This new street was smack in the middle of Abu Rummaneh, a neighborhood so named because of the pomegranate tree that once shaded an unknown holy man's tomb and shrine there. After the French evacuation from Syria—al-Jalaa' in Arabic—it was officially renamed Jalaa' Street. But no one called it that. People preferred the old name, as it had settled in their memories and they had grown too accustomed to it to accept the change.

It was Bahjat Bey's good luck that the government inaugurated a wireless radio station that very year along with an affiliated institute for the study of music. The institute brought his dear friend Shaykh Omar al-Batsh to Damascus from Aleppo to teach the art of the *muwashshahat* songs and poems.

Shaykh Omar was a man of many talents. Not only did he hold more than one thousand *muwashshahat* poems in his memory, but he had also managed to compose new sections of these poems, which would later become famous, something not even Sayyid Darwish was ever able to do. Alongside this, he had learned the art of traditional Sufi dance from Saleh al-Jadba, his teacher in Aleppo. Shaykh Omar brought these dances from Sufi shrines out onto the musical theater stage. Once in Damascus, he began spending time at his old companion Bahjat Bey's house. Together with their group of friends, they were able to recover echoes of the old days in Aleppo, echoes that grew louder and took on a life of their own as they were conjured up by Shaykh Omar, the genius of the traditional arts. Needless to say, Omar al-Batsh took the place of honor at these gatherings, priceless oud in hand. The last Ottoman governor of Syria, Jamal Basha, had gifted him the instrument as a young man. Shaykh Omar would settle into his designated role, tune its strings, and sing.

Whenever new guests joined the Thursday evening gatherings at Bahjat Bey's house, he would implore Shaykh Omar to recount the tale of the famous meeting he'd once had with Mohammed Abdel Wahab. Decked out in his usual European-style suit and Turkish-style tarboush, he would begin telling the story in his melodious voice, emphasizing his pronunciation of the letter "gim":

"It was the year 1934 when the famous musician Mohammed Abdel Wahab visited Syria to give concerts in Damascus and Aleppo. At his first show, he was shocked to find the hall nearly empty when he arrived. There were only about a dozen people there, no more. He sang reluctantly—he was used to performing in front of huge crowds. But his singing was nothing short of perfection. Afterwards we all flocked around him and left him somewhat perplexed when we told him that he had passed the test: his next concert would find

the hall filled with people who appreciated great art.

"Abdel Wahab made a mental note of our little test, so as to turn the tables later on. His plan came to fruition when we invited him to attend an evening celebration of local music from Aleppo, to hear our great musical masterpieces. Upon hearing our request, he asked us—and Shaykh Ali Darwish can testify to this—if we could play him an original, pure 'sikah' muwashshah!

"Everyone listening was stunned by the impossibility of his request. There were no original, pure 'sikah' muwashshahs that were not mixed with what the Arabs call 'khuzam,' and the Turks, 'huzam.' In fact, a pure sikah is nearly impossible to make into a muwashshah! Still, I bravely accepted the challenge, announcing, 'Tomorrow night we will all gather and I will play you one!'"

"At the end of the evening, Shaykh Ali Darwish harshly scolded me for my bravado: 'You know very well that there is no original, pure sikah muwashshah! What have you gotten us into?'

"'How could we let Abdel Wahab be in Aleppo and not play him something marvelous?' I retorted, and we all set to work. We worked together all night until I created two muwashshahs. I composed them and set them to music myself as original sikahs, with no huzam. I summoned my group of singers and they memorized the muwashshahs. The following evening, at our concert, they executed them beautifully. Abdel Wahab was dazzled. He was as overjoyed as if he had just learned the principles of musical composition that very evening."

After finishing the story, Shaykh Omar al-Batsh would tune his strings and sing one of the *muwashshahs* he'd just described:

> A doe-eyed woman captured my heart
> Lalalalalalalala ya layl

> With her eyelashes,
> Lalalalalalalala ya layl
> And her eyes, her ebony eyes
> Lalalalalalalala ya layl
> Her honey-coated lips are a heavenly libation
> … But none of these can I ever acquire

On those lively evenings, troubled by nothing but the omnipresence of political conversations, there was a five-year-old girl in the crowd. She sat with her mother and siblings in a little room next to the main hall, listening to the songs and finding it hard to keep still. She'd move right up to the door and sometimes she'd even sneak in to observe the scene. Other times, she'd dance in an out-of-the-way spot, neither bothered nor bothersome.

Years later, this child would learn to play the oud. She would also perform the traditional Sufi *samah* dance from Aleppo with her girlfriends in the annual talent show at her school, Dawhat al-Adab. The audience would be especially impressed when she began to intone Ibn Zaydoun's *muwashshah*, "I Didn't Desert my Lover out of Anger," accompanied by a small group of Damascene girls. Her father's friend, Shaykh Omar al-Batsh, had put the poem to music. The applause was hearty when she began to sing, her voice tinged by the innocence of childhood:

> Oh essence of musk, oh sunrise at daybreak
> Oh slender branch of frankincense, oh wild
> gazelle
> Even if I were to hold onto some hope,
> beyond your simple acceptance,
> I wouldn't even want you to offer me that hope…

This young girl wearing short white socks, her fair hair gathered in a pink ribbon, would later become Mrs. Shahira al-Haffar. Today was her funeral.

I sat in the transit lounge, waiting to head toward the assigned gate for boarding. From behind panes of glass, I watched passengers and airline employees in non-stop motion all around me. I enjoyed observing the other passengers; their simplicity and spontaneity offered me clarity of thought. In the airport, they can exist outside of the gravitational pull of the worlds they belong to, or be at least in a transitory state of liberation from these worlds. Here most people are on the brink of opening new chapters of their lives. Airports are, after all, the dots connecting old stories to new ones. We Syrians may very well have our own special type of relationships with airports, for as soon as we have passed through the very last window of the very last passport checker, we are granted a new lease on life. Whenever the person checking passports announces that we are not wanted by any national or international security agency, a feeling of relief washes over all of us, even if we have never pronounced one political word in our entire lives. We always imagine that we might fall into the clutches of some security force or other, if only because our name sounds like someone else's!

The ground staff finally announced that our gate was open for boarding. I queued up with four other people in the line reserved for first-class passengers, following the calmly rhythmic, masculine footsteps in front of me. After the employees checked our passports, I noticed that the face belonging to the footsteps looked fatigued and resigned—a man, perhaps in his fifties, quite thin, and not too tall, with light brown skin and hair. He was dressed with a natural elegance, in blue jeans, a black shirt, and laceless black tennis shoes. By the time I was settling into my seat, I found he was already there in the seat beside mine.

My general mood that day made me unenthusiastic about befriending anyone on this trip. I was filled with memories of the good time I'd just had in Tunisia, where I'd been with people whose company I really enjoyed. We'd all attended a conference called "Arab Youth and Cultural Belonging," held in the southern city of Gabès, on the Mediterranean coast. Our evenings together were filled with unbridled laughter, and I embraced these evenings with open arms because of the months of misery I had just lived through. It was even hard to believe they were just months and not years. The war in Syria had impacted everything, and this was the first conference I'd participated in since leaving.

My neighbor in the next seat greeted me politely, even a bit amiably. He spoke with the sort of enthusiasm you might have when you recognize the other person. He seemed like he had something to say. A few minutes of calm passed, and then we were getting ready for takeoff. Each of us had drifted off into our own worlds—until that moment at takeoff that brings all the passengers together in an unspoken bond of anxiety. It is a moment that affects everyone, even the most seasoned traveler. That's when he turned, eyed me nervously a couple of times, and then blurted out, "My mother died today and I'm going to bury her!"

What else could I do but hold his hand during most of the flight—perhaps some empathy would flow through it from my heart to his. I wanted to hold him close to me, but we can't always do exactly what our hearts desire!

After I'd let go of his hand, he introduced himself to me: "Nasser al-Amireh, international expert in climate and drought."

Ummm… what do I know about the environment? The only thing I could recall about geography is what Edward Said once wrote, "Geography is our number one enemy!"

But then I remembered something that helped me step into his world. Just a few months ago I had attended an academic conference hosted by the Jordanian Society for Scientific Research, and the conference panels had covered a number of topics including health, economics, education, and climate change.

As life coaches always say: expose yourself to as many random things as possible. Attend a conference no one else attends, read books no one else reads, speak to people no one else speaks to, believe in the possibilities of chance. So it was at random that I chose to attend the climate change panels, while most other people there had opted for the panels on economics and education. The first presentation was by an Indian professor, Dr. Mana Shiva Kumar. To build on what I'd learned in his talk, I decided to listen to all the other papers in his session too—from ten o'clock in the morning until four o'clock in the afternoon. I really appreciated Professor Kumar's paper about the little errors we make every day in relation to the climate. We make these mistakes unconsciously, unaware of their consequences, he said—an accumulation of natural disasters. We sat together at lunch and talked. He was surprised I was attending a panel so far from my own area of specialization. The next evening, I picked him up at the hotel and took him to visit Amman's old downtown and the Roman amphitheater. We ate *kanafeh* at Habiba's and drank coffee on the balcony of the Jafra Café in the middle of the old city. Professor Kumar told me that our areas of specialization were actually not so distant, that it is in fact in areas closer to my specialization—not his—that the problems with climate change begin: in culture, not geography. Solving issues of climate change must start with people changing their mentality and how they address the problem of limited resources—not by sending secret messages to the clouds, waves, and wind.

Perhaps that geography-filled day was simply a trial run, preparing me for the later contemplation of Dr. Nasser al-Amireh's life journey!

Our plane landed at Queen Alia International Airport; we'd both been in transit through Istanbul on our way to Amman. Our conversation had veered between the general and the personal. I found out that Nasser had studied at the University of California at Santa Barbara. He was divorced from an American woman with whom he had three children—two boys attending university in the States, and a girl who lived in Amman with her grandmother, Nasser's mother, who had passed away the day before. Nasser told me that his mother was from al-Sham, in the way that Palestinians and Jordanians refer to all of

Syria as "al-Sham," even though she was from Aleppo. She was actually a member of Aleppo's well-known Haffar family. Nasser now worked in Dubai at a center for the development of its arid regions. After listening to these details about his family, I pondered Nasser's daughter, the girl who had been living with her grandmother. What would happen to her now that her grandmother had died? I was flooded with sadness and empathy for the girl, but before my emotions took hold of me completely, Nasser's question rang in my ears, "Are you separated as well?"

I found this question very strange. Did I show the telltale signs of a separation? Or had my companion on this journey been seized by his baser desires? To borrow geographer's terms, his question was fit to scale. Though it was limited in scope, it gave away the actual scope of the space that we come to occupy in other people's minds.

So I tried to be clear, straightforward, and concise in presenting myself to him. I wanted to leave enough of a space for a natural relationship between adults to develop, the kind of deeper, less fleeting relationship in which each person truly recognizes their own worth as well as that of the other person. After some thought, I said to him:

"I'm Joumane Badran. I am a Syrian living in Amman and I have a doctorate in cultural anthropology. Right now I'm working with a Dutch humanitarian organization. I'm not separated from anyone. I've never been married. But I have lost someone before, about five years ago. It was incredibly painful. Believe me, Dr. Nasser, this ordeal whose concrete effects you're dealing with right now will soon turn abstract and lodge into the deepest recesses of your heart, leaving an indelible mark. Nothing will ever be able to remove it—it will become an integral part of your personality, your outlook, evident even in the way you walk. Of course, you may be able to hide it from people, but it will remain an outward sign that proves that you've lived, experienced things, and suffered."

I stopped myself there before what I was saying turned into a sermon, for people who live through traumatic experiences are often consciously and deeply drawn to consoling others. Often they are shocked at their own maturity, proud of their painful wealth of experience, in the way that only someone who has shown courage in the face of great distress can be. Once I'd laid those ideas out to him, I relaxed. I'd already disclosed them with my body anyway, by holding his hand for such a long time. To me, this wasn't just an arbitrary act, but it demonstrated an important, justifiable kind of empathy.

Before we each went our separate ways, navigating through the sea of passengers, Nasser asked for my phone number. So his sadness had not totally consumed him—he was still aware of certain things! He punched my digits into his phone and called me right away. His number showed up on my screen, ready to be saved. Little did I know how much I would come to depend on that number, once I saw what life had in store for me.

I poured myself into my work for ten straight days, looking for recognizable parts of my inner self that the war in Syria had stripped me of. I plunged into information and statistics, stories of refugee and migrant women, of women fleeing from bombardments—women whose ranks I had belonged to mere months ago, and whose ranks my sisters Jude and Salma still belonged to. Whenever this thought managed to penetrate the surface of my mind, I would find myself debilitated by a feeling of depression. I'm not here to offer anything to anyone. I'm only here because I fled when academics working in Aleppo started being directly targeted in the war. A colleague of mine, Dr. Muhammad—a history professor with whom I shared an office in the Faculty of Humanities—was injured by a sniper's bullet while walking home from the university through the Bustan al-Qasr area. There was no shortage of contradictions in my situation. I felt lucky I'd found a safe haven and a well-paid job, but I also felt defeated and my conscience was tortured by the knowledge that I had left Baba and my sisters inside a vortex of danger and suffering.

In this sea of confusion, I had the memory of Nasser's profound, warm gaze flooding me with joy. I allowed myself a wide smile and didn't stop it from radiating all across my face, hoping it could sweep away all the tragedy etched in me, leaving nothing but happiness in its wake.

As I expected, Nasser phoned me after the shock of his loss had subsided. The sweetness of solace left him feeling lonely as he started experiencing the patience that accompanies bereavement. He called me searching for a different kind of comfort, one I know very well. He needed the comfort of words.

We agreed to meet one evening at the Blue Fig café in Abdoun. My relationship with places here in Amman is still awkward and limited, when compared to Aleppo. There, I had my own spot at a table that was always kept for me. I would go there for different kinds of meetings and I knew everyone who worked there. They paid special attention to my guests and me, they knew what I did and didn't like—when I wanted to write, when I wanted to meet friends.

Nothing could equal sitting on the terrace of the Baron Hotel in Aleppo—not the Ritz, not the cafés on the Champs Elysées, nor even the sidewalk cafés in Prague. A relatively small building in the heart of downtown Aleppo, even the street on which it stood took its name, Baron Street, in 1946, to honor the hotel's nationalist reputation during the French Mandate period. At the time, the street had been called Gouraud Street, after the French general who took Damascus at the battle of Maysaloun, stepping on Salah al-Din's grave, and pronouncing his infamous words: "Saladin, we're back!" The Baron Hotel itself was built back in 1906 with thirty-one rooms and two bathrooms. The Mazloumian brothers later built a third floor that had a bathroom in each of its seventeen rooms.

To the east, you could see the famous Azizieh neighborhood, a bastion of the bourgeoisie, especially the Christian bourgeoisie. Elegant cafés and restaurants—like Wanes, Shalal, and Cordoba—lined the sidewalks from where you could see the green shrubs and flowers, which had been planted along the banks of the river Queiq after an infestation of sandflies threatened a leishmaniasis outbreak. Artists, writers, businessmen, and statesmen met in these restaurants, going out late to listen to music by nameless Armenian bands, skilled in creating nostalgia for the forties and fifties when people in Aleppo danced to the sounds of popular tangoes and waltzes.

The Bab al-Faraj clock tower was located to the

south of the Baron Hotel. The Bab al-Faraj gate is a unique landmark of Aleppo's historic old city. As people always say, "You don't know Aleppo unless you've been to Bab al-Faraj," even though there are six other remaining gates to the old city. The national library stands in front of the clock tower, a destination for those who love reading, research, theater, and the arts. Between the hotel and Bab al-Faraj Square there are narrow, parallel streets leading to the Bustan Kul-Ab neighborhood, or "Bustan Kalib" pronounced with a local accent, where people sell auto parts and farming equipment. There are also many cheap hotels there, the kind with names like the Suez Hotel, Unity Hotel, and the Syria and Lebanon Hotel where a number of rooms share one bathroom. It also houses restaurants serving Armenian-style kebabs, pastry shops, and nightclubs—the most famous of which are the Moulin Rouge and Crazy Horse. Women from all walks of life—from those wearing hijabs and niqabs to airline hostesses—walk through these streets, the lower parts of which bustle with mostly Russian and Ukrainian working women and a few local ladies of the night.

If you sit on the hotel's terrace, you can see the Arab Writers' Union on the other side of the street. It's situated in an old apartment that hosted many lectures and literary evenings over the years, saving us from the monotony of academia. The Kindi Cinema is located on the next street over. It displays sexily enticing advertisements for outdated box-office failures. Teenage boys linger in front of it, munching on falafel sandwiches, their eyes glued to the pictures of tempting naked women. But they usually leave soon after, heading toward the old buildings all crammed together, or toward the clothes and shoe shops that line Quwatly Street, their windows perennially displaying attractive sales and offers on Syrian-made products or cheap, mediocre-quality Chinese ones. This cinema was never short on patrons, no matter what kind of films it was showing, since there were almost always young women and men—teenagers, almost-adults, and sometimes university students—desperate to find a private place to meet. The usher would light the way to their seats with a small flashlight and they would file into the back rows, flirting and then moaning as they exchanged kisses and quick love affairs. The usher would unfailingly shift his gaze away from them, plunging them into a safe darkness, the film playing in the background of their consciousness, the very same movie that had witnessed these encounters countless times. "Kindi" Cinema, "Quwatly" Street—no one wondered about these place names found in nearly every Syrian city.

On summer evenings, we used to sit on the large open terrace at the hotel's entrance, slightly separated from the street by a few steps of the same stone as the low wall surrounding it. The words "Baron Hotel" hung over the main entrance behind the terrace, in elegantly thin neon-blue lettering. We'd move inside to the lobby that was a cross between a lounge and a bar in the winter months and have intellectual, social, and political conversations in front of the marble fireplace, which was just as faded as the black and white checkered floor. I had never once gone up to a room in the hotel. Back in the day, the rooms had been filled with famous people, and the hotel owners had maintained them to look as they had when those people left, even naming the rooms after their respective occupants. I knew those days were past, yet each time I was there I fully expected to see Agatha Christie sauntering down the stairs at any moment and sitting down right in front of me, or Gamal Abdel Nasser standing on his large balcony waving at the crowds, or Turkish, British, and French military officers hatching their conspiracies that were still secreted away in files from the two world wars, huddled over a table behind us. Inspired by the diffuse power of this place, which can sometimes feel like a secret cave, my friends and I also used to hatch our own personal conspiracies and make up our own myths and legends. So many personalities have gathered here; you can still hear their secrets echoing through its hallways, still see that special glimmer of past lovers' eyes, their knowing laughter, their unfulfilled love stories, and the gush of their warm tears traveling through time from those tender days in Aleppo.

In the winter of 2000, I met Sami up close for the first time in that very bar. He was sitting with a group of Russian men and women, drinking and laughing loudly. It never occurred to me that I would run into a young man from Raqqa here. His face was familiar to me because we'd studied at the same school and his brother was in my year—when we were in seventh grade, he was in tenth. One evening, I was having dinner with Najwan, a girl-friend of mine from university. He approached me confidently, shook my hand, and introduced himself. I was not in close touch with anyone from my small town, though many people came to Aleppo for their university studies. I was not part of their circle because I was not interested in the way people from Raqqa developed relationships with each other so quickly. Yes, they supported one other and plotted things together, but on the flipside, they got too involved in each other's private lives and intruded where they should not have. They all seemed to be under the impression what happened in Aleppo, stayed in Aleppo. But the fact is that secrets did travel back to Raqqa, and very quickly at that. The town was only two hours to the east so their secrets would actually arrive well before they did.

Sami's confidence surprised me, as did his spontaneity. He said that he remembered me from our school days. We exchanged a number of glances and smiles, and then he went back to rejoin his friends.

Sami had studied software engineering at Moscow State University, and then came back to work at the thermal power station located mid-way between Aleppo and Raqqa. I remember feeling cold while we were talking, and his fancy, black leather jacket that hung down over his hips. It was lined with a collar of thick gray fur and cinched by a wide belt around the waist. I felt like burying my face deep in that fur collar. He had brown skin, a large rectangular head, and wilted eyelids tugging down at the corners. Large and broad, his nose was his most distinguishing feature. As my auntie used to say, "A big nose is a sign of character!" His mouth, on the other hand, was tiny, round, and wide-lipped. It seemed smaller than it should have been in relation to his other features.

The next day, I met Sami in the very same spot, with his very same friends; they appeared to be staying in the hotel. We exchanged greetings, sat together a while and reminisced about our school days, some friends, our shared acquaintances, and the countryside. The conversation between us developed in the same way you open Russian matryoshka dolls, one from inside the other. Big conversations led to smaller ones, and then even smaller ones, topics of conversation growing ever more personal. Sami and I were very well suited to be together. Often when people share similar objective circumstances, their mutual attraction is granted more room to develop both logically and easily. This is how we first grew close.

He would visit me at the university, we would drink coffee together in the evenings in the quiet Shahba neighborhood, talking and talking. Then he started wanting to spend weekends in Aleppo. We would go out at night and spend hours talking and strolling through the area in front of the citadel, and eat at the Dar Zamaria restaurant in Jdeideh, where they served meatballs cooked in cherry sauce, where oud players who'd tasted the fine art of music with their mother's milk played the traditional songs of old Aleppo.

Sami brought joy to my life, which had up until then been dominated by my academic research for my master's program. He had opened up a tiny door within me through which ardent, intense feelings seeped. But these feelings were ultimately short lived, like fireworks. He was kind and charming, but he wasn't very clever. On his first visit to my office at the university, he pursued me with a poem by Pushkin. Taking my hand in his, he recited it in a calm, beautifully husky voice, while staring deeply into my eyes: "Love, love / O' hear my cry / Send once more to me / your visions. / And in the morning, Entranced anew / Let me die / Unawakened."

I later found out that all Arab students are taught this famous Pushkin poem in their first preparatory year of

Russian language classes, before they go off to pursue their academic specialties. When I told my girlfriend Najwan about this, she scoffed, "Of course! Who did you think he was, Mayakovsky?" I was embarrassed by my own naïve eagerness.

Sami waited for me to defend my master's thesis before officially proposing to me. For the two years that we were together, he'd rented a studio for us to meet in near the university. I spent hours there in his arms. It all began with such passion and ardor, but soon the brilliance of our time together dulled. I absorbed him quickly. I memorized every part of him—I could predict all his jokes, reactions, and silliness. He didn't have any hobbies! This was the first time I learned that there were people out there who didn't have hobbies. He never read a book unless it was for school, and he only managed to get his degree by chance. He would ask me to talk to him about what was in the newspapers, books, and magazines that I was forever reading. At first he would listen to what I was saying and nod his head. But he didn't pay much attention to my studies or my work. He thought I did this simply because I hadn't gotten married yet. His concerns were limited to us being together and having a house and a car. I couldn't understand this kind of love, but through him I discovered that it is a genuine, secure kind of love—far removed from any false pretenses.

Love shouldn't require ambition and suspense; you shouldn't need to expend great effort to convince the other person to be with you. It should be enough to want to stay together, to want to keep that person safe, to be all at once the strongest support and the softest refuge. This is what Margaret Brandt, one of the most important feminist writers in the world, learned from her years of volunteer work helping the women victims of war in Guatemala and Nairobi. Professor Brandt married a nearly illiterate man who repaired steam-driven fishing boats. She lived with him in a little house on the Caribbean coast for forty years. She told me that she loved him without any theories or reasons why. She never cared about the cultural differences separating them. She also said that it was normal for people not to be alike, for all people have their own different passions in life. If you love someone, you love now, you love them later—no matter the circumstances. She lived with her husband happily because he offered her love and security. He was generous, and there was no part of his companionship she wished to avoid.

I withdrew from Sami's life, but it wasn't easy. I didn't have any excuse to offer, my only justification was that I wasn't happy. This was difficult to explain to others. I felt that he was smothering me. I could feel the bars of a life in prison with him closing in on me before I'd even entered it. After long nights of insomnia, endless tears, and a conscience tormented by a person who was considerate to me until the very end, I decided to leave him. Of course, he didn't believe it and he didn't give in. This phase took five or six months of give and take, of supplications and pressure. But in the end, the desire to emancipate myself overtook everything else. I left him an alcoholic and he left me sick with a perpetual knot of guilt.

Tareq was Sami's closest friend—they spent a happy childhood together as neighbors, in the same grade at the same school. In the afternoons, they used to make bird traps, or chase after half-moving cars, hanging onto their sides until the driver found them. Tareq was a clever boy, self-confident with a good sense of humor. He always knew what to say and how to say it in the best possible way. He was originally from the countryside near Raqqa. His father was an imposing and difficult man, the math teacher at our school. Tareq used to like to show the other students that he shared the misery caused by his father's harshness.

One winter day, Tareq threw a piece of rubber into the classroom's heater. The room was pervaded by such a terrible smell that opening the door and windows wasn't nearly enough. All the students started coughing and some of the girls acted as if they were suffocating and on the verge of passing out. This is how Tareq managed to get our lessons suspended for the rest the day. After the investigation, the students' opinion was divided into two factions: those who accused Tareq and those who accused Sami, who was with him. Sami did not speak a single word in his own defense, while Tareq desperately tried to fend for himself and his future, which he claimed a suspension for this incident could destroy. He wept bitter tears that everyone believed to be sincere, seeing as he was an excellent student. As a result, Sami was suspended for three days and returned with his father the doctor to sign a pledge that he would not do it again. On another occasion, Tareq cut up the pages of his notebook and fashioned them into a long tail, which he then attached to the substitute Arabic teacher's behind, as he walked up and down the rows of students, earnestly reciting Ibn Zaydoun's poem, "I saw you in Zahraa, And I was yearning for you / The horizon is endless and the earth's surface is calm and peaceful."

The students burst out laughing so hard that their teacher was left bewildered, until he discovered the tail hanging off his backside. He flushed scarlet with embarrassment and exasperation, then he slammed his book down and stormed out of the classroom. Naturally, suspicion hovered around the row where both Tareq and Sami were seated. Sami wouldn't give up his friend and refused to be a snitch. Tareq made himself seem innocent, shooting deliberate glances at other students he seemingly suspected. Sami was suspended from school for a week, and his father came to fetch him.

When it was time to apply to university, Tareq got a high enough average to get into the software engineering program at the University of Damascus. Sami had not been lucky enough to get sufficiently good grades, but his father's money allowed him to enter the program at Moscow State University, where many Syrians—especially from Raqqa—went to study before private universities opened in Syria.

The two of them worked together in the thermal power plant until they were both presented with equal opportunity to become the head of the pumping section. At this point, Tareq ratted on his friend to the military police, informing them that Sami was still using his military service deferral for having gone to university. The usual postponements of service and conventional forms of bribery were no longer as successful as they used to be, due to the unrest that had erupted throughout Syria, spreading from Deraa to Homs to Deir Ez-Zor. All deferrals had been called up to military duty, and in fact they postponed the release of soldiers who should have been discharged from duty, until further notice.

Sami's call up to military service was to the country-side in Homs, at an electric power plant. There, he was killed in an armed confrontation between the regime army and the free army.

In his years at university, Tareq had been an active, brilliant member of the Baath party's branch office at his college. He often represented the party on official occasions. After graduation, he was transferred to the Raqqa city division. His ambition was to enter the leadership, and he become the secretary of the party's branch in the province, always saying that working in the branch's secretariat was a wonderful destiny that anyone from the countryside would relish!

After this, he started traveling frequently to attend training courses in development, media, and human rights. He started to act like someone with money. When the revolution against the government and the spread of heated demonstrations and defections began, Tareq appeared on the Al Jazeera satellite television channel from Istanbul. He was now an official spokesperson for the revolutionary alliance, denouncing the regime's dictatorship, announcing the deterioration of the party, and predicting the victory of the revolution.

Nutoraki Baghdad Station

I decided not to put a lot of effort into my appearance, so I wore beige cotton trousers, a white linen blouse, and a pastel-colored Majorca pearl necklace—as if I were getting ready for an evening out with close girlfriends.

Instead, I met up with Nasser. This time he was more dignified. He truly was *Dr.* Nasser—not the sad, confused man I had flown with that day. He wore gray trousers, a white shirt, a navy-blue blazer, and his hair was combed down to the side and fixed in place with gel, revealing his large forehead. I thought that he looked a lot like my grandfather on my mother's side.

Nasser and I were totally coordinated in our appearance—simple, elegant, and authentic. We embodied contemporary, bourgeois aesthetics. We sat down and relaxed on the comfortable leather sofas at the Blue Fig café, overlooking the beautiful homes and villas surrounding us. A short distance to the north, the flag atop the Syrian embassy waved confidently in the wind, conveying business as usual, spreading the message that what was going on in our country was nothing but a bad dream.

I don't know why I was comparing him to my grandfather. Perhaps it was the Brylcreem in his hair. It immediately made me think of my grandfather's red jar of the stuff which forever remained in its place—even years after he'd passed away—on his nightstand, above which hung a tapestry depicting Venetian gondolas. The windows of that room opened up onto two streets in the Nutoraki Baghdad Station neighborhood in Aleppo—I still don't know what the word "Nutoraki" means. These windows tell stories of love, dreams of art, travel, and success, all stimulated by the sounds of trains coming from many stations—Istanbul, Latakia, Qamishli, and Budapest, trains always chugging away in the direction of life.

Baghdad Station was one of the most beautiful neighborhoods in 1950s Aleppo. It had three large, parallel streets, intersected by another that linked it to the public garden. There was a statue of Abu Firas al-Hamdani there, surrounded by fountains and all different types of trees—willows, elms, and cypresses—as well as blooming roses and wildflowers in brilliant reds, yellows, and purples. Blue and white jasmine bushes climbed high over the walls, their perfume wafting well beyond the iron bars seemingly erected there for the greenery to climb, all across the seventeen sprawling acres of green space. There were wooden benches scattered throughout the garden, and an enclosed children's playground. Another section housed cages for peacocks, where all noise was strictly prohibited. They would strut around and periodically spread their feathers for spectators.

But this was not always the case, because they were so vain and coquettish. Meanwhile, a swan swam around its own private lake, not even noticing the crystal blue water it was so accustomed to. The lake was surrounded by statues by famous Syrian sculptors such as Jack Wardeh and Waheed Istanbuli, and these statues would become increasingly well known with the passage of time.

Willow trees lined the streets of the Baghdad Station neighborhood, where none of the buildings were more than six stories tall. Their branches crept through open windows on the first two floors, peering in at their inhabitants, stealthily winding into bedrooms and curling up around cups of morning and evening coffee. The Christian, Muslim, and Armenian families that made up Aleppo's haute bourgeoisie lived there: the Dallals, Saqqals, Kayyalis, Martinis, Sabbaghs, Mudarres's, Aqqads, Traboulsis, Attars, Antakis, Mukarbanas, Hallaqs, Hamawis, Marjanas, Qanaas's, Sarkissians, Izmirians, Sawahims. The more popular, overcrowded quarters where the petit bourgeois and proletariat lived lay in the areas to the east—Sheikh Taha, Siryian, Ashrafieh, and Sheikh Maqsoud. The latter is where Kurds from village areas like Afrin and Azaz congregated, as did Armenians and Turkmens as well as Arabs coming to the city from regions to the east.

My grandfather's house was on the first floor. It had windows that overlooked the street, but no balcony. In these old buildings, balconies only started on the second floor. In the summer we'd open the windows right onto the street and fall asleep to Aleppo's evening breezes, fragrant with beauty, joy, and life. The footsteps of people walking by lulled me to sleep, their murmurs lost between waking and slumber. Sometimes I would hear the beginning of a story only to finish it in my dreams. The first proverb I remember was told by an old woman passing by under the window. Crying, she proclaimed, "Children will always reciprocate a mother's selflessness with heartlessness." My dream that night finished her story.

Our windows opened to the west, where the director of the railways lived in a house adjacent to the passenger terminal. It was a large, one-story house, surrounded by a beautiful garden blooming with fruit trees—apricots, plums, almonds—and many varieties of red and yellow roses encircling a small fountain. Behind the gray stone walls there was another wall of pine-nut trees. On the right side of the main door there was a little wooden room for the solider who guarded the house with an automatic rifle that never left his shoulder.

Basel, the son of the railway director, used to study civil engineering. He was also in love with my auntie Dalia, who was studying English literature in the Faculty of Humanities. He used to follow her to the bus stop in front of the public garden every morning, where she waited for the bus that would take her to the university. He drove a government-issued Mercedes that his father had procured for him. As the winter rains grew heavier, Dalia began to find the Mercedes increasingly appealing. Basel started passing by the garden to pick her up at the bus stop, drop her off at the university, and then swing around to pick her back up and return her to the same bus stop at the end of her day.

One evening, Dalia's brother came back home, hysterical. The roads in nearly all of Aleppo had been closed and my auntie was still out. He went to the university campus searching for her and returned panicked and desperate, since a few days earlier the Muslim Brotherhood had stormed the Faculty of Humanities, entering the lecture halls with support from their student cadres. He made his way back home with difficulty, since people were on the streets mourning the minister of the interior, Adnan Dabbagh, who had passed away under mysterious circumstances.

His solemn funeral procession passed in front of the public garden. Everyone at home ran to the sitting-room window to look out at the distant crowd and its spillover to the main street, where the coffin was being borne on the pallbearers' shoulders. The minister of the interior had secretly married the singer Mayada El Hennawy, who had now inherited an enormous fortune from him. This created huge problems with his family that didn't end, it was rumored, with her attempted murder by an unknown gunman.

Mayada El Hennawy wasn't simply a singer of her generation, but a true diva—as they call women who inspire people. The poet Ahmad al-Jundi from Salamiyah once said wittily, "I kiss the television whenever Mayada El Hennawy comes on." And when Ayham, our neighbor's son in the first grade, would make a big fuss and anger his father, he would be punished by having to walk to school instead of getting a ride in their car. This would allow him to stop in front of the Nada Barbershop, which had a big poster of Mayada El Hennawy hanging on its door. He'd get lost in her sorrowful, faraway gaze, in those features of hers that could make even a stone melt out of passion. The boy would stop there for a long time—perhaps a half-hour—and contemplate her perfect marble-colored neck, before Nada the barber would come out of the shop and shoo him away.

My auntie Dalia loved Mayada El Hennawy too. She loved her songs, her looks, her transcendental sorrow, and her crystalline skin through which her soul shone through so brightly it seemed ready to transform her into an angel. Dalia was convinced she looked like her, and we all agreed. She had the same ponytail, wore the same colorful clothes, and copied her makeup and fingernail polish. Whenever Mayada released a new cassette tape, Dalia had it the day after it came out.

That evening after the funeral procession, Dalia phoned. She said that she could get from the university to a girlfriend's house in the Sulaymaniyah neighborhood on the back roads, and that her friend's parents would bring her home as soon as the roads were safe again. But in fact my aunt was right next door—she was calling from the house of the railway director. She hadn't gone to the university that day at all, but instead spent it with Basel in his room.

Traffic on the main road leading to the train station always calmed down after midnight. The Western Road had been built at the end of the 1980s, in order to lead to the Tishreen Bridge. The area sunk into a pleasant quiet until the 2 a.m. train from Damascus arrived. Then silence fell over the area again until 6 a.m. when the train from Latakia arrived. Between midnight and the arrival of the Damascus train, Basel would bring the man who guarded the door to their house a bottle of Juwayyid *arak* and a kilo of grilled kebabs. In the meantime, Dalia would make sure everyone was sound asleep, close the door quietly, and slip down the stairway next to the right side of the building. She would then cross the street and enter his house, heading straight for Basel's room through a side door that opened onto the garden, and that you could reach without having to pass through the main door.

Basel loved Dalia with all his heart. Whenever he saw her, he would kiss her hand eagerly and sigh deeply. Dalia was beautiful. She was thin, blonde, and fair. Her eyes had a lively hazel hue. She always used to wear high-waisted, straight-cut Lee jeans and a tight blue, white, and red checkered shirt that she would cinch in a knot in front or at the side of her hips, to show off her breasts and slender waistline. She looked like she'd walked right out of the show *Virginie*. Her long nails were luscious and manicured, their red polish shining as she turned the pages of books she read at her little desk, while eating her favorite paté sandwiches that Basel brought her every evening from shops like Somer or Sirop. I would swiftly and silently race down the twenty steps to take the bag from him, so she'd share some of her sandwich with me. On Fridays we'd save it until midnight to eat while watching *The Love Boat* on TV.

One night that summer, Basel invited her to an evening concert at the Aleppo Citadel—it was a performance of *The Nutcracker* by the Russian Bolshoi Ballet. Basel had free tickets that his father had received, in the way that important state employees received free things. Dalia told my grandmother that her friends at university would be there and convinced her to let her go. My grandmother consented, on the condition that she would take me along with her. Dalia had no choice but to agree.

We walked up to the theater in the citadel on a fine July evening. The breeze was calm, the sky illuminated by tranquil stars, the moon as clear as everything in Aleppo: its stones, its roads, its industry, its businesses, its people's attitudes. Aleppo didn't have many secrets.

I fell asleep to pleasant breezes, to the brilliant music of Tchaikovsky, and to the soft sounds of the dancers' steps. Dalia in her red silk dress rested in Basel's arms; he kept her naked arm wrapped in his, kissing her neck from time to time, nuzzling his nose into the wisps of her blonde hair that she'd washed with apple-scented Hamol-brand shampoo. I awoke to the sound of a thump. Basel and Dalia were leaving, she dragging me by the hand. Sitting with us in the very same row, reserved for guests of the railway director, was a woman in her thirties and a girl around six years of age. The woman was beautiful indeed. She was tall and well built, with blue eyes and blonde hair. A slit in her black silk skirt revealed soft, pink thighs. Diamond rings glittered on her fingers. Her daughter's extremely careful neatness and tidiness resembled her own. That evening Basel discovered that this woman, Ghada, was married to his father and that the little girl was his sister! He was playfully chatting with the girl at the event and asked her name. Their last name was the same, their father's name was the same, and their fathers had the same job. It turned out that Basel's father had married Ghada, an employee in the central administrative office, and kept their marriage hidden because she was a Sunni and he an Alawi.

After the ballet, many small things in the railway director's house changed. Basel started blackmailing his father in exchange for his silence about his marriage to the rest of the family. Many small things changed in my grandfather's house at around the same time. My auntie Rajaa came back from

Saudi Arabia. She had married one of her distant cousins, the son of another auntie, Sumayya, who we called "Um al-Ikhwan," meaning Mother-of-the-Brotherhood. Rajaa wore a hijab and whenever she came over to my grandfather's house, she started preaching about Islam in way peculiar to her. By the end of that summer, the hijab had become a new theme in my grandfather's house. My grandmother had also started wearing it, as did Auntie Dalia, who spent all of her time in bitter fits of tears, regretting the days she had passed in Basel's arms, in brazen surrender to him.

Basel started to cover himself up too, but in his own way. In fact, it was in the way urged by Dalia, from whom he'd started receiving sermons and warnings, while drowning in his miserable psychological state. He participated in prayer sessions, rarely leaving the nearby Tawheed Mosque.

The bright red Aleppo sun set every evening behind the railway director's house in Baghdad Station. The taxi drivers knew the arrival times of all the trains and would throng onto the station's sidewalks at those times, leaving as soon as the gray and red luggage carts with the three letters emblazoned on the sides—SRL, short for Syrian Railway Lines—started breaking away.

At the beginning of the new year, Basel and his family left that house. They packed their suitcases and walked into the train station entrance right next door. They boarded the train for Latakia, never to return.

Dalia did not say even one word of farewell to Basel. The night before they left, she had closed all the windows to the house overlooking the street to the west. Just like that, all of the bedrooms in my grandfather's house were suddenly plunged into total darkness.

Dalia said that Basel was crazy. She said that like all sons of government officials, he cared about nothing in life except cars, drivers, and guns. Once, when he was waiting for her to get off of a public bus, he asked her, "Why is everyone riding this bus wearing green? Isn't that strange?" But at that time, all the public inter-city buses had a green adhesive plastic stuck on over the glass. Another time, he told her that he wanted to use his car to cut into the line of people queued up in front of the People's Co-op, waiting for oil, cooking fat, and Kleenex just to see them fly up into the air—the ladies' skirts becoming upside down umbrellas, and men's shoes falling on their heads. Yet another time, he told her that they were poor because their driver was poor, their servants were poor, their guard was poor, and they only had one Mercedes—the rest of their cars were Peugeots. The governor and people who worked in the Governorate were the rich ones, they only drive Mercedes!

Dalia said that after Basel learned about his father's marriage on that night at the citadel, he took her onto an empty train car at the station. He had decided to kidnap her and, brandishing a gun that turned out not to be loaded, threatened the train driver so he would take him to Jibreen Station, about fifteen kilometers to the southeast. The driver yielded to his threats, Dalia crying and begging him to stop.

When Basel found religion and started to pray, he went to the mosque, did a doubtful *wudu'*, and stood in the second row. A man in front of him was wearing a white *dishdasha*. Because Basel was still new at getting into the rhythm of the bending and kneeling down, his head got stuck in the robe of the man in front of him, and he rammed into his backside. The horrified man screamed, and Basel couldn't get his head out of the man's clothes. He said that he'd tried to pull himself out, but everything had gone dark all of a sudden and he couldn't breathe. The other men praying were greatly disturbed by this. They followed him as he fled from the mosque and beat him up.

Nasser was friendly and warm. We both caught ourselves trying to avoid exclaiming with childish excitement, "It's like I've known you forever!" although that was probably the most appropriate expression to describe how we were feeling at that moment. He told me directly that he was extremely fatigued, but that despite his sadness in the past few days, he would conjure up my words, my smile, and the touch of my hand, and make them into "a cloud that shielded him from the harshness of time." I found those words beautiful and touching.

Our conversation turned to Aleppo. As he spoke I tried to search for something to say other than the cliché, "It's a small world." He told me that his great-grandfather's house where his grandmother Shahira grew up was that elegant villa with the pink stones that overlooked the northern side of the public garden in Azizieh, on the Baghdad Station side. His great-grandfather was the lawyer Bahjat Haffar.

"What? The villa in front of the fresh juice shop called Kan ya Makan?" I felt slightly but pleasantly dizzy and was silent for a moment.

If you only knew, Nasser… I can tell you how many bars are on the gates surrounding that garden, the colors of the chairs on the balconies, the kinds of potted plants lined up atop its large walls. I could tell you about the eucalyptus tree in front of the little door on the side street, where I wasn't allowed to go when playing with my cousins outside.

Perhaps your mother was the lady who always wore bright red lipstick, a housecoat, and curlers in her hair when she went out onto the balcony to ask us to move away or to lower our voices. I would sit on the edge of the villa's wall, my back against the iron railing, my feet resting on a big knot in the trunk of the eucalyptus tree.

Nasser kept talking as I gave him more and more evidence that we were speaking about the same place, laughing in disbelief, shocked at the coincidence. I asked, "Do you know the Kayyali's house? They are your neighbors."

"Do you mean Mrs. Ra'ifa? Yes, of course!"

"Ra'ifa is Nana Umm Bashar, my grandmother's sister. My grandfather's house is in the big building in the middle of the neighborhood exactly facing the garden—the Joseph Nassour building."

"No way, I don't believe it! You live above Abdou, the bicycle repairman…"

"You know Abdou too? Unbelievable!"

"We used to pump up our bicycle tires there before going to ride them in the garden."

"What happened to her?"

"Who?"

"Mrs. Ra'ifa."

"She died. She had a stroke and then passed away."

"Oh, poor thing, may God rest her soul. Her son Bashar, didn't he and his wife live with her?"

"That's right. They left that house and moved to the

one in new Aleppo. The old house was rent controlled."

"And your house, I mean your grandfather's house?"

"My grandmother owns it and she still lives there. The neighborhood is safe, even with everything going on now, so my aunt and her family have moved in with her too, because their house is in Mogambo, which has heated up."

Mrs. Ra'ifa, as Nasser called her, or Nana Umm Bashar as I was used to calling her, was an lifelong neighbor of the Haffar family. She was a young bride when Nasser's grandmother, Madiha Khanum, lived in the villa. I remember her well. She used to come around and drink her morning coffee at her sister's, my grandmother's, place. I used to love waking up early on summer days, which we spent in my grandmother's house in Aleppo, so I wouldn't miss her and her lovely stories. In the late fifties, when I was around ten years old, I remember her leaving home once wearing a summer jacket over her light blue, or pink, nightgown, which had slipped off her narrow shoulders and covered her wide rear end, a lace collar exposing her small, thin breasts—breasts that had nourished five girls and two boys.

She sipped her coffee with great pleasure, served in my grandmother's little china cups decorated with scenes from *Romeo and Juliet*. She told us everything my uncle wouldn't about what was happening between the government and the Muslim Brotherhood in Hama. She said, "They came to search the Birqadar's house. The owner had hidden his gun in the portable heater, which was still set up in the living room from the wintertime. The officer and his soldiers entered their house and turned it upside down. They asked him if he had any weapons. He said no. But his son who was only four years old had seen his father hiding the weapons, and he told the soldier, '*Ammo*, there's a gun in there!' pointing at the heater. They took his father away to prison right then—he'll be put away forever." Nana Umm Bashar stopped for a minute and then sighed, murmuring, "Oh yes, may God free us all from slavery." After she had emptied out her collection of daily stories, she would leave my grandmother's house and go to Nasser's mother, Shahira's house. Shahira would have woken up by then and put the coffee on to wait for Ra'ifa Khanum's visit.

Nana Umm Bashar had two sons, Bashar and Fateh. Bashar was a doctor, a general practitioner, with no specialization. A long-time Baathist, he was appointed the doctor responsible for overseeing the hygiene of restaurants in Aleppo. This was a prestigious post because Aleppo is a city known for its cuisine, a special Mediterranean blend of Turkish and Arab flavors. As a result, Dr. Bashar had a lot of work, and also held a lot of authority. He was responsible for licenses and violations of health and hygiene. He was the person from whom everyone needed approval, starting with mobile sellers of licorice and *sahlab* to owners of sandwich shops, to the managers of restaurants in the fanciest hotels. Therefore, Nana Umm Bashar almost never cooked, since cooked food from all of the restaurants in Aleppo was delivered to their house on a rotation. There were always different modes of transport stopped in front of her house: bicycles whose drivers carried trays wrapped in cellophane, motorbikes carrying dishes in paper bags, one stacked on top of the other, and cars belonging to specific restaurants that would bring food and drinks of all kinds. Her lunches always had grilled meat and raw *kibbeh*—for dinner you would find *sujuk* and *shawarma* sandwiches.

For breakfast there would be *mamounia*, pastries filled with cream and pistachio, and all kinds of other sweets from baklava to ice cream with fruit, and sweet *mahalabia* pudding, with nuts. No matter the evening, there was always a table for her at the Aleppo Club, the al-Jalaa' Club, or the Siropian restaurant. Her relatives and guests held the same privilege as well.

Her second son, Fateh, left home young because he refused to partake in the money, influence, and illegally smuggled food that his brother brought home. He cited the Qur'an to his mother, "But if they endeavor to make you associate with Me that of which you have no knowledge." His aunt Sumayya's sons, who occupied prominent positions within the newly revived Muslim Brotherhood, had influenced him. They opened his eyes to his brother's sins, constantly wagging their sharp tongues behind his back. They used a subtle mix of intimidation and seduction to encourage him to join them and become an active member of their group.

Fateh stayed away from his mother's house for a long time. She didn't see him at all until just before violence hit Aleppo in 1980. It was one June evening that was so hot it felt like the gates of hell had been opened. There was a curfew that evening, and Fateh had to move ten machine guns and ten hand grenades in a separate wooden box from the house of one of the leaders of the organization in the Hullak neighborhood to another location about twenty-five kilometers to the south. He came home, took the keys to Dr. Bashar's private Land Rover—with a special green license plate showing it to be state property and therefore not subject to searches—and put the box in the trunk. He carried out his task safely. A few hours later, the artillery training school in Aleppo was raided, and about one hundred Alawi military officers were killed. After this, Fateh left for Turkey and studied chemistry at Istanbul University. He got a doctorate in science there. He married his auntie Sumayya's daughter and became the brother-in-law of the same men who pushed him into the organization. Afterwards, he and his family left for Saudi Arabia where he discovered the secret of embalming and mummification, which he later worked on for a long time. At one point, he prepared a special chemical mixture and took it home so that no one in the university laboratory where he worked could steal it. He poured it into an old tile-cleaning fluid bottle and left it on the kitchen table. It so happened that a maid was mopping the floors at that very moment and unknowingly poured the chemicals from the bottle, which was labeled as cleaning fluid, into a bucket. Her hand suddenly became hard and stiff. Before what he'd done had a chance to stain his reputation, Shaykh Ammar—who took on outcasts, people with troubles, and especially those with harsh sentences, that could even extend to the death penalty—presented Fateh's side to the authorities. He asked them to pardon Fateh and take advantage of his genius in serving the homeland—only, of course, after Fateh had paid off the Shaykh with a sum proportional to the weight of the accusation against him.

Fateh had two sons. Years later I met them at my grandfather's house when the family was finally allowed to enter and leave Syria freely. The boys had come back to study at the University of Aleppo, after having graduated high school in Saudi Arabia. They were strange looking, with long, unkempt hair and faces full of inflamed teen-agers' spots that they left untreated. They wore jeans that they hitched up over their stomachs so the hems would end above their ankles, keeping them pure for prayers, according to my grandmother. They looked different than the people who lived on our street at this time. My grandmother always invited them to eat with us at different gatherings, at Ramadan *iftars*, at Eid—they were her sister's grandchildren after all, and they had grown up abroad. When they would come to her house, I used to hide in one of the back rooms or go out, because she told me that they didn't socialize with or even like to see women who weren't wearing the hijab. And that was perfectly fine with me.

In December 2009, CNN broadcast a tape showing an al-Qaeda training camp in Yemen. The camera had obviously been told to zoom out, and it was so far away I couldn't see the acne pits left behind on the face of that person standing in the desert, behind a boulder, shouting at someone behind him to open fire with a Kalashnikov. It was Fateh's younger son. It really was him—there was no way I could be mistaken. He was the reminder of all kinds of convictions about life that I didn't share. Whenever I bumped into him on the street or at the university or even at one of my grandmother's relatives' houses, he glared at me with harsh, accusatory looks, always forcing me to prove my worthy intentions toward God, religion, my family, my femininity—the list never really ended.

When Nana Umm Bashar died, we didn't know whose side she was on... Was she on Fateh's side, or Bashar's? She cried over them both, called out for them both, and asked for good luck, success, and victory over their enemies for both of them. During my university years when I lived with my grandmother in Aleppo, she would find many large reference books strewn across my desk. She once asked me about them and so I read her aloud a passage about pleasure and intimacy, riddled with sexual terms and taboo words. She was completely astonished, laughed wholeheartedly, and exclaimed, "Yiiii, show me, show me! Is that actually what's written? Is this really what you're studying? Is this what qualifies as good literature... porno?"

From that day on, she always asked me to open up to page fifty-nine of the Damascus Scientific Academy's edition of *Happiness and the Pleasures of Wine Drinking* so she could see for herself and read with her own two eyes the wonders that were printed in this book, giddy with her new discoveries. Often, when she came, she was carrying the weight of the world in her heart—what troubled her especially was her separation from her sons: Bashar, who'd gone to prison for taking bribes, and Fateh, who had once again disappeared in Saudi Arabia. She would ask me to play her Iraqi traditional *mawwal* music, so I would get out my tape recorder to play Nazim al-Ghazali singing Abu Firas al-Hamadani's poem, "I say as a dove is weeping beside me... oh my neighbor, dove / don't you feel as I do?" Then Nana Umm Bashar would turn her head, sway gently to the tunes, and break down in tears, her whole body trembling.

A few days before she died, my grandmother woke up angry. She didn't speak to anyone and didn't bring me coffee in bed, as was her habit every morning. I asked her what was wrong but she didn't answer. I insisted, and she started crying, saying she'd dreamt of my grandfather who'd passed away ten years earlier. In the dream, he'd

left her and married her sister Umm Bashar. She was em-
bittered and felt exceedingly jealous. When Nana Umm
Bashar came to drink coffee, my grandmother was still
angry and wrathful sparks flew from her eyes. That same
night, Nana Umm Bashar suffered a stroke; she died a few
days later. My grandmother cried a lot, as did I. She told
me, "Thank God your grandfather married her, took her
with him, and left me."

When I left Aleppo, Najwan had just given birth to her third
son. She had married a food industry engineer, a partner
in a preserves factory located on the road to Kafr Hamra,
which led to Azaz on the Turkish border. After the attacks
and battles between armed groups on the countryside north
of Aleppo intensified in January 2012, her husband's factory
was robbed, dismantled, and moved to Turkey, to be sold
there as scrap or be rebuilt by what had started to be called
factory pirates. They dismantled dozens of factories and
moved them into old Ottoman houses. Some media outlets
claimed that businessmen from Aleppo joined these groups,
demanding that their own factories be dismantled so they
could re-open them there. Najwan's husband was not one
of them. Indeed, by 2014 he had lost his entire savings. He
started selling hummus and *ful* that Najwan had prepared
in their kitchen from a wagon out in front of their house.
I used to be cautious in inquiring about Najwan's political
views; she always had something quite unexpected to say.

We became friends in our first year at university.
She'd come back to Aleppo from the Emirates four years
earlier to study in secondary school, and when the time

came she enrolled at the university. Her family had roots in the countryside. During the events of the 1980s—when she was only seven years old—her father had been imprisoned on the charge that he belonged to a banned group. She still remembers the civilians storming into their house brandishing guns. They arrested her father at dawn in front of his wife, mother and father, and all her siblings. He didn't resist arrest. No one heard anything from him ever again. In the five years following his arrest, both people who knew him, and some who didn't, tried to intervene. They paid great sums of money for the least bit of information, women gave all the gold they had only to find out if he were alive or dead. The news came by way of a prisoner who had met him in Tadmor jail: he had been executed. Afterwards, Najwan's mother married his bachelor brother who had been living with them in the Bustan al-Qasr neighborhood, so that the family wouldn't be separated—the three young children and their beautiful young mother who hadn't even reached thirty yet.

One September evening in 1995, there was a knock on the door. It was none other than the prisoner, released after fifteen years in jail, gone in search of his wife and children at his now deceased parents' house. They were brutal days. Everyone experienced wildly inhuman pain—even the two children whom Umm Najwan had with her brother-in-law, now husband. They all decided to stay with the brother-in-law, and traveled with him to the Emirates, leaving Najwan's first husband alone in the house that had been transformed into a Qur'an school.

Najwan was able to overcome any barrier that had been placed in her way. She was goodhearted, hard-working, and loved school. She continued her studies and got a master's degree. Wearing a hijab didn't stop her from mixing with colleagues and professors in the university, or from going on trips and to parties, just as her past didn't stand in the way of her future. She said to me once, "When I wasn't able to put my memories in order, I left them behind. It was just like having to organize a dirty, chaotic room filled with suitcases. You don't even know where to start so you just leave, in despair, slamming the door behind you."

Nasser opened up wonderful, deserted places in my memory that I never thought I would be able to revisit. He reminded me of a time when I felt like the future couldn't come fast enough. Once I was back there, mentally, it was a funny thing indeed—I felt like I had been completely projected back into the past. Nasser made this happen.

That house, the Haffar house, was always bustling with handsome young men in white shorts and colorful shirts. Now that I think of it, Nasser must have been one of them. I used to love that house. I loved the warm yellow lights emanating from the crystal chandeliers, hung from the high ceilings. I loved the antique pictures carefully arranged on the wall exposed to the street. Even more, I loved the big old eucalyptus tree with its branches climbing toward the second-floor windows, shielding the family from the eyes of nosy onlookers. I used to seek refuge in its shade on swelteringly hot July days, when returning from a long walk in the Azizieh neighborhood or Tillal Market Street. I would get a tamarind juice from Kan ya Makan and savor its bittersweet taste while standing under that tree.

Mrs. Shahira grew up in Damascus and graduated from the Arabic literature department in the Faculty of Arts at the university there. She married Mr. Adham Amireh, the son of her father's friend who had been an important economist in Palestine in the days of the Mandate. They had come from Haifa to Amman, where he was one of the people who founded the Arab Bank and designed its economic policies. Adham, Nasser's father, followed his own father's footsteps in working for the bank after graduating from the Polytechnique in Paris. He passed away of a heart attack when he was in his fifties. After his death, Shahira's visits to Aleppo multiplied, for she had bought out her siblings' share of her father's villa. Nasser would accompany her on his holidays from the Islamic Educational College in Amman.

The last time Nasser visited Aleppo was before 1982. Violent events broke out that year between the Baath Party authorities and the Muslim Brotherhood, for whom the Sunni stronghold of Aleppo was a major incubator. After that, Nasser left for America and his mother followed him. She returned and lived out the rest of her days in Amman after Nasser married there.

We talked for hours and hours, reviving the spirit of the past—the scent of jasmine, honeysuckle, and linden trees, the damp fragrance of the steam rising from kitchen windows in the ancient houses near the Baghdad station. Having a shared memory with someone does not necessarily result in shared feelings. But Nasser shares something very important with me. He shares Aleppo—my second memory, half of who I am.

A Kingdom Ruled by Girls

On the morning of August 28, 1963, massive crowds poured onto the National Mall in Washington, D.C., and gathered in front of the Lincoln Memorial. Civil rights advocates in the United States had come to listen to a handsome young Black man, whose eyes radiated the suffering of the prophets. Wearing a suit and a crisp white shirt, Martin Luther King Jr. gave a speech to a quarter of a million men, women, and children. He used captivating language about changing the history of the most powerful country in the modern world:

> I have a dream
> That one day this nation will rise up
> And live out the true meaning of its creed
> "We hold these truths to be self-evident;
> That all men are created equal."

On that bright morning, from the marble podium that had become a pulpit for freedom, only three microphones were needed to broadcast that voice of courage and its sublime utopian invocation, for the whole world to hear for decades to come. His voice echoed through the syca-more and cherry trees. The world saw the tears of men and women shimmering in the reflecting pool across from the dome of the Congress building.

> I have a dream
> That one day on the red hills of Georgia
> The sons of former slaves and former slave owners
> Will be able to sit down at the table of
>   brotherhood.

A young Syrian Arab man stood amongst these crowds of people. He was well-built and brown-skinned, with black hair. His dark eyes were brimming with life. He craned his neck to listen to this pastor's speech, hanging on to every word with pride and a feeling of importance. He realized that he was experiencing a crucial moment in history. The man's name was Suhayl Badran, and he would later become my father. At the time, he was a student at Boston University, the same university where Martin Luther King Jr. had studied. He had just entered the architecture de-partment after having completed his first year of studies there with distinction.

> I have a dream
> That one day every valley shall be exalted,
> Every hill and mountain shall be made low,
> The rough places will be made plain,
> And the crooked places will be made straight,
> And the glory of the Lord shall be revealed,
> And all flesh shall see it together.

My grandfather was an important landlord in the Euphrates Valley. He owned vast tracts of land where dozens of peasants lived, working the land with their families. My grandfather expanded his business from selling his abundant crops to buying and selling farming implements—from grain to tools and machines—and his efforts made God's land thrive. My grandfather the feudal landowner was nothing at all like the Grand Dukes of Czarist Russia or the slave owners in the American South. He did not even really resemble the feudal landowners in Aleppo and Latakia, those who flogged peasant workers with whips, made them work for food and shelter, deflowered their daughters, condemned them to debt, and then exploited them for that debt with the land that they owned.

Hajj Ali Badran was the feudal landowner according to the customs of the region, not according to socialist theory. He didn't inherit land from his ancestors, who were the teachers and judges of the tribes in the area. He was a translator from Persian and Turkish, working within the constraints of the Ottoman state, and in doing this work was able to save money. Like so many other people, he used this money to buy tracts of land on the banks of both sides of the Euphrates. This was lucrative because a lot of land was available, there were so few people on it, and these people had no consciousness about owning anything beyond what they might use for their basic needs.

The family's wealth came from my grandmother's side; she inherited her father's land and gold. She is the one who encouraged her husband to buy land. She trusted him in this way—he had an adventurous mentality, especially since he embarked on his first adventures with her money, and most of them were successful.

Between the years 1915 and 1965, Hajj Ali plunged into new developments: he built the first grain mill in the region in order to meet the people's need for meal and flour. He later transformed it into a mechanical mill. As the number of people grew along with their desire to settle down in Raqqa and its surroundings, he built a huge kiln for firing clay and transforming it into bricks.

At that time, the world was producing new political maps. The two world wars were responsible for this. Syria found itself in the eye of both storms and they resulted first in rounding up everyone who resisted the Ottomans and agitating for independence, and then, afterwards, challenging French colonialism. Most of those political mapmakers were descendants of feudal families and they composed the ruling aristocratic class. This rule continued because the system of social class division was central to the history of struggle in Syria. Hajj Ali Badran was one of these rulers, as well as being the representative of the National Bloc in Raqqa and its surrounding regions. Before these violent political birth pangs of 1920, my grandmother's own womb had produced my uncle Yusuf. He was born after the battle of Maysaloun, a battle in which Yusuf al-'Azma, the Syrian Minister of War under King Faisal I, was martyred. They named my uncle after him, and they ended up sharing the same fate. More than forty years later, he became a minister in the separatist government, which followed the unity government between Syria and Egypt.

After my uncle Yusuf, my grandmother did not give birth to any children other than my Auntie Layla, so my grandfather married two more wives. They gave birth to five sons and four daughters. After that, my grandmother wouldn't let him come near her.

The French forces demolished Raqqa in 1936 with unprecedented fury. The family moved and spent ten days in a shelter on the road to Deir Ez-Zor that was originally a storehouse for margarine, oil, and dried fruits. It was there, and for the first time after more than ten years of separation that my grandfather came together with my grandmother. She fell pregnant with my father.

My uncle Yusuf graduated from medical school in Damascus at the end of the Second World War. The rest of my uncles, his half-brothers, worked on their father's vast lands. My grandmother sat in her room overlooking her garden, which was blooming with pomegranate and quince trees, sipping unsweetened coffee from a copper pot. Her traditionally tattooed hand turned the dial on her British Cambridge radio, seated in its wooden case. She waited for the news report that would announce how the Minister of Health, her own eldest son Yusuf Badran, had been able to deliver the first batch of polio vaccine for children to Syria. The news report also announced that the share given to the Eastern region would be enough to vaccinate ten thousand children. This was the vaccine invented by the American scientist Jonas Salk and introduced to the world in 1955. It consisted of an intramuscular injection of an inactive dose of the children's polio virus. On that news bulletin, my grandmother heard the Egyptian BBC Arabic service broadcaster, Hassan Abu al-Ela, say, "America will become the leader of the world, and Europe will chase after it." So my grandmother insisted that Suhayl study in the States. Only America would do.

Baba, Suhayl Badran, went to Boston—with the strong footsteps of an elephant, the soaring wings of an eagle, and the lighthearted song of a swallow. Since he had a long and lasting inheritance, he developed an intense desire and burning passion to succeed. Mama, who had surreptitiously read his memoirs, said, "He was a bulldozer of love and desire, he found lovers in every beauty he laid eyes on."

He finished his studies with two master's degrees—one on the restoration of ancient cities from Boston University, and the second in urban planning from the University of California. After that, he worked on projects in the Tennessee Valley in the American South. He saw America slowly inch its way toward world domination, building around thirty dams, which completely changed the look of the country. It created the largest hydroelectric power plant in the world, generating sixty billion kilowatts a year. However, what attracted the interest of Suhayl Badran were the subsequent development projects. They entailed major transformations that were to serve the main project, bringing life to previously marginal places. Instead of remaining forgotten, these areas now witnessed people settling in with houses, schools, camps, gardens, clubs, tourist resorts, and cultural centers, which in turn encouraged venture capitalists to compete in developing them. Suhayl had experienced the dreams and sheer force that come with being a twenty-something, that time when one feels capable of taking on the world, of challenging the limits of the impossible. At the moment of the dawn of my existence, as he always calls it, or the moment of historical abandonment, as my sister Salma always insists on calling it, Baba decided to return from this expanding world on the other side of the seas to Raqqa—his original stomping ground, lost between the desert and the country-side, carrying all the possibility of resurrection. Baba says that secrets reside in the infinitely small things, of which big things are born. He says that perfect shapes such as circles can only be seen as dead shapes, for they hold no possibility of hidden potential.

At the time, he had been reading the memoirs of Ralph Waldo Emerson, who wrote a spiritual record of the American Dream that reflected his unbridled imagination and ascetic vision. Emerson had gone to Europe in the nineteenth century to live in the glory of the old world, only to find it drawing its last breath after having reached its intellectual, scientific, and philosophical pinnacle. He recognized in his country, "America," a latent power waiting to explode in the zero hour. So he quickly retraced his steps, rushing back home to preach about the free world. This sentiment was somewhat mirrored in Suhayl Badran's eyes, for he saw America as a world that was on the brink of ful-filling its promise, while the zero hour was in his own native land of Syria—hers was the promise whose fulfillment he wanted to believe in. Raqqa and the Euphrates River Valley would be the new cities on the horizon, just like the cities in the Tennessee Valley. Syria was being built at that time within the framework of the 1970s Troika Movement and the political passions and positions that arose from fighting against the feudal families, including Ali Badran's family. Although the Baath party considered these feudal families to be reactionaries, Suhayl Badran believed that those thoughts shouldn't stand in the way of building homes, and that what was needed was for lanterns of love to shine upon margin-alized groups in society.

Suhayl signed on to work as an engineer on the Middle and Lower Euphrates projects, the latter of which ended in the village of Tabqa, forty kilometers to the west, where they built a dam. The dam was a dream that would illuminate the furthest village in Syria with electric light, not to mention the resulting developments—schools, hospitals, public gardens, open-air cinemas, sports clubs, and thousands of hectares of dead lands revived in the Syrian countryside around the Jazira province. Suhayl jumped through the bureaucratic and administrative hoops held up by Damascus and navigated the patronage system, all of which was usually far removed from the realities of the people and places at the mercy of Baath Party officials who controlled millions of dollars. More important than anything else was the fact that Suhayl the engineer knew every inch of these lands by heart, he knew their soil and water, their joys and sorrows. Much of this land and his grandfather's property were actually expropriated by the revolution and the trend toward nationalization.

Nationalization was like a fatal bullet that struck many landowners whose fiefdoms were dismantled and granted to the state, which then distributed them among the peasant farmers under the slogan, which we sang out in school, "The land belongs to those who work it." At home, my auntie Layla let loose all her curses upon those who did this. They turned her life upside down, took her father's property, and made her equal to the farmers who used to bring her butter and honey for her breakfast, who chased away the swarms of mosquitoes before waking her from her nap on the brass bed set up on the balcony of the summer house, in the fields that overlooked the Euphrates.

In the year 1963 my grandfather died of nationalization. He had a heart attack when he saw all his ideas,
sweat, and dreams become the property of others, legiti-
mated by what had been said by Gamal Abdel Nasser, who
was striving to be a knight in shining armor at the expense
of a few hundred landowners. The regime established by
the Syrian revolution followed his lead: taking land from
those who think and work—to give to those who my
Uncle Ibrahim, who watched over the land, decribed as
people who "attack women in the fields during the harvest
seasons and then proceed to bathe in the river."

The engineers, managers, and even the laborers who
used to work on these projects viewed Suhayl the engineer
as a feudalist, an ally of capitalist culture who had studied
in one of its great centers. To them, this was a virtue in
the form of an accusation, as most of their experiences had
been with socialist states. At the dawn of the 1980s, they
began to line up with their children in front of the little
window of an enormous white building in the Rawda
neighborhood of Damascus, an American flag waving
high above it. They were there holding letters of reference, introduction, and guarantees from Suhayl Badran the
engineer, which would ensure their children's successful
interviews with the American consul so that he would
issue them a visa for the United States.

The first building that Suhayl restored after he returned
from America was the villa where I was born, brought up,
and spent my childhood and adolescence. It was over one
hundred and fifty years old. My grandfather had inherited
it from his father, then my father swapped with his siblings,

giving up some of his inheritance in exchange for the house. Baba took on the restoration of our house like he did everything that needed to be renovated. He kept the identity of things, building around them with a harmony that soothed both the eyes and the soul. Mama lent him a great deal of help with her urban vision that was based in deep readings of philosophy, art, and French literature. My father had met my mother through her maternal uncle. He had studied with my father in Boston, and invited him to a dinner party at the Saad Club in Aleppo when he got married. Baba met Mama and fell in love with her there. Mama had been married before, to a captain of the high seas—and scion of one of the important bourgeois families in Aleppo. But she separated from him after less than a year of marriage, since he insisted on her accompanying him on his journeys at sea. She suffered from seasickness and hated the months when she had to set sail with him. He loved her so much that he couldn't be parted from her for even one night. She found him selfish and thought he didn't understand her suffering. So she left him. She married Baba only a few days after they met.

My grandmother opposed the pairing because of my mother's previous marriage. But my aunt Layla, who was taking care of my grandmother during her final days, had a lot of influence over her and told her that this happens even in the world's best families—Jacqueline Kennedy was married to John Kennedy before Aristotle Onassis, after all! My aunt Layla was addicted to reading magazines like *Maw'id, Shabaka*, and *Ruz al-Yusuf* whenever she could get them, fueling her interest in celebrity news.

Our house soon had two wings. The Eastern wing

was antique, built out of old-style bricks and restored as if it were a building from the eighteenth century that had only yesterday dusted itself off. Its ceilings were dotted with Abbasid-style domes and vaults. It had an office, a reception hall, and a vast dining room that opened onto an inner courtyard blooming with flowers and lemon and citron trees planted around a large swimming pool with a blue granite bottom. The West wing was modern. The bedrooms were divided between two floors, with a little inner staircase connecting them. It went from the attic all the way down to the main door of the house, which opened onto a simple outer garden planted with jasmine, white jasmine, basil, and red roses. There were straw chairs whose seats transformed over time into ones made of colorful plastic wire, one of them blue, the other red, the third green.

All of our household belongings were precious and carefully selected. Each had its own specific memory. The reception halls were decorated in the Louis XV style, the living rooms copied Harrods, and everything was crafted by the best-known furniture maker in Aleppo, Leon Massabki. The chandeliers in the reception halls were made from pure crystal that Baba had brought with him from Austria. The lamps in the other rooms were bronze—three were antique oil lamps, dating back to my great-grandfather's day, that Mama had found cast aside in the house's basement. She took them to the Hamawi shop in Aleppo and had them turned into electric lamps. All the carpets were Persian, of course—our family wasn't open to Chinese or German rugs, no matter how antique they were. We had two very large Persian carpets, three a bit smaller, and five more from Kashan. My father inherited his rugs from my grandfather, who in turn inherited them from his father and grandfather, and so on. The vases, cups, and ashtrays made of silver, white, or colored crystal were carefully arranged on the sideboards and tables and in the windows. My parents brought these things back from their many travels—to Poland, Bulgaria, and Czechoslovakia. The paintings on the walls were also hung with obvious care, originals by Syrian and Arab artists, most of whom were friends whose paintings Baba loved to acquire from exhibitions held in Damascus, Aleppo, and Beirut: Louay Kayali, Fateh Moudarres, Saad Yakan, Waheed Mugharaba, Sharif Muharram, Tammam al-Akhal, and Fawaz Younis, who was from Raqqa.

The most expensive piece decorating the large reception room in the antique wing was the National Bloc walnut-wood wardrobe, which was a meter and a half tall, a meter wide, and a half-meter deep. It had two shutters on the bottom and six drawers on the top—three on each side. My grandfather had stored his political documents related to the National Bloc in it when he was the regional representative, making my father a witness to the political history of his family. When he came back from America, he thought it looked like junk because my auntie Layla had put old newspapers and dust rags in it. Leon Massabki restored it, first staining it a dark brown color. He re-drew its designs in gold, put new bronze handles on its drawers and an expensive piece of gray- and black-veined white marble on its top. He also installed old brass locks in the shapes of animals—a turtle, a bear, and a snake—which Baba had bought in the old souq in Muscat, Oman. An original red velvet box was placed as a centerpiece. It impressed everyone who saw it, for it held pure 24-carat gold jewelry with the name Suhayl

Badran engraved on it. It was a memento of his having received first prize from the Arab Cities Association for his restoration of Raqqa's ancient city walls in 1984.

Though our house never was lacking in maids, there was one type of housework that my sister and I always took it upon ourselves to do, something we were very good at: polishing the antiques and cleaning the rugs. The maids each had their own different fates—Rahima the Kurdish woman who was later murdered, Jamila from Nouriya who used to say that her brother had given his kidney to the singer Samira Tewfik. There was also Sabah who was an Alawi and later married an army officer. But their fates were never tied to polishing the antiques. Mama used to say that was our work, that it was no work for servants, that we should ponder the spiritual importance of what we held in our hands, that these objects should carry our fingerprints. A little bit of water on the crystal and then wipe it with a dry cloth; wipe the bronze and silver down with a cotton cloth moistened with a special liquid from Beirut. The oil paintings had to be dusted with a feather duster to preserve the integrity of their colors.

The way the house looked from the outside did not betray the luxury inside, which was consistent with my father's architectural vision to make it harmonious with the simple houses of our family and other neighbors in the area. My uncle the minister's house was five down from ours, and it looked like a grand palace, on display to people walking in front of it who would step off the sidewalk and cross to the other side. But the most intimate house was my uncle Faisal's. He was my youngest uncle, the son of my grandmother's co-wife Hajar. His house was always full of life and the joy brought to it by his Italian wife and three sons. Faisal had studied fine arts in Rome.

Faisal always had wandering eye, even in his youth. From the time his mother died, he was always in the servants' quarters. When he was seventeen years old, my grandmother once found him in the basement, lying on top of her servant Rahima, who confessed it wasn't the first time. He was sent off to Rome and Rahima's family came from Afrin to retrieve her. Then they killed her. My father said that it was the blood of feudalism that had awoken in Faisal's veins. My grandmother disagreed, claiming instead that he had inherited the blood of his vile mother, referring to her husband's late second wife. My aunt Layla reminded her that they had found my uncle Yusuf as a boy after he had undressed one of the maids, laid her out on the terrace, and marked her body with charcoal lines, sure that he could perform surgery on her. My grandmother answered Layla sharply, saying that at the time he was not even ten years old, was determined to be a doctor, and did this for purely scientific purposes.

Uncle Faisal married Natalia who was Italian, and like him was a free spirit. She lived in Raqqa for a few years and spent her days running through the neighborhood after her sons, who were full of naughty boyish energy, throwing whatever she could reach at them—a shoe, slipper, or something from the house—and screaming in broken Arabic, "Badran is bad boy!" My aunt Soueida, one of the famously unmarried ladies in the neighborhood, lived next door to them. She would wake up to the sound of this shouting and leave her house wearing only the short dress that women in Raqqa usually wear under their long outer dresses. Braless, her breasts swinging like a portent of a sure battle, and struggling to put on the headwrap that kept slipping between her fingers, she would shout, "Follow that crazy woman, she'll kill her own sons!" The three boys would escape into Auntie Soueida's place and take shelter in her house, like it was a burrow. Natalia would reply, "Soueida is bad boy too!"

Auntie Soueida was very light-skinned, short, and fat, with a huge backside that her ample traditional dresses did nothing to hide. She plaited her hair in two short brown braids. She used to go out and sweep the sidewalk in front of her house every morning, in such a way that passersby could clearly see the crack between her thighs—the fabric of her dress would unfailingly bunch up there. This made her the focus of attention of both the children and grownups who lived there or were passing through. It turned out that she couldn't wear any underpants because they gave her a rash, so she decided to do without them. This she announced in front of everyone. Mama strongly disapproved of such behavior. She thought it was inappropriate, and that Aunt Soueida was excessively ignorant. I told her that she prayed, fasted, and read the Qur'an. My uncle Faisal said that she was a model of a revolutionary woman, indeed a progressive example of the "*sans-culottes*" who appeared in Paris during the French Revolution and included hardworking women who fought against aristocratic traditions while wearing short trousers suited to horseback riding. This group was one of the foundations of the worldwide women's movement.

My aunt Soueida's directness and revolutionary des-
potism were a source of joy and admiration to me. I would
sit in the doorway to the neighbors' house and contemplate her constant movement, which was not hindered in
the least by her heavy body. She used to shout out to me,
"Jo-Jo, don't sit on the steps in front of the door, that's
where the jinns have sex and you're bothering them." She
was the only person in the world who called me Jo-Jo
because nicknames were forbidden in our house. I would
shudder at the sound of that and carry myself elsewhere,
thinking, "With all of this open space to choose from, why
do the jinn insist on doing their deeds only on the steps in
front of the door?"

My uncle Faisal had gone abroad with his family to
teach art at the University of Baghdad when he received
a tempting offer to go to Rome through friends he'd
met while studying there. It was difficult for people who
weren't Baathists to find job opportunities at the University
of Damascus or the University of Aleppo. Influenced by a
strange mix of existentialism and Marxism, he challenged
private land ownership, feudalism, and reactionary politics.
However, he lived off of the income from what remained of
the land my father left him. The last time we ever saw him
was when we bade him farewell in 1983. He was imprisoned for a full year then because of his continued contact
with Iraqis after the complete severing of relations between
the two countries. He left for Rome, and from there to
Baghdad, where he got his doctorate. He didn't leave Iraq
despite the wars that enveloped it. He was also never able to
return to Syria after being accused of belonging to the Iraqi
wing of the Baath party. Nostalgia for his country pervaded

his spirit up until his death. He died in Iraq mere months before the Americans invaded.

In 2005, I flew with Alitalia from Casablanca to Milan to attend a conference on Mediterranean women's legends. The flight attendant extended Captain Qays Badran's greetings to the passengers. The name was confirmed in four languages. The pilot was my cousin Qays, Uncle Faisal's son. I asked to meet him, and he came out to my seat in the middle of the flight. We embraced for a long time. He was intense and handsome—a lot like my father. He had the fiery Badran looks. I fell in love with him and wished I could stay with him forever. In Milan, he introduced me to his Italian wife. He told me that they all had moved to Italy after the American occupation of Iraq, and that his mother Natalia had died a year ago, electrocuted while decorating a Christmas tree.

A Descendent of Carmel-Heim

Nasser returned to Dubai. I was very happy with how things were. At work, I was distracted, but when I closed my files in the evening, an image of him would be abruptly conjured in my mind, spreading light and warmth all throughout my body. We did not communicate through any of the devices at our disposal—no phones, no email, no online messenger. We left our communication to time. I was satisfied by the intimacy we had created, and he seemed satisfied by the feminine solace I provided, as he put it. But painful news from Syria shook me out of this bliss, and I re-entered a cycle of anxiety and depression. I called my family in Raqqa to check on them. When the lines were cut off, I resorted to Facebook so I could ask my friends who were able to speak to their own families by satellite to check on them. People could go to satellite phone centers in the city, like Thuraya, to make and receive calls from their loved ones and see how they were doing. So I could pass on my family's landline number, someone would reach them that way, and they would then convey generally reassuring messages from my father and one of my sisters back to me. Our lives had become very difficult.

The elegant studio rented for me by the organization I worked for was located in the Rabieh neighborhood in West Amman. I lay in its spacious bed that was attached to the wall near a large window through which I could clearly see both the sky and the small garden across the street—it was a small forest of trees surrounded by barbed wire. The apartment's other window overlooked a branch office of the Arab Bank, the Mawardi Café, and a shopping mall. I rarely looked out that window; when I did, it was mostly to see what noise was coming from that direction. There was only one enclosed room, which had a bed and an en-suite bathroom. The rest of the space was all open-plan and formed one expansive sitting room. Furniture divided it into a sleeping area, a sitting area with two small sofas and a large Bergère chair, a small office with a table, chair, and filing cabinet, an American-style kitchen, and a bathroom.

When I arrived, small reproductions of famous paint-ings hung on the walls and vases with fake flowers filled the room. The first thing I did was to throw them all away and replace the paintings with those I had brought with me, originals by real artists. Whenever I had a bit of money saved, I would buy an oil or acrylic painting signed by an up-and-coming artist making their way in the art world. Some were also gifts from artist friends I'd made in remote areas of the world where I'd traveled for my anthropological research into how art manifests traits of peoples and cultures.

Because I left Syria so quickly, I wasn't able to bring

everything I had wanted to with me. I had to make do with an antique oil lamp, a picture of my family, and a picture of myself with Nikolai Ceausescu, the former Romanian leader who was executed with his wife Elena by firing squad in 1989.

According to the appraisers, the antique oil lamp dated back to the Abbasid era. We had found it with a group of objects when we installed an inground swimming pool in our backyard. The objects included cups, vases, serving plates, and little ceramic dolls. Many objects still preserved their original shapes. We also found a large trough made of white marble, its base adorned by carvings of olive branches. Baba thought it was likely a Byzantine-era baptismal font, and that perhaps a Christian family had owned the land and lived in our house years before. Some of our relatives spread a rumor that we'd found gold. Jude supervised the digging, hoping to find her imaginary treasure every night. But that never happened. In fact, if any of our family had dug under their own houses, they too would have found the same kinds of things that we did and possibly even more. Earthquakes, landslides, and other movement over time jumbled the earth's layers, mixing together traces of people belonging to all eras of history. An investigating committee placed the treasures we'd found in our town's local museum. We kept only one vase and the oil lamp, which looked like Aladdin's magic lamp. We asked that they leave the baptismal font so we could make it into a fishpond. But that was illegal, according to Baba.

I was very skilled in collecting donations for charitable causes, and I kept the receipts in several notebooks: one for five-lira donations, one for ten, one for twenty-five. I would give a receipt to the person donating by tearing one end of the paper out of my notebook and keeping the other end as evidence. I then could easily compute my revenue. There were many causes to donate to in Syria in those days—the Palestinian intifada, Sudan, South Lebanon—and many people collected for them… on the roadside, in shops, in trade unions, and in government circles. We could even get permission to leave school to collect. I spared no one: not my mother and father, nor my uncles, the neighbors, or my classmates. Collecting for charity kept me busy. I amassed huge amounts—once I managed to get one thousand liras. As a result of my great efforts, I was chosen by my school to go to Damascus as part of the welcome ceremony for Nikolai Ceausescu, who was making an official visit to Syria. I arrived at the ceremony with my classmate Maya, who was also chosen to participate because she was the daughter of an important government official. I heard the stage director ask his assistant to bring him a pretty girl to present Nikolai Ceausescu with flowers. Excited, I rushed toward the director and told him I wanted to present the flowers. He scrutinized me: not yet ten years old, I was wearing a short navy-blue skirt, a white shirt, socks embroidered with silk threads, and new shoes. My hair was tied back in a bun atop my head. He told me, "You will present him with the bouquet, but don't come too close to him, unless he tries to give you a kiss."

Maya dropped her hand. She shot threatening looks at me, because no one had the right to upstage the daughter of an important state official, especially not by usurping the honor of presenting comrade Nikolai Ceausescu with flowers. Our school chaperone tried to intervene so we could trade places, but the stage director was firm in his decision. The bouquet of red and white flowers was large and fragrant, surrounded by a cushion of mature green leaves, whose color continued to brighten the photograph even after so many years had passed. Our important guest arrived at the Officer's Club Theater and I was in front of him even before he sat down on his chair. I held my small body up straight to come near his highness. White-haired and almost seventy years old, he bent down to greet me. I still remember the many spots I saw on his hand, which he rested on mine as he took the flowers from me. He resembled my grandfather so much that I forgot the theater director's warning, so I came nearer and nearer to him. A cool scent radiated from the skin on his neck as we exchanged two strong kisses.

Maya invited me over to her house four years after my historic meeting with Ceausescu. She played me the footage of his tribunal, which at the time was banned in Syria, on her video recorder. Ceausescu and his wife Elena faced a committee of inquiry made up of the leaders of the revolution. I could not believe the strange charges being brought against this man who smelled of fresh snow atop towering beech trees, and who had kissed me with great affection. He and his wife sat there looking disheveled, like two poor, miserable parents lowering their only son into the grave. They defended their final moments ferociously. They insisted that that if they had to die they would do so together. Up until the tribunal's final moment, they couldn't believe what was happening or that they were truly being tried as dictators. Nor could I, especially when

I remembered the dark spots on his pale hand. Elena shouted, "Don't touch me! Why are you tying me up? I was your mother! I am your mother!" Her earsplitting shrieks sliced the air as would the truth. Nikolai was more composed. I cried from my insides out, and the guard who led them to their death was crying too. Next we heard the gunshots and then the camera hovered over their lifeless bodies. The revolutionary doctor approached, closed the leader's eyes, and announced his death.

Maya's father died in Damascus a number of years after he was transferred there. When I went to give my condolences, we sat in an opulent reception room in a villa on Rabia Hill in one of the capital's suburbs. I put my handbag down on the table next to me and looked around at their lavish furniture. The base of the table looked like the Byzantine baptismal font we had found in our backyard and the tabletop was a round plate of beveled glass. A photograph of her late father in a gold frame tied with a black ribbon rested on the table. And next to it there was a cup of bitter coffee for me to drink to ensure his eternal peace.

When night falls over the Rabieh district, the garden in front of my bed becomes a wind tunnel. Noises howl through it, like the screeching and wailing of cats. The trees transform into ghosts and I curl up in bed. I escape into the sky, which is more familiar to my eyes. I've stared at this sky so much, it felt so close—its stars were sparkling pieces of candy that I could reach if only I could stretch my arms far enough. It was the same sky that was above our house.

Ever since I met Nasser, the world outside my window no longer provided the backdrop to my pre-sleep musings. He did. I would give my mind free rein to think about him, unmonitored, unchaperoned. I would turn him into an idea. Other times I'd make him more concrete, into a cave I'd take shelter in, perhaps a pillow, sometimes even a pampered little boy. I knew it was figments of my imagination, fantasy. But it came from my mind, and the mind does not create fantasy from a vacuum. No, fantasies are derived from raw material, like that given to me by Nasser during those pure and genuine fleeting encounters we'd had. I would go over our time together, picking and prodding at my memories, at his words and features, imagining our next meeting that I awaited with patience. Every morning I would wake, content.

Less than a month later, Nasser called one evening saying that his plane had just landed and that he'd like to have dinner together if I wasn't already busy. As I was hanging up, I bit my lip hard, overtaken by the excitement of this wonderful surprise. We moved each other without having to proffer wise words, without acting with enigmatic caution. A short phone call from the airport sufficed. This meant that we were brave enough to risk a great deal to remain true to our feelings, and that we were resilient enough to handle any possible effects of our sincerity.

At eight thirty that evening I found him waiting for me in the lobby of the Intercontinental Hotel. He hugged me like a father who had recovered his long-lost daughter, and we walked together to eat dinner at Burj Al Hamam, a place of many future meetings. We soon immersed ourselves in conversation.

"You saved me," I told him. "You really saved me. I'm just so... tired!"

"I know you must be. The news is really bad. Raqqa is in ruins. How's your family?"

"They are in a difficult situation. The bombardment is very close to where they are. Elements of many different factions have infiltrated the civilian population. But up until now, they're still better off than many others."

"Won't they leave?"

"Baba insists on staying."

He raised his eyebrows, about to say something, but then went silent. I continued, "When we were little, and we used to talk about wars in distant countries—death, torture, displacement, disease, destruction, poverty, humiliation—we always believed that those places were far away and would remain so. It never occurred to me that this could one day happen in my country."

"I don't know Raqqa at all, I've never even visited it," he said. "Once we went on a trip to Jaabar Castle, but we never reached the city. They say that the entire region is full of archeological sites and that the Euphrates is beautiful."

"Exactly. Civilizations have been built on top of each other there since the tenth millennium BC. There are still archeological ruins there, dating back to the Roman, Umayyad, Abbasid, and Seljuk eras. It even had an active presence under Ottoman Rule and the French Occupation. But then no one remembers it any more—even the government forgot us. They pay Raqqa no attention unless they need to think of a place to put a government official whose pockets are empty and need to be filled. Now that the government needs to lighten its load, it has abandoned Raqqa and handed it over to the extremists, in the same way that you'd give a dog a bone. Now our land is being used for their battles and sick whims. All of them are gathered together there: the Free Army, the Nusra Front, and the Islamic State. I actually refuse to distinguish between them—to me, they all wreak destruction. The worst of them is the one they call ISIS. Even al-Qaeda has repudiated them for their savagery and the world wants Raqqa to put up with them!"

"Maybe the government has planned a strategy to finish them off."

"Any solution will be borne by us, and us alone. Even if they've decided to gather them all together and do away with them in one holocaust, it will kill civilians—my family and my fellow Syrians. Or they'll abandon the province of Raqqa completely and let it become part of a single patch of territory with Mosul, with Turkey sponsoring the plan."

Loud laughter ascended from a table nearby. I turned around and saw a group of five men and two women, one of whom I knew. "That man is an academic at the University of Damascus. Lately he's been a fierce opponent of the regime. Syrians are everywhere... the man next to him has also become a star on political talk shows. They bang on about democracy, an egalitarian state, and before that about freedom. I honestly don't remember the names of their new parties and political tendencies. To me, they're all the same. They're spreading throughout the country, ruining peoples' lives, and now here they are at the Intercontinental laughing away, while at this very same moment people are dying because of them. I'm here because of them too."

Their presence so close to me soured my mood. The air grew heavy. Nasser scrutinized them. "Which group is the best?"

"Each one is worse than the next. Victims became executioners. Some of them benefited from the regime and lived off it for years but then turned against it. Some of them were dependent on those abroad. Then there are the poor, the ignorant, and the absent."

"You're exaggerating, Joumane. There's no lack of patriotic, brave, and noble people in any given group."

"They're immature people, have a limited perspective, and have jeopardized millions of lives."

"Why don't we simply say, they call freedom slavery?"

I felt steam coming out of my ears. I didn't like to have these kinds of conversations with him, and today of all days! So I took a deep breath and pressed my fingertips into my eyelids, to help me absorb my irritation. "Since when did the bourgeois support revolutions?"

He laughed, throwing his head back, the veins in his neck taut against his pale skin. "Have you forgotten I am a refugee? Refugees are not subject to the same class divisions that characterize settled communities. We are a class in and of ourselves. The refugee is a rebel by nature, unless proven otherwise. So who do you support then?"

"I am with our house, of course!"

He nodded his head, looking deeply into my eyes. He'd understood me perfectly.

The source of my annoyance at the next table gathered their things and left. The atmosphere grew pleasant again, and the positive feelings of our meeting settled around me once more. A shared history between two people only begins with a conversation, never before. It must begin there, no matter what they have shared or not—tensions, resolutions, or reactions to things. Through our conversations, Nasser and I began to create a special little history that we nurtured amidst the grief gripping the world around us. We built a house of words: the basement held the memories of the inaccessible things we loved. Everything on the ground floor was bright and safe; our conversations would come and go as if we were passing through familiar rooms. Atop our imagination was an attic open to a certain sky.

"Why should we be the victims of other people's battles?"

"Who is *we*?"

"*We* is Raqqa. Perhaps Raqqa itself is good. And then it is poverty, ignorance, marginalization, corruption, and destruction that engendered this violence. This is what led people to run to untested saviors. Why did all the apparatus of the Syrian state, including the army, simply withdraw from this place? Raqqa had always been somewhere that resisted its marginalization and found a way to live well. People in Raqqa always treated each other well. We had simple, loving family times, and lived the good life staying up late, with music, food, wine, and poetry. People from Raqqa always woke up in the morning to the sounds of traditional Arabic music, like *mawals* and *atabas*, and fell asleep to the tales of Abu Layla al-Muhalhal. How could they simply transform one day into a society of Taliban?

"Our women won't stand for it—no one can liberate us, because we are born free. Women are liberated without ideology, without theories—they walk through the world as directly as an arrow that has total confidence in the wind that carries it. They wear clothes that have nothing to do with either tradition or modernity. They buy potatoes on the very same road they take to buy jewelry at the gold souq. They hurry off to their modest jobs looking the same way they would if they were meeting the president. Strangers are perplexed to observe a collection of scenes that for us simply constitutes daily life in the street—a woman who has come from a nearby village to Raqqa's most crowded street, wearing traditional Arab clothes and carrying a big pot of yogurt on her head, balancing it with one hand, smoking a cigarette with the other. She takes a drag, exhales, and walks toward the center of the market. She doesn't worry about whether she's sitting or standing; she doesn't need a guide to instruct her about what other people deem to be key issues, lost in an excessive concern for etiquette. If you've ever passed in front of the medical clinics of Quwatli Street or Tell Abyad Street, you know it's normal to see women take out their breasts and offer them to their hungry children without any reservation. The only people who look at these breasts are strangers. City people may find this backwards and ignorant, but it's actually a kind of freedom. It's a way to free themselves of the judgment of people who see themselves as superior, as anthropologists say."

"What do you mean, 'people who see themselves as superior'?"

"Those outside of the system, that is to say society, and who take on forms of authority."

"Ha!"

"How will such women submit to these new customs, put on the niqab, go out only with a male chaperone, have restrictions imposed on them? None of these things are part of their customs or lives."

"We are living in a tinderbox," said Nasser. "When the first match is struck, the whole thing will burn down. Baghdad, Cairo, and Tripoli burned. Now Damascus, and Jerusalem before it. All the icons have fallen."

I interrupted him sharply, saying, "This is not important to me. My house is neither in Damascus nor in Jerusalem."

Nasser was shocked at my violent tone. His face froze with the impending feeling that he had said something wrong. I too froze for I knew that I had spoken more directly than decorum usually dictates. I changed the tone of my voice and apologized with my facial expressions. "I am very sad that all of this is happening, but my only icon is Raqqa."

My frankness in that moment made any polite pretensions fall away. Nasser replied to me directly, "As for me, I have no city that can rise or fall. I have nothing for anyone to fight for, to the point that it doesn't even occur to me to mention it—either to others or even to myself. I don't know how a person can have a city they belong to and feel attached to, like their parents and grandparents and great-grandparents before them. My origins are in one place, I grew up in another, my life is scattered between many different places. My fate is that of a typical Palestinian. Our family's roots are in Marj ibn Amer. Most of our family lived near the Haifa Port, after leaving their agricultural lands in the Eastern plains because of a disagreement with a feudal landlord who had registered their lands to another family. Most of them started selling grain to make a living.

"My great-grandfather was the first family member who had a clear vision for the future. He studied at al-Azhar. His son followed him into the teaching corps there, during that period when Palestinians competed with each other about their sons' educations. In the second half of the nineteenth century, my father's father moved to Carmel-Heim. He was one of the few people permitted to live in this new German neighborhood that was built at the foot of Mount Carmel for the Ottomans to welcome their German friends to Haifa. They created it as a canton that would develop the area. My father's grandfather was an Arabic language and history teacher in the German school there. My grandfather studied at that very same school and then was sent to Frankfurt for a year. Afterwards, he became a manager at the Anglo-Palestine Bank's Haifa branch."

Nasser leaned back in his chair and started typing on his mobile phone screen with both hands. He then turned the phone to show me an enhanced black-and-white picture he'd saved. Two men wearing Western suits and ties were shaking hands and holding a small, dark velvet box. The box held a bank note with the words Palestine Currency Board written on it.

"This is my grandfather and Sir S. S. Davis, the Treasurer of Palestine, holding the first Palestinian pound. It was issued in 1927 by British Colonial Office's board."

I studied the photo, looking for traces of Nasser's features in his grandfather's face. They had the same broad forehead. He also perhaps inherited his stature from him as well.

"In 1947, when the United Nations proposed that the solution to the Palestinian crisis was to partition Palestine into two states with an international administration over Jerusalem, Haifa's fate was to become a part of Israel. So that is why we left."

He said this and cast his gaze into the distance, far beyond the tables behind us. I couldn't turn to see what he was staring at, but I could see the light reflecting from the pools of water that had formed in his eyes, mirroring the rose bush swaying behind me, like a Renoir painting.

"My father told me about how, as a boy, he used to go to the eastern side of the city, where his most beloved place, the train station, was. This place connected him to what would be a major milestone in his future, his marriage to my mother, who was from Damascus. This same place later connected me to Aleppo, because the train in Haifa was part of the Hijaz railway line, which connected it to Deraa. The station was established in 1908, and work on it was completed in the year of the Nakba. But no sooner did that happen then the Hagana blew it up to prevent Syrian goods from entering Palestine. Today, it is a railway museum that houses only two locomotives.

"When he was young, my father took many trips with his parents on that magical train. He would eagerly wait for its whistle, and a few minutes later would wait for a sumptuous meal to arrive, prepared by the Wagons-Lits hotel group, also known as the Orient Express. It would usually consist of a meat dish, cooked in white wine and stir-fried with spinach—my grandfather's choice—whereas my father, only a child back then, would order the chicken breast with lemon, basil, and garlic Provençal sauce. The meals would be served hot with a fresh green salad made of lettuce from local farms, a cheese plate, and a selection of seasonal fruits. The adults would drink coffee with liqueur, and the children, orange juice. All this entered the train on service carts, with stainless steel covers and white towels. The china was decorated with a picture of two golden lions facing each other against a blue background, the emblem of that ancient Belgian company that monopolized mobile food services during the First World War. Whenever I ride the train, I still imagine my father, only a boy, sitting in front of me, ordering his favorite dish. That's why I loved Baghdad station and my time in Aleppo. Whenever the train whistled near your grandfather's house, I would rush to the balcony and try to make out the features of the passengers through the large glass windows. But the train moved too quickly, and of course it wouldn't reach Haifa."

I didn't want to disturb the well-ordered beauty of the picture Nasser painted, so I didn't tell him that this train's journey out to the provinces was not as neat and tidy as he'd imagined. They didn't serve any food, and the dining car was nearly always empty, but they would permit you to bring the food you wanted along with you. He didn't realize that the era of the "train set" in Syria was the last time that this fast train with comfortable seats was running. Syrians were indeed thrilled with it for a few years, but when the unrest broke out, railways were damaged, there were explosions in some areas, and many trains fell prey to terrorist operations—so the trains stopped running everywhere.

During that dinner, it dawned on me that I should have studied geography instead. With Nasser, I discovered that I really loved that subject and that it was even something of an obsession of mine, though no one had ever noticed it, least of all myself. Maybe it's because I had specialized in cultural anthropology—an area bearing a striking similarity to human geography. If Nasser had taught me this subject in my early school years, he and I could have drawn alternative maps of this terrible world. If Baba had bought me that globe I saw in the window of a bookshop on Jeanne D'Arc Street in Beirut's Hamra neighborhood, I would have no doubt settled on geography! Then, Nasser and I could have studied together the political entrapments that geography draws up.

I was four years old, standing in front of the shop window in Hamra, pointing at the globe behind the glass. It shone blue with gold lines woven all around it, delimiting areas and regions. I shouted: "The world, the world, I want the world!" His hand in mine, Baba dragged me away, exasperated. "We will buy you the world in Damascus… in Damascus!"

Nasser continued, "I tried to visit Palestine once. I wanted to go to Haifa, Jerusalem, and Yafa. When I actually made the decision to go, people I knew reproached me: how could someone like me possibly agree to go to Israel? To beg those people in the embassy, at the borders, and at checkpoints to visit my own country? *If you do this, you will be a shameful disgrace.* I would be normalizing relations with the enemy, especially if I allowed my passport to have an Israeli stamp. In all honesty, these arguments didn't actually convince me. The way I saw it, all I wanted to do was visit my country, visit Palestine. But with all of these comings and goings I ended up changing my mind. I guess I was just so used to not being there that my desire to go simply wasn't enough.

"Joumane! This was perhaps the first time I declared to myself that *my* city is a place where I can live with dignity, where I am unconditionally safe, where I can get the best education, where I can earn a salary based on how hard and how long I work. This is what my definition of 'my country' has been for a long time now. You may find this too pragmatic, you may think it means that I don't belong, or that I am rootless, as is our custom to say. Perhaps this makes me a nationalist extremist, or even a traitor. But I'm being honest. I'm saying all of this based on my life experience. More than sixty years have passed since my grandfather left Haifa with his son, my father, in 1948, becoming refugees in Beirut, and from there moving to Amman.

"I followed them by leaving in turn. When I was sixteen, I left Amman for Beirut and enrolled at AUB. I studied geology since there was no geography department. Then I went to UC Santa Barbara, in California, where I studied natural geography and got my doctorate. I met a woman there. We married and had a family. I had never experienced any real collapse in my life until I separated from Corrine. She made me more introspective in my relationships with women. Corrine is a sea-turtle expert; she established a national association dedicated to preserving this endangered species. She is a profound person, very calm and giving."

I tried to form a mental image of Nasser's wife while he was speaking. I imagined her as a beautiful woman with long blonde hair, wearing a white cotton dress and sitting by the sea, with a turtle by her side. I felt oddly jealous of her. I knew nothing about turtles, except maybe the story about the turtle that won the race against the hare.

"We had three children and raised them, just like people do all over the world. I was happy that we had a settled life. We were able to save up enough money to provide our children with financial comfort, with fun and happiness. But after our two boys went off to university, Corinne started to slowly withdraw from our family circle. I didn't pay much attention at first—I know how women's moods fluctuate, especially when they reach middle age. But the changes in her began to worry me when she became distant from her daily tasks, distant from the routines of the children's lives, especially Sarah's, who at twelve years of age was very close to us both. Corrine entered a period of serious depression. It was enough for me to just approach her for her to burst out in unwarranted fits of rage. She wouldn't even let me stand next to her. Physical closeness was no longer tolerated—we kept as physically distant from each other as possible. I knew from my long period of intimacy with Corrine that she was strong enough to express anything that was happening to her. But she wasn't brave enough this time. It was around that period that we went to her parents' house in West Virginia for Christmas.

"One evening, she was sitting at the fireplace, distractedly looking at the long, wooded path in front of the window. The path was covered in snow that had been falling for days. She called me over and asked me to sit across from her. She spoke to me in a tone I'd never heard from her before. She was calm and firm, and seemed to have prepared herself well for what she was about to say. 'Look at this snow Nasser! We are so happy to see it, we anticipate it from year to year, but as soon as it is all piled up here we get bored with it. Its mood doesn't change, it doesn't surprise us, and we've memorized all its fluctuations. We know what it will do at the beginning, in the middle, and at the end. It storms, we spend a few days at home, then it calms down and we go out. Snow is beautiful, but we long for spring. Our bodies seek the warmth that will absorb the damp. I've spent my life immersed in a world of wonderful creatures. I follow them from shore to shore to protect them from extinction. I've strained my hand writing letters to raise awareness about their world. Whenever I arrived at the truth, more distant facts were laid out before me. I sometimes forget that whatever I do, nature is stronger than me. It alone has the power to preserve or exterminate the turtles. Neither my desires nor my science can stand in the way of that.

Preserving one group of turtles doesn't mean the survival of a species threatened with extinction. What does the world care if the turtles lay eggs or not, if they live or die? I sell my passion and my time to fishermen who use nets to catch fish, but instead catch a turtle that injures itself, to a child on another shore who takes a turtle home and it dies far from the sea, to workers on ships who can't control the oil leaking from their cargo. But the turtles don't pay attention to any of this. They lay their eggs on strange islands and then leave, going far away. The newborns have to take responsibility for their own lives and use all their strength to climb out from deep within the sand, and then swim away into the sea. No one shows them the way. They know it. Nasser, you spent your life observing the movement of the wind and waiting for clouds. You wonder if they are full or empty. But despite all the technology in your field, you can't stop them or create them, nor can you take them from the west or bring them back from the east. You observe, that's it—you record your notes, you take measurements. The most you can do is warn us of storms, so we pile up at airports, or advise us to use our wheat wisely when making *fatayer* because there won't be much this year. You can caution us to fill the red buckets stored in the garage with rainwater to use for our daily needs, so the water bill will be a little less this season. You say that you are protecting people from illness, death, and shortages, but you forget that what you work on for years can be blown away by one fire, one chemical experiment, one nuclear explosion.'

"'What's the point of everything we do? You can't stop an earthquake, you can't stop a deep freeze from destroying a season of crops, you can't protect a forest from fire. Why didn't I ever talk to you about all of these contradictions? How can you accept one phenomenon and reject others? You accept a total lack of winter rain, but you can't accept a snowstorm in the summer! You should either accept or reject all transitions. This is how we can reject determinism. Therefore, just as you accepted my love, my cooperation, and the effort I made for your sake and for the sake of our family, I am now asking you to accept my desire to leave without a fuss. I am telling you that I have tired of you always being an observer. You are a good observer. But it has become destructive for me to observe my body losing water and to watch my soul wilt.

I want a source of energy to revive me, and encourage me, an energy I am able to reach toward. Have you ever seen a tide rolling in, with another behind it, and another behind that?'

"I loved Corrine with all my heart and at the time I could not understand what she was complaining about. I believed that I had been the best husband possible. I told her, 'I observed you becoming more mature, beautiful, and successful. I observed our children grow up and show their love for life. I've observed our complicity in this every day, with every failure, and every achievement.'

"She would get really annoyed whenever I mentioned the stability of our life together. I had nothing to say and no way to defend myself. How could I defend myself when I hadn't done anything wrong? But this is when I realized that we were different, that our differences lay in our mindsets. She had an adventurous way of thinking, which would disregard everything for the sake of desire. And my way of thinking was more systematic, putting its stock in examples. We couldn't arrive at a compromise because people of different mindsets don't make compromises. What I saw as typical, Corrine saw as deviant, and so on.

"So, my wife…"—Here I admit that his use of the word wife gave me pause—"became like a turtle in her nature and she started measuring human life by the lives of those ugly creatures. Have you ever really looked at a turtle's face, Joumane?"

"No."

"It's like an ancient human face, one nature wouldn't forgive. Corrine says that the lives of all creatures can be summed up in the lives of turtles. They leave their children to the forces of nature, to be killed by jellyfish. Whoever deserves to live on, lives on. The one journey the turtle makes outside of her true home in the sea is to lay her one hundred fifty or two hundred eggs on a safe island, burying them in warm sand, and retreating. She then returns to the sea once more. This journey of only a few meters on dry land is full of danger, since everything surrounding the turtle—eagles, lizards, crabs—is lurking, waiting to kill it. The mother turtle wants only to go back to the sea. She will never see her children again. If she ever came across them one day in the ocean, she wouldn't know them. Turtles are slow. They carry their green houses on their backs, with their memory in them. The only challenge to turtles reaching the water is speed. Ultimately, the houses they carry on their backs, filled with all their memories, are their demise. They can't just leave them behind to gain speed. Half a kilometer per hour on dry land—the water is so close but yet interminably far!

"Corrine had even measured her pregnancies by the standards of the turtle world. If the temperature of an incubator's environment rises, the hatchling will be female; if it decreases, then the hatchling will be male. She arranged for cold environments for her sons' pregnancies and her daughter's in warm weather. She was right every time."

As Nasser was recounting the story of his previous life with Corinne, I wondered how he could have been with a woman who calculated her pregnancies in this way. This must also mean that their physical intimacy must have been similarly calculated. How could I be so jealous of a woman I didn't know? Then again, how could I be so naïve? Of course I was jealous, she was his wife.

Nasser continued, "Many sleepless nights followed this conversation. It seemed to me like a marker, announcing the beginning of the end. That's when the idea of another man started to haunt me, or rather consume me. Had Corinne known someone whose light shone brighter than mine? Had mine begun to fade due to habit and familiarity? Was her love growing toward a new light, sprouting new leaves and a new life away from me? The idea alone made me very anxious, and plummeted me into the depths of jealousy, anger, and exhaustion. And what would happen to the children who had lived their lives in such domestic harmony? I don't know who Corinne was with. Perhaps she wasn't with anyone, perhaps there wasn't another man, but she was sure that she didn't want us to be together. If I wanted to be harder on myself, I might say that her not wanting me was such a strong desire that even when I proposed that Sarah come and live with me, she never opposed the idea. Now she is living on one of the Galapagos Islands in the Pacific Ocean where the largest green sea turtles in the world live.

"It was a harsh turn of events. It felt like I was falling into a bottomless pit. I was afraid of being alone. I was afraid for the children. But our children are stronger than we think. They dealt with this change calmly. It would have been silly not to follow in their footsteps. I decided to leave North America and moved to the Center for Geographical Studies in Dubai. That is how Dubai became my city."

"Oof, that's a lot… You're quite an experienced old man."

He laughed out loud, and his voice cut a path between his memories and his sadness. His laugh was sweet and sober; he didn't care about the few wrinkles around his mouth, or the dark ceramic fillings in his molars. I meant what I said: at that moment I'd noticed that Nasser was not a young man—he was in his late middle age. He'd experienced family life; he'd had a wife and his children were at university. Perhaps his emotions were depleted, and he'd grown immune to many of life's temptations, which I still yearned for. He responded wittily, "But if they don't erupt, old volcanoes leave behind warm waters that cure illnesses. The best crops grow in fertile soil!"

This time I laughed.

He presented me with a red rose that he'd swept out of the glass vase on the table. He signaled to the singer in her light blue satin gown, holding her crystal-encrusted violin, and she began to play a Farid al-Atrash song on warbling strings: "Why is the world beautiful when you are with me?"

Things that I thought only happened in books and films were happening to me, right then and there.

"You listen to Arabic music!"

"Of course! It's the legacy of Shahira Khanum. You forget that Mama was a competent oud player."

Later I learned how much Nasser loved Arabic music. He would hum classical songs whose words even I didn't know. He knew the different types of scales and the names of all the singers and composers. Once we were walking downtown and went into the Buhkaria market. There was a shop that sold instruments, and a young man sat there, tuning his oud. Nasser urged me, "Come, come..."

We sat next to each other on two bamboo chairs in front of the tiny shop. He called over a boy carrying a shoe-shining box and took off his shoes to have them shined, while surrendering himself to the tunes of the oud. I was exhausted. He held me in his arms and I dozed off while listening…

The owner of the shop made us tea and at Nasser's request, the young man started playing. "The fair ones, they wronged me, and the innocent dark ones, I hope they are fair with me." Nasser told me it was a song by Abdul Ghani al-Sayyid, an amazing singer who was not very well known. He bought an oud inlaid with mother of pearl and gave the oud player more than fifty dinars. I told him that was way too much. He replied that this was his mother's favorite song, a special song from his childhood.

Nasser's geography was painful but interesting. It was full of intrigue and came with secrets and longings. He spoke about a country whose names were now only printed in books of history, sociology, or nationalist education. It had never occurred to me that I might ever meet someone who had lived in Palestine, or experienced the stories of its people. Our curricula are only concerned with inevitable, natural phenomena: citrus fruits on Mediterranean coastlines, first harvest vegetables in the Jordan valley, olives on mountain terraces, Egyptian cotton. Teachers assure us every year that the Euphrates rises from the Taurus Mountains and the Nile from Lake Victoria.

I found my experiences insignificant compared to the kinds of transitions that Nasser had lived through. But mine were still fresh, my scars were still forming inside me. His scars were thick and deep in comparison. I withdrew from the conversation for a while, turning my thoughts

inward, going over the details of where I had come from—
my house, my school, my neighborhood; Mama, Baba,
Jude, and Salma.

Nasser ran his finger along my cheek and my body
trembled. I returned to the present. "I am a foreigner and
all alone," I said. "I don't know what will happen to me
between one day and the next. Will I ever see my family
again or will I lose them forever? Will my aunt Lamia and
I share the same fate? She lived with her Iraqi husband in
Baghdad. Then one day they closed the borders between
the two countries and, just like that, we heard no more news
of her. On her side, Auntie Lamia had children. On ours,
her father and older brother died, unbeknownst to her. No
one was able to tell her these things—even birds couldn't fly
across the border between our two countries. The dispute
between the two wings of the Baath Party made communication impossible. Any Syrian who met an Iraqi, even on
a sidewalk in a faraway city, was accused of being an agent.
Any Syrian who met a fellow citizen who once had gone
to that country would disappear from the face of the earth,
especially if news of it reached Colonel Jabbar, the person in
charge of the Iraq file in the Eastern region. Colonel Jabbar
is an icon of the oppression of that era: he could make even
a married couple separate, could confirm that you were in
Baghdad when in reality you were in Khartoum, all while
letting you know that the gifts you are handing to him—
whether it's the women in your family's gold, kilos of cheese
and ghee, or stacks of cash—will not be turned down.

"But these gifts will do nothing to return you home
when the report written by your neighbor or colleague
at work, or your cousin on your father's side, is juicy—if

it so mentions or connects you to Iraq in any way, even in passing. My aunt Lamia would never have married an Iraqi had she not contracted tuberculosis. She went to the Bhannes Hospital Center in Lebanon for treatment. That's where she met Hassan Sharrad, who owned one of the most famous cinemas on Saadoun Street in Baghdad. He was also undergoing treatment. They grew close, as would any man and woman with something moving in common, be it an identity or a tragedy. It thrilled her that one man could be in charge of all these films, actors, and action—and that so many people would come watch, breathlessly waiting for the opening credits. Such was the image she had conjured up of the cinema. Sharrad loved her because she looked like Soad Hosni, a beautiful and innocent young actress. When he asked her about the dowry she wanted, she told him, "I want a reserved seat in the cinema where no one else is allowed to sit, regardless of whether or not I attend the show." And so it was. My auntie Lamia lived through many wars—the Iraq-Iran war, the Kuwaiti occupation, the defeat and the embargo, and then the allied forces' entry into Iraq.

"During the fall of Baghdad, the cinema collapsed under a bomb and with it my aunt's permanently reserved seat. Her husband had already passed away. Up until my uncle Faisal eventually left Baghdad with his family, he was Lamia's last source of comfort. When they too left, she was ravaged by loss. When, finally, there was a rapprochement between Syria and Iraq and our passports no longer proclaimed, 'Travel to all Arab countries permitted, except Iraq,' we learned that our aunt Lamia had been reduced to dust, along with all the others in the cinema. What, you think my experience will be different, either slightly or totally? No, my fate will be the same as hers—I'll die a foreigner, all alone, far from my family."

I talked on for quite a long while, but I didn't feel like Nasser was getting bored. Though the trove of stories I was carrying was small, it was filled with precious facts, drawn by the clash between the misery of the past and our noble intentions for a better future. Nasser opened my right palm and started to draw delicate circles on it with his thumb.

"Loneliness, Joumane, is not a path taken by one person alone. We all take it, but the misery lies in the fact that, though in it together, none of us recognizes the other. Friends along the way are many, but they are too occupied with their inner torment to deal with what's outside. If we would only peer out of the prisons we build inside ourselves and looked around, we would find a friend right there beside us. Our loneliness begins the moment we leave our mothers' wombs, because we begin to distinguish things by geography. These distinctions didn't matter before: our mother is our only geography. We can bear loneliness in life because there is always someone or something to guide us—relatives, hobbies, school, other peoples' experiences, even a bird flying overhead. But our loneliness manifests itself most strongly the moment we die. We all face death alone, no matter how many people we surround ourselves with. And then we move on to an unknown geography, while others remain—even if temporarily—in more familiar ones. They have maps and a compass to guide them. Cities at war are all locked in singular and strange battles with themselves. Wars change geographies, they lose track of habit, familiarity, ways forward, emergency exits. War is disruption. It takes a long time to form, like any pressing environmental phenomenon—global warming, for example. Similarly, the causes of war accumulate historically. When the spark is lit, the distribution of air masses changes, the distribution of rainfall changes. Some areas become arid, others are revived. Similar things happen to people in the shadow of war. Some of them grow poorer, but others thrive and benefit from the chaos. Ice is melting, sea levels are rising, temperatures are increasing, coasts are eroding, the banks of rivers are flooding, and islands are disappearing. There is always a social class who benefits from this devastation. Only those engaged in it have work in a war. Everyone else waits, whether they surrender to it or go mad. Geography alone determines the battle."

Nasser looked unmovable, like nothing could affect him. He was tough, and this toughness was impressive. I wondered how his wife ever left him. How could she run away with someone else (if this is indeed what happened)? He was a strong man, a confident, good-hearted man, with the most profound look in his eyes. I remembered how Khulud, our neighbor in Aleppo, intense with her red hair always brushed upward like a Russian doll, used to say, "You can only tell who a man really is when he's wearing his pajamas."

His palm still touching mine, Nasser said, "The best way to belong to a place is to try to actively make an impact on it, to change it for the better. We begin by changing the life of just one person. This applies to both positive and negative change. Changing elements of the environment affects the overall balance of life. Forestation, for example, increases the amount of green area, increases the chances of rainfall, and therefore increases the amount of water in the flatlands. This sustains life. We must develop the skills to make change. Education is the main thing because it allows people to open closed doors. Joumane, you have everything you need to feel that you belong, not just because you have knowledge, but because you are different."

I didn't want to ask Nasser what he meant by "different" or why he said that. It was enough that he did. There are times when even one additional word can be destructive—it is important to know when enough has been said. That's why I suggested that we pay the bill and leave. I realized later that Nasser was fond of logical challenges. One time, we went to the mall together, to buy some things I needed for the house. As we were leaving, we were stopped by someone working for a tourist office. He claimed that we could win a trip to Hurghada, if only we could correctly answer a few questions:

"Name one of the new wonders of the world."

"Petra."

"What's the longest river in the world?"

"The Nile."

"What was the last family to rule Czarist Russia?"

"The Romanovs."

"Who was the British Prime Minister during the tripartite aggression against Egypt?"

"Anthony Eden."

"What gets bigger the more you take away from it?"

"A hole."

"Who invented the principles of Islamic law?"

"Farabi."

"Who was the heroine of the film *Two Women*?

"Sophia Loren."

Nasser held my shoulders and pulled me close, softly put his hands on my head and whispered, "I love this head so full of lovely things!" That's when I realized I had entered into a mental challenge with him.

Nasser and I had begun to build a shared history together, a positive one, for it had started with a precise set of understandings and the honesty and bravery a transparent relationship between a man and woman requires. This does not mean a full disclosure of emotions and desires, as many believe is the case. What is more dangerous than that is revealing our true beliefs about what the other views as sacred; it is indeed what we fear to do even in the silent safety of our own minds, lest we lose respect for each other as we struggle to unhypocritically put into words our understanding of things like homeland, treachery, and identity, and to do so to someone who is still a stranger. This is all the more true when you are faced with an extreme security situation, in which violent political confrontations are built atop other, already problematic ones. Showing your basic values to someone doesn't make you brave as much as it reveals to you what you truly desire. With Nasser, I experienced other types of beautiful feelings, not just the passion that joins a man and woman. There is a lot to be said about joy, about friendship and familiarity. I loved being with him, everywhere, all the time—just being with him full stop. I loved laughing with him. I loved crying with him. I loved speaking with him, feeling safe and reassured. Just that, simply that. On days when I'm not with him, I become like a passionate writer... I devote my daily life to writing, and then the day passes with my pages still blank!

Narrow Corridors

I hoped beyond hope that—somehow—I'd be able to get out of my visit to the Zaatari refugee camp. The very idea of going there felt like a stone was being cast straight into my heart. It would have been unprofessional of me to retreat and not go. Then I'd be reduced to a defeated woman sitting behind a screen, scrolling through her Facebook feed, uselessly condemning the state of things. I also knew that I would need at least several visits to complete the reports on the situation of women in armed conflicts that I'd been working on.

Ours was one of about four hundred organizations from eighty countries that contributed to the formulation of minimum standards for disaster response, specifically in setting up refugee camps. Heading north to the camps was just a work obligation for my office colleagues, Tamara and Peter. For me, however, it meant getting to know another side of myself. Were it not for a decision someone had taken at the right moment, I myself, or any member of my family, could have ended up in those camps. Just a short while ago, the people who are now in the Zaatari camp were ordinary, even powerful, Syrians. They had houses and possessions, shops, jobs, plots of land. Then, in the blink of an eye, they became the weakest people in the country. They were displaced by bombardments and the gangs that attacked them in their homes—either because of their stance on what was happening, or because of their religion or sect.

The camp itself was spread over even ground. It resembled a solitary, false beacon of safety and trust, so close to our war-torn homeland that everyone could see the smoke incessantly rising from it. Our first challenge was reaching the refugees and getting the authorities to allow us to communicate with them. Then, in order to do my work, according to the guidelines in the international NGO manual, I had to find out what the refugees were able to do for themselves before I could evaluate their needs. The camp was still being assembled. It was a self-contained city made up of desperate people on behalf of whom hundreds of others were working, each with their own personal tales of catastrophe, tales they were striving to make up for, forget, or flee. It seemed akin to the way countries were supplying the camp with aid while they were the ones who played a major role in displacing them to begin with, only to reassemble them later, plastering the refugee label on them. States kill with one hand and pay blood money with the other.

A viewer from above would look down at the camp and see what looked like yellow LEGO blocks, assembled on the dusty ground. These were the refugees' tents, aligned one next to the other on a matrix of parallel roads, which served as the camp's "streets." Each yellow tent carried the UNHCR logo, each carried a story, a mix of truth and pretense. Some people were forced to leave their homes, some left them because the situation in the camp was better, and some didn't have a home to begin with. It was a world of victims, rapidly transforming, rapidly splintering, so they were made into victims of victims, into torturers, thieves, merchants, preachers, social and political activists, into poets and lovers.

I gazed over all this hurriedly, willing my eyes to capture all the details for myself, worried that someone would notice, stop me, or forbid it. Later on, when writing up my reports, I would have to recall the prefabricated bathrooms—square plastic boxes walled in on three sides, and the fourth, to which the users turn their backs, open to the ground with a hole covered by a sheet of plastic. People take care of their needs and spray water out of small umbrella-shaped dispensers to clean themselves. I would have to recall the white plastic square-necked buckets scattered everywhere, which served multiple purposes: washing, cleaning, drinking, moving water, and rolling asphalt on the streets between the tents. I would have to recall electricians supplying network lines; the two adjacent tents that were transformed into a mosque; a donation box sitting on a table at one of its entrances, watched over by a young bearded man wearing a short *galabiya*; the reception office, the security guards.

I walked down Street #5 and saw that it was one of the streets in the camp already completed. People were inside their tents and their children were playing outside in front of them. They looked closely at every passerby, incorporating them into their lifelong memory—the memory that will accompany them forever, inspiring their writings, their drawings, their stories. Far in the distance, you could see prefabricated houses and caravans, reserved for the camp's staff, lined up on parallel streets. These prefab houses seemed to reinforce a stark difference between the staff—the strong, powerful, and generous, and the refugees—the weak and vulnerable. Even the staff didn't realize that they should stop holding their work-shops and putting on banquets in fancy hotels when there was a ceasefire or when a treaty was signed. They didn't realize they were acting just like politicians do. There must be someone to convince them that what can be said in the Kempinsky Hotel can also be said in a tent made of cloth—and with more humanity at that.

Volunteers are deployed from many quarters. They work on organized projects, trying to confront the camp's gloom with their fresh humanitarian drive. But after a while, they too will surrender. Some will be killed by the bullets of one of the warring sides. Others who have suf-fered from the administration's corruption, its bureaucracy, or jealousy will flee. Those who think that humanitarian work is like running a private business or a political party will derail every new and creative idea. The names of those who came up with these ideas will be obscured and effaced. Those young people who found themselves by "giving back" will discover that teamwork is a noble idea in theory, but it fails in practice. They'll discover that they are all human beings and that this game is no different than football. They'll learn that, despite knowing all of this, the desperate people here will still cling to the volunteers, will follow their confident gazes, believing that their confidence lies in the fact that they are stronger and more knowledgeable. But the main difference between them is that the volunteers can act with the logic of someone who knows they will return safely to their families at the end of the day. The others, however, can only act with the desperate logic of those who have lost any sense of safety. They have even lost the legacy of their own creation story, and so must search for a new one, a story weaker than an UNRWA tent and one with no pegs to hold it up.

An older woman walked out of her tent. She lifted up her russet brown dress and tucked its hem into her leather belt, exposing a pair of men's woolen trousers underneath. The trousers were tucked into her dark nylon stockings inside sturdy plastic boots. Her head was wrapped in a black cloth, which also covered the sides of her face. She held onto a rope on her tent that was attached to an iron rod, shouting at the young volunteers distributing cardboard boxes from a small van.

"I don't want any more cooking utensils! I have more than enough—come and take them. I only want to know what's going happen to us when rain starts to fall."

Of course, no one could answer her question, not even the Secretary General of the United Nations himself. The young volunteers ignored her question, deposited the box in front of her tent and moved on.

A tall, full-figured young woman emerged from behind the older woman. She couldn't have been more than twenty years of age. She was wearing a dark blue wool dress that hung to her knees, with jeans under it. She had on heavy gray plastic boots, like those that industrial cleaners wear. She had covered her piled-up hair with a gray scarf. She had copper-colored skin and wide, dark blue eyes. This young woman smiled right at me as I slowly approached their tent. She had strong-looking white teeth. As I approached, the older woman—who I assumed to be her mother—yelled at me, "Journalist! We have nothing to say. Leave us alone."

I didn't have a camera with me; I was taking pictures on my mobile phone. But perhaps my notebook and pen in my hand were signs enough. No doubt so was my gray vest, emblazoned with the symbol of the organization I worked for, its many colors symbolizing "solidarity." I noticed that the older woman had an accent that wasn't Syrian. I also noticed that no one crowded around me as people usually did in the camps. The children were busy with their games, chasing each other around. Small groups of them spilled out onto the dirt, holding meetings as if they were grown men.

I told her that I was a doctor and I'd come to see about what they needed. The title "doctor" helped me a lot since people assumed I was a medical doctor and would start complaining about their ailments until they discovered that this was not necessarily the case.

The woman didn't care for me much. I followed her into her tent and her daughter said, "Please, sit down."

I lowered my head to avoid disturbing the laundry that was hung out on a blue plastic cord stretched between the tent supports. Inside, everything was clean and neat, as would be expected of any Syrian country house, except of course that they were refugees and thus had no furniture and no decorations. They had only the pantry essentials, such as cheeses, olives, pickled eggplants, and jam preserved in jars, and whatever was left of their refugee kits. They had sets of worn foam mattresses that could be used as seats. It seemed that they had managed to get more than their share of those since they had stacked them in two layers and had even fashioned some of them into pillows and cushions. In the corner, I spotted a makeshift kitchen equipped with a small gas stove, cooking utensils, pans, a coffee pot, a pitcher for water, a jar of frying oil, and unopened bags of sugar, rice, and tea. Everything was tidy and in its place. Next to where we were sitting was a gas heater, a television, and a satellite receiver. The woman barked at her daughter, "Sabrine, make the doctor tea."

Sabrine lit the small gas cooker and filled a pitcher of water from the white plastic container while I searched for a way to get through to her mother, who was still keeping her distance from me. She poured the sweet tea and put a leaf of fresh mint into each glass. The mother took a packet of Gauloises out from under a pillow, offering me a cigarette. "Pass me the lighter, Sabrine," she ordered in her now clearly Egyptian accent.

I took the cigarette she handed to me, hoping to break the ice somewhat. "Are you Egyptian?"

"Yes."

"What happened to you?"

I was oddly surprised at feeling a small weight lifted from my shoulders as she confirmed her nationality to me. She took a long drag of her cigarette and puffed the smoke up in the air above her, forming a white cloud. I followed it cheerfully.

"I used to be Egyptian, but I became Syrian thirty years ago when I married Abu Hassan."

"Why didn't you go back to Egypt? To your family?"

"I don't have a passport. I haven't renewed it for a long time and I don't have family there. I don't know anything about them or where they are."

As the conversation flowed, the older woman and I started to settle into each other. Sabrine's friendly movements and intelligent comments nudged us in that direction.

"Sabrine is more of an Egyptian than a Syrian name."

"Yes, I named her after the actress and singer Sabrine. I loved her round face and thought my daughter's was just like hers—I loved her voice and shining eyes and voluptuous body." Sabrine started humming a famous song by her namesake.

She really did have a lovely voice. Her mother followed up, "I also have Mervat. Abu Hassan loves Mervat Amin. Hassan was named after his grandfather and we named our other son Hussein."

"Where are they? Is everyone here?"

She took another deep drag on her cigarette and the deep blue of her eyes flashed—an able woman despite the worries of war and being a refugee.

"Hassan and Hussein—God give them strength—are in Lebanon. They have been working in construction there for years and send us money. They had finally come back to start a project at home, but with the first incidents, they left again. Mervat is with her husband in Sahnaya, near Damascus. Her husband is a police officer and their area is safe. Abu Hassan, Sabrine, and I came here. We left Meliha where we had a house, land, and fruit trees we could live off of. But some infiltrators broke into our house. They told us they were anti-regime revolutionaries from the Freedom Brigades—what freedom, I don't know! They took over the whole place. They settled into the house and said we could stay. But how could we stay there in a house full of men, just us and our daughter who is a young woman? Abu Hassan said, "They'll turn us into servants. It's better to leave the house and come back later—they can't take the walls with them!" Then the regime started bombing the area with rockets from a nearby base. We left on a moonless night, together with our neighbors, Abu Hassan's cousins. We moved through the orchards until we reached the Deraa agricultural road. It was a difficult journey full of patrols and checkpoints—one for the regime, one for the Free Syrian Army—and we paid five hundred liras at each checkpoint until we reached the village of Ghazzaleh. We spent the night there with relatives of my daughter's husband. If the road to her house had been passable we would have gone there. We had spent nearly all our money, so we couldn't cross the bridge over the Lebanese border. It turned out to be closed anyway, so we called my son Hassan. He told us to go to the Jordanian border and they would take us to a camp where everything was free. Then we could put our affairs in order when they let us enter Lebanon, since we are Sunni Muslims."

A girl who I guessed was about fifteen years old came in, calling for Sabrine. She gave me an embarrassed smile, pulled Sabrine by the hand, and the two of them went outside. Umm Hassan and I continued chatting. She kept trying to speak in a Syrian dialect that I felt didn't work well with her Egyptian accent.

"Listen, my girl, I've lived a long, hard life," she said. "More than thirty years ago I went to visit the al-Hussein mosque, on the holy night commemorating his birth. I went there from Damietta with my first husband and we camped outside the shrine for two nights. We'd been praying and praying for God to bless us with a child, but after three years of marriage I still couldn't get pregnant. When we got to the mosque itself the crowds were as thick as on judgment day—lights, music, and people from all kinds of places, speaking with different accents and dialects. Arabs and foreigners, people from the Delta and the countryside, people selling sweets and beans, beggars, the disabled, the sick, pretty young women. I was swept away by this world. It was like nothing I'd ever seen before, and it was full of other people who seemed as awestruck and joyful as I was. I held tight to my husband's hand. I was crowded out by so many men and women larger and taller than me and I had to push them away with my other hand. We were forced to start searching for a way out of this unbearable crowd. We walked and walked, pressed up against people and never reaching the end. I grew absolutely exhausted from all of this, all the while still praying to God and the blessings of Hussein, Zaynab, and the holy family for a child. Moments later I felt a lovely chill—a frisson that began at my hand and moved around to my back, then my womb and then lower down. I told myself: this is Hussein giving me a gift. I held tighter to my husband's hand and my whole body relaxed. When we finally made it out of the crowd, I turned to my husband but he was not there. I was holding another man's hand. I searched for my husband and couldn't find him. This other man trailed after me, not letting go of my hand. "I was here searching for a woman. God has blessed me, as has our honorable master Hussein," the man said.

"We didn't spend long negotiating. This was a blessing I simply couldn't ignore. I left with him and we went to Ghouta. From that day onwards, I abandoned everything related to my previous life. I had grown up as an orphan and my brother had married me off to a relative of his wife. I'd never really loved my husband—so much so that my body refused to carry his child. It was only when I came to Syria with Abu Hassan that I got pregnant with Hassan."

"Wouldn't you be better off going back to Egypt?" I asked, the naiveté of my words shocking even me.

"Egypt is also in a mess—it's a mess all around. Everything is destiny."

Sabrine came back inside, a playful smile on her face. She pulled a cardboard box out from among a number of other boxes. She tried to hide whatever she was handling from me, but I saw that she was taking a number of plastic bags filled with what looked like yellow dough. As she was leaving the tent, her mother shouted after her, "One hundred lira a bag, and not a penny less!"

Soon, Sabrine was back, announcing that she had sold seven bags. Once she realized that her mother was indifferent to me knowing what they were doing, she was no longer worried about speaking openly in front of me. She threw the money in her mother's lap and her mother sucked her teeth, dissatisfied. "All these women and only seven bags!"

It turned out Sabrine was selling sugar. They always had it in abundance because one of the camp's workers

was flooding her with extras taken from the aid pack-
ages, vying for her attention and approval. She cooked
this sugar into a depilatory paste and sold it to women
in the camp. She said her clients even included some
international aid workers; she removed their hair with
great professionalism, adding milk and mint to their mix.
Her mother noticed my surprise and pointed out, "What,
did you think refugees don't care about their appearance?
They like to have clean, shiny, smooth skin too. All of
these men here pass most of their time with women!"
She laughed hesitantly, as if testing my sense of humor.
"They know how to entertain, how to help pass the time.
Remember, time here passes slowly. The atmosphere is
cold. Souls are trapped here and never really relax except
when body is pressed against body. We have only each
other, and sugar is abundant…"

Of course I knew that people don't stop having sex;
sexual activity even increases in such crowded settings.
This is recorded in dry, scientific, informational language
in our camp guidelines manual. This is one thing that camp
workers are meant to know—along with the formulas
for how to distribute birth control pills in refugee camps
where sexual activity is higher in harvest seasons. In many
camp settings, this season offers more natural chances for
the mixing of the sexes. But this had all just been presented
to me anew as a real-life occurrence. It was about sudden
desires that are shaped from molten tragedies and inherent
human needs. This was all bigger than my own experiences, bigger than what I read in manuals. To help me recover
from my shock, Umm Hassan made me an offer. "OK,
come along tomorrow and Sabrine will give you a good

hair-removal session. Your husband will be happy—you'll never have been so smooth before. And I'll read your fortune for free." She pulled a little green package from between the two mattresses and opened it. "Look, this is from Shaykh Mohideen's shrine in Damascus. It is never wrong." She cupped the shell she was holding between her hands and shook it. It emitted a strong whisper. She held it close to her lips and muttered something. Then she held it in her right hand and threw it before I could tell her to stop. I normally didn't like these folk superstitions even if they were just for fun and entertainment, but this time I gave in. I scrutinized her face as she stared at the shell lying in front of her. Her features were frozen and lifeless; a frightening light shone from her eyes.

"You will fall seriously ill. But if you survive, you will live a long life."

I smiled but my lips were contorted. I turned. What she had said shook something deep inside me and my lower lip inched up to cover the upper one. As if that were not enough, she added, "I once told a man his son would leave him, and he would go mad. His son fell asleep and never woke up and then his wife lost her mind."

I stood up abruptly to leave, as if she had just kicked me out. I was so keen to get out of there that I left without saying goodbye, without thanking her, without setting a time for our next meeting. I just wanted to get as far away as possible from that dusty tent and from the weight that had suddenly settled on my shoulders.

It was a cold October night, and the desert cold is nothing to scoff at. No wind or rain was forecasted. The sky was clear and the stars shone like the eyes of a stray cat.

Our tent resembled the refugees' tents. Located on the first parallel street south of the camp, ours were no different from the others' at all—we had the same mats, mattresses, and ingredients to cook and eat. We had few possessions, but we had the freedom to come and go from the camp, according to our work schedules. We had homes to return to when we pleased. But the question of home was entirely different for me. Among all the workers in the camp, I was perhaps the closest to the world of the refugees. My real home was far away, further away than the homes of any of the refugees here. If they all had left their hearts on the other side of the border, my situation was more dire: I was the only Syrian who hailed not from a city or province—but an Islamic State. My family was still resisting the idea of having seceded from the republic, just as they were resisting the idea of being refugees. Always with firm faith, Baba declared, "Everything is destined. Whatever is happening to me here could happen any-where. I will stay put in my own home." Salma affirmed, "I feel the same." At one point, Jude proposed that they move to a safer place, Latakia for example, but the other two quickly persuaded her that they should stay.

I shared my tent with two German volunteers. In the evening, they opened up their laptops and began preparing their reports. Everyone here was busy preparing reports.

I had my warm blue sleeping bag with me. It was a gift from Sami, who had bought it for me in Moscow. I opened it up intending to sleep outside in front of our tent. People rarely sleep out in the open, contemplating the stars, like in adventure stories. Despite my unfamiliar location on the ground, the sky looked very familiar. I could see the heavens. If I could have drawn a line between the stars fixed in the sky above me, I would have reached Ursa Major and Minor. It looked exactly like the sky in Raqqa before a storm, or even after one on those nights we'd come home after a cousin's wedding. Everyone in the neighborhood would already be asleep and the cold northern winds would invigorate us as they brushed against our faces, still warm with the excitement of the evening. We would walk ahead, crunching cold, dry gravel under our feet. My auntie Layla would whisper, "Walk more quietly so you don't wake the jinn up from its dream!"

Three young volunteer security guards walked by me, inspecting the tents that had to be quiet by ten o'clock, when the main camp lights were turned off. One of them shone his flashlight on me, confused, demanding, "What are you doing? You have to be inside the tent!"

"I'm looking at the stars."

They laughed. "That's not allowed. We must ask you to please abide by the rules."

"It's strange that a person can't even exercise her freedom outside in this space."

The rudest of the three said, "All these people packed into tents are here for having demanded just that—freedom!"

The cynical volunteer workers left. I hadn't let that young man provoke me and I complied with the rules. Sometimes people make no distinction between kinds of authority. Authoritarian desire can eat humans alive and take unexpected, inhumane forms. I stopped believing in authority, teamwork, committees, and reports a long time ago. They are all negative, misleading terms.

My bed was halfway into the tent when I spotted a tiny, ghostlike figure running by. I knew it wasn't an animal approaching the tent because I heard a young girl's voice. "Miss… Miss Joumane!"

"Who's there?"

It was Zeina, a thirteen-year-old girl whose tent I had visited earlier that day. I had met her family and we talked at length. She had told me that she didn't want to go back to her village, but that she would leave this camp one day no matter what, and she'd then be done with the smell of boiled eggs that clung to woolen blankets and made her stomach turn.

"My uncle's wife Doha is about to have her baby!"

Her family was composed of three brothers and their wives who lived with their many children in tents next to each other. Doha, who was about to give birth, was a young bride in her twenties. The women in that tent made brightly colored straw trays of different sizes. Earlier that day, Zeina had given me a blue, white, and red one that she'd woven with her small hands. I took it from her, feeling like a tourist who had just acquired a masterpiece. I'd forgotten in the moment that I'd seen countless others like this every so often in my own town, being sold at the women's union, at rural development associations, festivals, and popular markets.

One of the women had told me that their house wasn't far away, just across the border in Deraa. Their village was called East Ghariya. It was near the international road to Jordan. They had fled continuous shelling by both the state and the armed opposition: "The skirmishes hadn't stopped for a week. We left with only the clothes on our back, our papers, and some money. We left our homes in the care of a neighbor who stayed behind. We took all the children and Doha, who was entering her ninth month of pregnancy. None of the men were with us except for her husband. They all work as drivers between here and Saudi Arabia. None of them could come back since the beginning of the bombardments because the borders were closed.

"We heard that they had opened a safe passage for three hours to let civilians out, so we just left. We rode in the back of a truck, crossed the unofficial border, and turned ourselves over to the Jordanian patrols. We had no water or electricity. Our supplies had run out, and the children were hungry. We wanted a break from the sound of gunfire and bombs falling... we just wanted to sleep."

Now Zeina screamed at me, "We need a doctor!"

Earlier I had noticed that the gynecologist who had been sent in by one of the international NGOs, Dr. Minhal, had signed an exit permit for two days and left the camp. But I didn't tell her because I wasn't authorized to share that information. I accompanied her to the clinic, and one of the German women came with us. She documented every step we took, as if she were going to write about every bit of her experience in the camp after leaving. We found the clinic volunteers playing cards by the light of a gas lamp. They only knew first aid but said that there was an obstetrician at the clinic on Street #7. It was relatively far to get there in the dark, so they said they would go and bring him to us.

Zeina and I went back to her family's tents. Doha was in labor and screaming loudly. Her husband had gone to sit on the ground outside, staring into the darkness. He had surrendered—to her voice, to the night, and to the experience of the women around her, just as he had surrendered when he left his home. When the powers of the world around you grow larger, and you grow smaller, what else can you do but surrender? Doha seemed bewildered by all the women bustling around her. I asked them give her some space and let her breathe. Thinking I was a doctor, they obeyed. But of course they were more experienced than I was; I had never even seen a birth before. But I repeated words I'd heard before, "Breathe deeply and push." I held her hand, another woman wiped her sweat, and the rest prayed. It was a primitive scene I'd watched on television dozens of times. Without even the most basic knowledge, I carried on. Of course, everything I was doing went against the rules of my job and my specific responsibilities. I told her that thousands of women give birth in fields and on the street every day. I told her that that my mother had birthed me on the road when we were traveling. This was a lie. Shortly afterwards the doctor arrived, and Doha safely gave birth to a baby girl. Tears flowing from her eyes, they decided to name the baby Joumane, after me, even though I'd done nothing but talk.

"I want her to be a doctor like you," Doha said through her tears.

This brand-new Syrian baby girl will be told the story of her unusual birth; it will become a legend she will grow up with. It will allow her to see herself as different and special, just like we did when we heard our grandparents' stories of the famine in World War I, the French occupation, and the October War.

It was nearing five in the morning when the two young volunteers from the clinic accompanied me back to my tent. The breeze at that time of morning didn't comfort me, but it did carry the familiar scent of cardamom-infused coffee. Someone had woken up and was starting their day with a national custom that being a refugee did nothing to deter. I got in bed and a wave of fatigue washed over me. The sounds of a serious conversation filtered through the air into my tent, the voices betraying the age of the participants. They must have ranged between childhood and adolescence. One of them was saying, "I always imagined him dressed in gold, a golden crown on his head, a gold cane in his hand. He shakes the cane up and down in the sky and he is very handsome."

Another said, "I think he resembles my grandfather Salah, but bigger, wearing baggy black trousers and a blue shirt, a red turban on his head. He squats down on his knees with a gas cylinder stabilized between them, shaking it to keep it lit. It doesn't rest on the ground but sort of balances on a point on the horizon."

The third spoke with a different tone and kept swallowing his words because he was laughing so hard. "Guess how my brother Adnan imagines him? He was on his way to Hamdi's shop and stopped to look at a container of that baby food, Cerelac. On the side of it there is a picture of a pretty woman with long hair. He said that this must be what God looks like."

"Of course! She has the power to feed him and for Adnan that's the most important thing in life!"

"My mother says that if we have questions about God, we should simply read the Qur'an. We should recite,

'There is only one God. God is patient. He was not created, he has no likeness.' Then we won't have so many questions about God and we won't be able to be tempted by Satan."

"No one knows what God looks like, but he must be very handsome and merciful…"

The voices of the children sitting behind my tent were like a lullaby steadily calming me to sleep. Their conversation was very familiar to me. Salma, Jude, and I had many similar questions about God. My Auntie Layla said God would always cherish us and this meant no one could let us down. Once, we were lying on the roof of our house in Raqqa on one of those summer nights when the sky felt very close. Salma asked, "If we put a ladder on top of another ladder on top of another ladder would we reach God? Is He behind this sky?" Jude answered her, "Maybe if we attached a rope to the moon and climbed it we could reach it." Mama stopped us, saying, "No one can reach God. Come on now, go to sleep and please say, 'Qul Huwe Allah Ahad. God is one.' Then close your eyes." It seems that all mothers have the same answers to questions about God!

When I returned to the camp two weeks later, I brought little Joumane some new clothes: hats, a white woolen blanket with silver threads, and little onesies that seemed like they would sooner fit a doll than a person. I also gave a box of sweets to her family. The baby had grown so much in two weeks. She took to her mother's breast with vigor. They presented me with her umbilical cord, wrapped in colorful cloth. Her father asked, "Please throw this into a school or university for me. I want her to become a doctor like you." I thought to myself, "I wonder where the cords of all these refugees were thrown when they were newborns? Did they throw them outside on the ground, making them destined to this life by their families' own hands? Every time I asked Mama about what happened to my umbilical cord, she used to give me a different answer—one time it was left in a school, once in a library, and once she simply rebuffed me saying, "Stop all this silly talk!"

It was around this time that I started experiencing coughing fits. It was a dry and persistent cough that would worsen at night, preventing me from getting a good night's sleep. I spent my days suffering from a mix of drowsiness and exhaustion that made it impossible for me to get work done. I figured that I had picked up an infection in the camp, but then I remembered that the cough had actually been coming on for months before that. I just hadn't really paid much attention to it until then. I wondered if perhaps it was the onset of the flu.

One day, I went to do some statistical research at the Ministry of Labor with my colleague Peter. The office of the minister in charge of granting permission to access the archives was on the second floor. The elevator was broken so we had to walk up. But after climbing just one flight of stairs, Peter said to me, "Joumane, you're in terrible shape—you're already out of breath!" I was actually having difficulty breathing and when we got to the minister's office, I plopped myself down onto the nearest chair. At first, I wondered if this was because I had stopped going to the gym. But my cough now came along with red spots in my phlegm. This shook me. My colleague Tamara told me that winter illnesses often produce bloody mucus.

I started paying closer attention to my body. The better I listened, the more frightened I got, and the more every tiny thing started to worry me tenfold. My sleep became very disturbed and I grew increasingly out of breath with every passing day, then the deterioration worsened and I could feel the difference in my body with every passing hour. It got to the point that I could not sleep in any position. I couldn't sleep on my chest without incurring terrible coughing fits. Sleeping on my sides was a little bit better because I would cough a bit less. The best position was on my back, if I lay stiff like a plank of wood. No cough syrup was of any use anymore, nor were the *zuhurat*, chamomile, za'atar or any of the herbs I tried to medicate myself with.

One night, I tried to deal with my fatigue by getting up to take a hot shower. No such luck; I finished even more exhausted than when I had started. The second I stepped out of the bathroom, I collapsed. It was one of the most difficult moments my body had gone through up until then. I tried as hard as I could to grasp the last scraps of consciousness, but they slipped through my fingers, and my shortness of breath got the best of me for a moment. When I finally got up, I went out to the balcony, clad only in my towel, and breathed in the heavy air that fought its way into my lungs. I lay back down on the bed and raised my legs up on a pillow, trying to take a few more breaths. From that point on, my own lungs would be what attacked and imprisoned me. Losing consciousness for some unknown reason is one of life's most frightening things—no one passes out without a cause. I was suddenly totally overcome by the notion that I had a heart problem, or that there was something terribly wrong with my left lung. I searched online for my symptoms. The answers I found were worrying and unhelpful. They began with anemia, ran through heart problems, and ended with lung cancer. Of course I automatically assumed the worst. But I didn't smoke, and I didn't work in the mines or in an oil refinery. Besides, lung cancer is much more common among men than women.

Morning dawned with a slowness I could only describe as provocative. With the first light, I was already at the pulmonologist in Jordan Hospital, all alone and without an appointment. He ordered an x-ray. I didn't even wait for the report. I took it right to the doctor and he clipped it onto the lighted board. Traces of alarm appeared on his face but he still attempted a faint smile. "I can assure you that your lung is OK. However, there is an enlarged lymph node between your lungs, which could be a problem."

"Cancer?"

"It could be just an inflammation."

"But cancer."

"Perhaps, but even if it is a malignant tumor, don't worry. We have good treatments for this and the cure rate is good, about ninety to ninety-five percent."

"Surgery?"

"No surgery, only chemotherapy. Let's start with an MRI. After that we'll send you for a biopsy to determine what type of tumor it is."

I didn't wait for someone to tell me that I didn't have cancer. I was sure that I did. In fact, in the wake of this shock, chaos, and isolation there was also something comforting in the knowledge that this was certain.

As I walked out of the clinic, I called Baba. The shock silenced him. His first reaction was to offer me naïve, false reassurances. He couldn't believe what I was saying. But, of course, he was unable to leave the house to come to my aid, as it was surrounded by military checkpoints of the regime, the Islamic State, the Free Army, and the Nusra Front. Even before I hung up, I realized that I was going to have to confront this all alone.

The MRI confirmed there was a mass of between nine and eleven centimeters in the lymph node between my lungs. This report pushed me deeper into an ever-expanding maelstrom. Death would be the least painful of the possibilities. I was terrified of the procedures that lay in wait—it would be safe to say that the road scared me much more than the abyss it would ultimately lead to. It was the harshest day I'd experienced in my thirty-three years of life. It was much worse than finding out about Mama's cancer, and tougher than the day she died. I remember perfectly how I arrived home that day feeling absolutely and completely lost. I collapsed on the chair next to the door without even enough energy to cry. My head was splitting open; my heart felt nothing at all. I looked at the request for the biopsy, which the doctor had ordered for the following day. I saw my name written on it in gray letters. This cannot be me. I was too weak to do anything. All I wanted was for someone to lead me to a definitive path, to a post-biopsy world where all the answers lay. As the saying goes, my legs were wrapped around each other in worry. That first night when I finally admitted my illness to myself, I really made this metaphor come alive—my legs were fused together in fear, and all my attempts to separate them failed.

We arrived at the hospital in Tamara's car right at noon. In the waiting room, I ran into an acquaintance with whom I'd had unpleasant encounters at work. I felt it was a bad omen—my mind was plagued by such existential signs. Peter took care of all the practical things I needed to do. I was totally lost, wavering at the brink. I just wanted to be done with this senseless charade. When I went into the imaging room, I could hardly catch my breath, consumed by an onslaught of coughing fits. The technicians gave me a partial anesthetic and put me under the imaging machine. The doctor started taking several biopsies from my chest, emotionlessly pulling tissue and fluid out of the mass lodged between my lungs. It was difficult to lie down completely; I had to prop up my head or be half sitting up. All this movement just increased my pain, and lo and behold again came the coughs. "God bless you!" the doctor said. When I heard the word "God," it had a strange ring to it—there was something new about it, closer to the soul than ever before. They took me to the recovery room where I waited with other patients for the anesthesia to wear off. There was a large bandage on my chest and black X marks on my pale skin. I could hear Tamara's voice nearby; she was speaking to her mother on her mobile, asking about her daughter. She told her we'd be back soon. She turned toward me after she hung up the phone and said, "It was a difficult day for all of us!"

I didn't smile. For her, it was simply another day that had passed. But for me, it would perhaps be the last good day I had left. I knew what was next would be even more miserable. The coming days would be like climbing rungs on the ladder toward death. Tamara would go home to her daughter, husband, and mother, but I had no family and no country to go back to.

"Rejoice wisely and mourn wisely," that's what my grand-mother used to say.

This is why, after the result of my biopsy turned out to be positive, I decided to not be afraid. I thanked God that I didn't have an unknown illness and that mine had a clear course of treatment, even if it failed. The doctor had prescribed some sleeping pills, but I decided not to take them. That was my first step in confronting my pain.

I didn't have just one panic attack. Panic took up residence inside me like a little beast living on the edges of my nerves, occupying my mind and imagination. My body became one with panic, and it could change with alarming speed. Every few hours a little red spot would sprout on my skin. At the end of the day, I'd have itchy red dots all over my body. They would later turn black and become permanent. My glowing, healthy skin became rough, spotted, hideous, and frightening. I was most ashamed of my chest and belly, where my pores widened so much they looked like alligator skin. I grew very thin in only a few days; I was a dried-out stick of sugar cane. My face was pallid and gloomy and the light in my eyes started to fade. The changes in my body were sudden and terrifying. I realized they were caused by the tumor spreading and poisoning my body.

I started gathering stories of people who'd had cancer and anything positive I'd ever heard or read about it. I followed websites that wrote about its stages, how it spread and how it was treated. The most important thing for me was to understand the best- and worst-case scenarios. What I found most reassuring was that this kind of tumor only spreads to the lymphatic system itself and doesn't go beyond it. The treatment for it is no different if you are at Stage IV or Stage I: the only variable is the number of chemotherapy sessions you have to endure. Most cases make a complete recovery.

At that time, I was closer to death than life. When people discover they have cancer, they think that they'll die the very next day. But as time passes and one is continually besieged by pain, people get used to the idea of death and of expecting it at any moment. What split my heart in two was not the idea of leaving the world too soon, but instead the idea of dying a stranger, far from my family and my country. Perhaps no one would even bury me for days. Even if I found someone to bury me, it would be amongst strangers' bodies in faraway soil. This is the ugliest kind of death. My glimpse of the end made me want to discover beauty. I spent a lot of the time of what I thought would be my now short life immersing myself in books about aesthetics. It was a painful paradox to learn about the significance of old Priam's lament for his son, the hero Hector, at the city walls of Troy. He saw death as beautiful. But this was not true of Hector's or my death—both were deaths against the movement of history. Beauty for him was a son burying his father in a solemn funeral, not the reverse. The dead should be honored with soil from their own land. I will not have this. My father won't even be able to bury me. He'll cry for me in his distant exile. The soil that will honor me will be another soil, not one containing the remnants of my ancestors.

It was all nerve wracking—the back and forth I had with myself, the dimensions of my illness, the transformation of the disease, my own condition, my doctors, my treatment. I refused to take tranquilizers despite the pain. Instead, I searched inside myself for the faith of the elderly. I soon found that mercy was at my fingertips. For me, this was no worse a solution than that of those who didn't believe in a god to have mercy on them.

I could hear my body crying out for medicine. My mind started to open up, preparing my body to receive the magic called chemotherapy that could heal the ill and change their destinies. I imagined the chemo seeping into my tumor drop by drop, burning every last cell and freeing my chest, which was gasping for air. It seemed to me that the more facts one learns, the more pressing a resolution becomes: the medicine mounting its attack, and I, merely existing, faltering between delusion and fear. My body was seriously debilitated, and I was too weak to move. It was so difficult to take a breath that I developed a stabbing pain in the left side of my chest and I could even feel the veins on my neck leading to my heart, tender and painful. The tumor kept growing. Soon it would kill me, so I called Nasser.

Three days after I called him, Nasser came to my house. I knew he was angry at me for not having told him about my condition as soon as I had found out. However, his compassionate, confident, and resolute words are what helped me keep myself together, preventing the final, ultimate breakdown. He was very good at hiding his own worry. He sat across from me on the sofa in the living room where I was resting. He held my hands between his and took a deep breath. Then he said, "All problems can be solved. People are constantly being exposed to cancer. It's become so common. And along with this increase in exposure has come an increase in the healing rate. This is especially true in your case, because we have some basic reassurance about your condition."

Those first touches, those first words that lingered in my mind once I had recovered from the shock of my diagnosis are what would stay with me to the end. I would forget everything else, and everyone else—who came, who went, who lived, who died, who were happy, who were unhappy. I only held on to what Nasser said and did. He was my protector, my miracle, and my salvation.

We spoke for a long time. I cried in his lap, he listened to me cry and answered me with tender kisses. He never tired of speaking, persuading me, and allaying my fears. He prepared a light dinner. I hadn't been able to eat for days and I only ate when Tamara and Peter forced me to. He spread butter and strawberry jam on toast and fed it to me, followed by hot tea. I felt better after I had eaten. What would I have done if Nasser hadn't been with me? It was nearly midnight when he led me to bed, and tucked me in. He thought I was asleep, but I wasn't. I just had no strength left. I heard the sound of a door closing inside the apartment. He was getting ready to leave. I got out of bed and stumbled down the hall with all the strength left in my fatigued body. I pulled his shirt from behind as he faded away. I knelt down at his feet and grabbed his knees, begging him not to go and leave me alone. I was afraid I would die alone.

It was the first time in my life that I had begged someone in such a humiliating way. He closed his eyes and he implored me to get up. Then he helped me to stand, carried me to my bed, and promised he would not leave.

Nasser went out the next morning and returned around noon. He had a black suitcase with him and a folder filled with papers. His suitcase held his clothes and some other things he needed. He announced he would stay with me. But how would this happen? Moving in here, but to what end? He told me that he was essentially moving to Amman anyway, because he had to help his daughter Sarah who wanted to move to the United States and attend university there. For now, he would be working for a consultancy center at the Royal Geographic Society. The discussion didn't go any further than that; I couldn't say a thing. I just kept crying. I felt like the weight of a thousand mountains was crushing my chest. His confusion was apparent, but he kept repeating, "We shouldn't cry, we should get treatment." He took out the folder of papers and handed it to me, saying, "Tomorrow we will take the first steps toward our treatment."

Nasser always spoke of "we," never of "you." We are going, we are getting treatment, we are eating, we are sleeping. I used to fight against my loneliness, my pain, and my despair with this collective pronoun. He used his knowledge of the city and all his contacts to get me an immediate appointment at the cancer center, so I would be treated as a citizen and not a foreigner. I didn't have any capacity for extra questions like, "Why are you doing this for me?" but a seed of gratitude was planted in my heart and it bloomed further with every passing day. I read the referral paper that allowed me to become a patient at the cancer center. My name was written on it and a number was circled, describing my situation, "treatment for lymphatic cancer." My name was no longer mine. I felt completely alienated from it. From that day on, I would no longer be Dr. Joumane Badran, but a number, a statistic, a patient at the cancer center.

Salma called me and said, "Joumane, don't be afraid. You are going to get through everything. Be like those women who crush their pain under their feet as they march forward. They're surrounded by snipers, rocket fire, bombs…"

"But they're not dealing with cancer!"

"You have lots of examples of people who've been cured around you," she said.

"I feel like Mama in her last days," I replied.

"They didn't have any medicine to cure her," she retorted. "Her situation was different."

"I'm all alone here. None of you are here with me."

I didn't dare tell her that Nasser was with me—Nasser, who had decided not to leave me, Nasser who was, all at once, my mother, father, brother, friend, and lover. If your lover is the one who is saving you from the brink of death, everyone else becomes white noise!

I passed the evening asking him simplistic questions that are typical of moments of weakness, questions we'd taken for granted not long beforehand. "Nasser, are the people who get treatment cured?"

"Of course, why else would they open these state-of-the-art cancer centers? Why would so many people research cancer? To kill people or to cure them?"

I added these sentences to my collection and went quiet. Afterwards, Nasser got me into bed and tucked me in. I don't know what he does in my house after that ritual is completed every night.

The costs of the treatment were prohibitive, and it was no easy feat to transfer money from Syria for the process is difficult and tightly controlled, especially when dealing with large sums. Baba gave John all my details, and within less than a week I already had the first installment.

John Dryer was an old friend of my father's. They'd known each other for more than fifty years at that point. They'd met as roommates when they were students in Boston. John's father was an important industrialist and his family owned mineral mines in Alaska, so, naturally, he'd studied mining. He had only visited us once in Raqqa, spending a full month in our home at the very beginning of the nineties. Baba went to pick him up from the airport in Damascus when he'd first arrived in Syria. When they got home, Jude, Salma, and I rushed out to open the door of his car and found a large man, very tall, who didn't look at all like Richard Gere as we had imagined he would. He had a funnily shaped big belly. He could never have enough bananas; he took them everywhere he went. Mama said, "Thank God he didn't visit in the eighties when imports were banned because of the belt-tightening policy—it was impossible to get bananas back then." We later learned that he had a potassium deficiency, and I cheekily noticed that his strange belly was actually shaped like a banana. We had a lovely time in his company—we visited nearby tourist spots, swam in the river, stayed up late, ate good food, and all our relatives came to meet our guest who'd come from so far away. John gave each of us an ounce of gold weighing ten grams—and mama one of thirty grams—that had been extracted from their mines.

He gave me lessons in financial speculation, and I had no idea what he was saying because I knew nothing of the language of finance. But I did learn to play poker and I taught him about the history of al-Andalus after having read about it in one of my orientalist paperbacks. I took him on trips to little remote alleys, and brought him to my girlfriends' houses, where he would unfailingly be invited by their families to try local dishes like meatballs with tomatoes, *hamis*, and *sayayyil*. When it came time for the celebrations of our victory in the October War, both Jude and Salma were participating in the opening ceremony. The secondary-school students all marched through the main street carrying the torch of the revolution. John prepared himself for this adventure, picked up his camera, and off we went. As they marched past us in front of the big municipal stadium, John started to take pictures. He waved to Salma and Jude, as enthusiastic as a child who'd finally come to an amusement park after having been promised it for a long time. Suddenly a short, thin man approached us. He was wearing gray trousers and a white shirt in dire need of ironing for him to look the least bit presentable.

He was holding a pen and a small notebook, a gun at his waist. He asked us to give him the camera. John was surprised and turned bright red. I told the man, "Speak to me, he's American." His eyes opened as wide as eyes could. He acted as though he'd found the true meaning of existence.

"And he's American too?"

"Yes, he's American."

He tried to yank the camera hanging around John's neck by force. He raised his voice, John started shaking and his belly swelled even larger. His ears were like elephant ears. He started shouting at me in English, "Call Suhayl, call Suhayl!"

His shouting really got on my nerves, which were already almost shot. I yelled at him to be quiet, and he was. John had already delayed his visit to us because of terrorism. Now it was presented to him in the shape of this petty security officer.

I told this young man who was only in his mid-twenties, "I'm not going to give you the camera, because it has personal photographs on it. We're taking pictures in a public place, where everyone is gathered, on an occasion dear to all of our hearts. It's victory day! We have to show the world how we celebrate our victory. Can't you see the television cameras recording it?" He started to calm down a little, but kept insisting that he take the camera. Then I lost my temper. I called him all kinds of stupid, and said to him, "For three weeks I've been trying to show my friend a positive, vibrant image of our country and now you come along and in one minute ruin this beautiful picture." He didn't seem to care much about what I was saying. People had gathered around us and we reached a compromise—he left the camera with us, but he took my ID card and said I would have to go to the security offices to get it back. This meant there would be an investigation. And at the time I was preparing for high school exams. John was rushing ahead of me on the road toward home, which he didn't really know very well, shouting in English, "Thank you, Tiger!"

John met Baba at the door and hugged him warmly, as though he'd just returned safely from war. He told him what had happened. Baba and I left to go get my ID card. At the security office, we met the officer in charge. I told him the details of what had happened. He let us know that the security officer's report said that I had a sharp tongue. We returned home an hour later with my ID card. We spent the evening eating kebabs, playing poker, with Dad and John drinking Mexican beers and singing in English: "When Johnny comes marching home again, Hurrah! Hurrah! We'll give him a hearty welcome then, Hurrah! Hurrah!"

John has called me Tiger ever since that incident. When he returned back home he sent me copies of stock market investments worth $3,000 that he'd made in my name as an expression of his gratitude for saving his life, as he put it. He invested them for me in the technology sector, which has gone crazy with speculations ever since.

With the second biopsy, which would be much harsher than the first, I began to rediscover words I'd forgotten: depression, death, wellness, sadness, distress, pain, health, body, truth, agony. All of this vocabulary took on real meaning with the bone-marrow biopsy—a needle plunged into the vertebrae in your lower back, sucking out some of your soul in liquid form. It was scheduled for Sunday at twelve o'clock. Nasser insisted on coming with me, despite the fact that the timing coincided with an important meeting he had to attend. He recorded all my appointments studiously, like a student who has decided to graduate with honors. He gave his number as my contact information, saying that he was my fiancé and the only of my relatives here in town, signaling that he was in charge of everything. He took my bag and stood in the corridor whenever I went into a test room or a clinic. When the biopsy doctor started telling me details about what he was going to do to my body, I asked him to stop. I didn't want to live through the experience twice. Those doctors were so far removed from the world of language and ritual. They didn't realize that speaking about the experience might be more difficult than the actual procedure. Nonetheless, they would keep chatting and asking me about culture and anthropology. The pain had made me forget all that I had learned before this chapter of my life was opened. When people here asked me about my life, my work, or my degrees, their expressions of sorrow would intensify.

The night I finally managed to get some sleep, I woke to the reality that I had to go for my PET scan. This was the passage to truth. I spent a night immersed in torment. I got out of bed a number of times, heading into the single room that we had decided would be Nasser's. He was deep asleep, but my sorrow was brimming over, threatening to erupt. I was jealous of how calm he looked, his measured breathing, his rosy skin. I didn't wake him up. He was in another world—a nearby world that couldn't cross into mine, no matter how close he came or what he did for me. He shouldn't be able to sleep so deeply! Did he come to sleep or to be with me on this critical night? When this night turns to morning we will be told how big the tumor is and how far it has spread. I won't shout. I won't wake him. I won't do anything. I don't want to be more of a burden on him than I already am. I don't want him to hate me, or to leave me. I need him desperately.

We left at eight. It was a dark, subdued morning in March, heavy with clouds. I didn't apologize to Nasser, like I had done every other time he'd come with me to appointments. This time I had a feeling opposite to gratitude. I felt a human's duty toward humanity. This requires everyone who knows someone going for a PET scan to be with that person, to support their friend. People avert their gaze as they pass by that terrible sign reading "Nuclear Medicine," imploring God to let them survive. But they should realize that this sign might someday be the one leading them to where they have to go.

It is truly a terrible place. Only patients, not those who come with them, walk through its doors. So Nasser remained outside the doors and I was left with the attendant—the sole person there who had any signs of life about her. She asked me to wait a second while she searched for my name on the appointment list. I didn't know how she could do that! Who would come here without a definite appointment? How could she talk to me in the first place, when the "me" that I knew is now broken into pieces? Which part of me will speak? Which one will wait? Which part enters and which exits?

I peered through the glass door behind me and saw Nasser absorbed in reading a magazine. I cursed him silently, then woefully took it back. The attendant told me that the nuclear material had just arrived from Syria. I didn't have the energy to feel proud or to think that the material that would help cure me was killing my fellow Syrians. It was like a Trojan horse the nations of the world left in order to destroy my country...

I found myself in a large room surrounded by five smaller rooms. One was for the injection, two were waiting rooms, another was for doing the scan, and the last was a washroom. No one else was there. It was eerily empty, and the doors were locked. One of the technicians came and gently guided me into a small corridor with a single chair. He said that he would check my blood sugar. He gave my finger a quick prick, inspecting my face, which showed no sign of pain. He was proud of his skill, but I didn't tell him that it did hurt quite a lot. I was saving my expressions of pain for the promise of suffering that awaited me. Ten minutes later, he injected me with a radioactive substance, concealed within a dark needle. After that, I was put in a little room that resembled one of Stalin's prison torture chambers, where people often lost the will to live. The nurse who led me there asked me not to talk or move so that the radioactive isotope could move through my body and not collect too much in any one spot. She told me to drink the glass of water that I had been asked to bring in with me.

This room was inside another room, which itself was in another room. It was silent and windowless, as narrow as a grave. Whoever enters will leave a changed person. It has two beds and two chairs. A woman who looked to be around sixty was lying on one bed, writhing in unbearable pain. Her suffering far exceeded mine, her body had reached the outer limits of what a body can take. There was a bareheaded forty-something Saudi man in a white silk *galabiya* sitting on one of the chairs. His phone rang and he answered reluctantly, ignoring the instructions not to. It seemed to me that the disease had robbed him of his logical abilities, and you could see the fear permanently etched onto his face. On the second bed lay a woman about my age, who was in better shape than the rest of us. She was wearing a black *abaya* and a black head cover. She had a newly done manicure with red polish—a sign of being cured, ignorant, or well adjusted! She said that she had Hodgkin's disease and had received the wrong treatment somewhere else. So she was doing chemo now for the second time and her hair had fallen out, again, for the second time. She had two young children who were with their father in the Emirates. "Thank God you don't have children. Children make it all so much harder!"

She handed me another glass of water, urging me to drink it too. "It's water from the holy spring at Zamzam." I told her I didn't want any. I was too preoccupied with the thought of the order of our deaths. Of us four, who would die first? First the woman in her sixties, then the Saudi man, then the Hodgkin's woman, and then me.

I urinated as I was asked to and went in for my scan. I wanted to be done with this whole drama quickly, even if it meant I would die sooner. I wanted to get out of this place and never see any of these people again.

Doing the scan was easier than preparing for it. They repeated it three times over the year I was in treatment. I came out like someone escaping from the gallows. Nasser was right there waiting for me at the door, holding my coat. I was once again filled with gratitude and buried my face in his chest, breathing in the smell of life with difficulty.

I lay down on the examination table. The doctor was nervous and I surrendered to him totally. This surrender gave me unexpected feelings of peace and power. Anxiety festers inside us even when we try not to panic, but what could the doctor possibly tell me that I didn't already know?

"You have cancer."

"I know."

"You are going to die."

"I know."

I'd thought about all of this over the past few days, and I rearranged what was left of my life with the worst-case scenarios in mind.

The doctor started passing his glove-encased hands over my nearly naked body, covered only with the blue tissue paper of a hospital gown. He touched my neck and suddenly stopped, shouting at his assistant: "I told you a thousand times, no bras for this examination."

I was taken aback by his unexplained edginess. I stood up mechanically, like a zombie, took off my bra in one second, threw it at the assistant, and lay back down. He calmed down and kept examining my ulcerated skin. I guessed that he was thinking about the possibility of other glands swelling, in my belly and thighs. He asked me in a low voice if I had experienced night sweats or fevers. I said no. He apologized for asking me to lie down because he knew my persistent cough made it uncomfortable.

I couldn't read any of his expressions as being positive or negative. After I put my clothes back on, he sat behind his little desk and I sat facing him. He didn't meet my gaze, but instead looked anxiously and distractedly at the blank computer screen in front of him. I was focused on his distractedness, and I realized how frightened doctors are of the gaze of a patient searching for signs of hope in their features.

Dr. Yaacoub's face was waxy and expressionless while he explained the nature of my disease. He stopped after every few sentences and asked if I had anyone with me. I told him my friend was with me. He had refused to let him come in before, but changed his mind after I told him I wasn't embarrassed to have him there and needed to have someone with me.

After Nasser came in, he continued talking about large b-cell lymphomas, whose causes are still unclear and which usually attack women in their thirties and forties. There are many factors that seem to cause them to grow, independent of genetics or viruses.

He also explained the treatment plan. Nasser took on the role of asking in-depth questions regarding the treat-ment. I followed their conversation neutrally, as if it were something that had nothing to do with me. I was reassured because I knew that Nasser would remember everything and repeat whatever I needed to know later.

Before this meeting, I had inwardly accepted the worst possible results. I only wanted to be finished with the crushing feeling in my chest. I wanted to breathe, move, and speak effortlessly like other people on God's earth do. At the end of the appointment, however, I increased my expectations and dared ask the doctor only one question, "Will I fully recover?"

He replied categorically, "Yes." And he added, "If you stick to the treatment."

Nasser exploded with joy upon hearing this. He held my hand that he knew so well by now, and then left the room at the doctor's request. The doctor told me, "You don't have any other tumors." I suddenly felt like I had made one more huge leap toward life. I asked him if the tumor had reached my bone marrow and he answered coldly but reassuringly, "It doesn't matter, you don't need to know all these details." His eyes were fixed at a point outside the window where you could see other hospital buildings that were under construction. He complained about this, saying, "All this construction is useless, lowering the price of the medicines is much more important!"

The only thing I cared about was my test results. I didn't care about his agitation, which had quickly regressed into a contemplative calm. He ran his gloved hand over his bald head and told me I could ask him anything else that was on my mind. However, I was too preoccupied with my own pain and suffering to have a conversation. I felt that I might speak to him at length some other day, perhaps after I was healed. Everything in my life was postponed, including my reckoning with life itself.

"Your bone marrow biopsy was clean," he informed me. "Your first treatment session is Tuesday." Then in English, he added, "Good luck!"

The doctor then left the small, dull blue-walled room. I believe I acted with extraordinary calm, allowing him to leave without the usual fuss.

He scheduled my first chemo treatment for four days later. His assistant came in to complete the procedures and fill me in on what to eat and drink. She also talked to me about the medicines I was prescribed.

"Will this treatment make my hair fall out?"

"Hmmm. Yes. The medicine will make your hair fall out, but it will grow back."

I spontaneously tugged at strands of my black hair and thought, "Will I live to see my hair again?" Then I let it fall back into place, like someone giving up something that wasn't theirs to begin with.

I lay back down in my bed, noticing it had clean, fresh sheets. It seemed that Nasser had hired a young Sri Lankan woman in her twenties to help look after me while I was getting better, until I could do things myself again. At that point, I could do nothing but say thanks.

I then decided that I had to come to an understanding with my tumor. Now that I knew it would be burnt up by the chemo, even if only partially, I started to wish for sleep. Outside the window, to the left side of my bed, was a large terrace that I could see through the iron grates. As soon as I turned my body, trying to find a suitable position to fall asleep, a gray dove flew by and landed on the terrace, making me smile. I made a mental note that at least, I could still do that.

But how awful is being ill? Disease has no morals and no mercy. It doesn't care about my youth, my body's freshness. It pays no mind to my powerful desire for life, joy, and accomplishments. Other peoples' experiences assaulted me, and I felt that all of them had imminently tragic endings. "Beauty always fades," al-Mutanabbi once said, and indeed mine seemed to have faded quickly. "The soil is filled with the beauty of all the captivating, doe-eyed women buried beneath it." I thought, my eyes will soon be food for earthworms, dust that fills neighborhoods, and then I imagined a quick succession of stories I had heard about the terminally ill, lepers throughout history, people who gather together and are burned outside of populated places. Soon my body will be like theirs. Then we have the story of the prophet Job. God replaced his true skin with old, decayed skin. But he was a prophet! I am merely human. I am weak. So why? Why?

In the hazy state between slumber and wakefulness, jumbled words reached my ears. It was as if someone was listening to a news report on more than one radio. Low voices and fragments of words: ISIL, Wiam Wahhab, Jumblatt, after a struggle with disease, regime aircraft have bombed the countryside north of Raqqa, patients in palliative care. Then the sounds of a guitar wafted out of the neighbors' house. "*You will come back home one day my son, defeated, with a broken conscience…*"

Why is this Abdel Halim song playing now? Why a song from the end of his life? Because he is like me of course—he was thin and weak… dark, pale, and desperate.

The sound of the guitar in my head didn't stop. But it didn't touch me either: the tumor had blocked everything beautiful out of my mind.

Among all these intense pictures was one of Dr. Yaacoub. His face seemed so familiar but it slipped from my memory like an egg white slips through your fingers.

My memory was exhausted. I lost interest in it, just like I'd lost interest in everything.

I fell asleep and woke up at around three in the afternoon. The image of Dr. Yaacoub came to me again. Nothing about him had changed except his physical size. Now I realized that I had known him as a young man twenty years ago. Was it merely a coincidence that I had been put in his care? Could it be a sign from the lucky star under which I'd been born? Perhaps this star would protect me on my path on this earth until I become nothing but the stuff of spirit.

The town of Genoa is in the north of Italy. In the south of the city there's a little village called Portofino that lies calmly on the edge of the sea. It could very well be the most beautiful place in the entire world. Hills covered in green, olive trees, vineyards, and castles owned by European noblemen are scattered on its foothills, some of which date back to the seventeenth and eighteenth centuries. Now they have been transformed into small hotels for tourists from all parts of the world. These castles look over a turquoise gulf, in which dozens of elegant little boats that belong to Portofino's fishing families bob with the rhythm of the waves. Fishing is the town's main profession. Next to these boats sway the majestic yachts of rich Arabs and Europeans. Beautiful, colorful naked bodies are sprawled out in magnificent elegance all along the golden coast, only a few meters away from the castles. The beaches of Cannes, Acapulco, and the Maldives can't compare. The Di Boticelli chateau is one of these magical castles that eventually became a twelve-room hotel. We used to spend a few days there every summer. My body first touched the sea in Portofino. And I first experienced my heart beating for someone else in Portofino as well.

After his master's degree, Baba went to work with one of his professors in a multinational engineering company based in Montreal, which took on major engineering projects from all over the world. That is where he met Mr. Boticelli, the CEO of Fiat Motors. The two of them developed a friendly relationship playing tennis together, and they both headed every evening to the court near the staff's living quarters. They would play together for about two hours. Before he left, Mr. Boticelli asked Baba to design a plan for the managers' recreation area at the Fiat company plant in Portofino. It was near the castle that he had inherited from his family. This man then hosted Baba's next vacation there. He completed his work and loved the place so much that he refused to take the design fee. Instead, he asked Mr. Boticelli to allow him to stay for a week every summer with his family in the castle. The man agreed immediately. This was one of the most wonderful events in our family history. My loveliest memories are of that beach—riding on fishermen's boats, grilling and peeling oysters like they did, throwing my little body into that delicious water, my fingers searching for a way to pull the sun down toward the horizon. Giorgio, the hotel manager's son who was two years older than me, was my best friend there. He used to take me on walks around the surrounding hillsides where the fragrance of peaches and plums filled the air. I sat behind him on his bicycle; we walked through the alleys of the quiet village; we climbed up to the top of the tower; we sat in the ancient church with its majestic Roman columns; we perched on the thresholds of ancient houses that smelled of the wine hidden in their cellars. Giorgio and I had our first kiss in the damp, dark basement of the hotel, its stone walls salt-stained in the shape of ghosts. I experienced extreme nausea after this kiss that extended well into the next day, along with a bellyache and diarrhea. To this day, I suffer from an aversion to kissing.

Nighttime revelers spend their evenings on the castle's terrace under the dome of the Portofino sky. Music plays and dancers meet on the dance floor. I always used to dance with Giorgio and would get upset when he danced with someone other than me, with one of the other young girls who were there with their families. Baba danced with Mama to Provençal rhythms and Shostakovich's second waltz.

At ten o'clock each Saturday evening, Dalida would mount the podium, carrying the whole world in her indomitable throat. She would open every nocturnal gathering with her most beautiful song, which I've played in the evening for many years, "I Found my Love in Portofino."

She stole the hearts of many people who came to this enchanted village from everywhere in the world, seeking joy in this ancient Roman corner of the Mediterranean. She would sing for two or three hours in Spanish, English, French, and Arabic. She greeted people and thanked them for coming with pure Egyptian expressions like, "Salaam, to you sir" or "A kiss, moon-face." All the Arabs who came would press her to end the evening with her customary Hebrew song, "Hava Negila." But as soon as the band played its opening chords, Baba's mood would always change. He would jump up in a hurry announcing, "The evening is over for us." We would get up with him and return to our room. Some of the other Arabs would get up with us, but the others would have been infected by the fervor of dancing and happiness. Baba responded, "The British in Egypt imprisoned her father because he was part of Mussolini's Il Duce group. Abdel Nasser expelled this group from the country, which is the only land they ever knew." Giorgio used to sympathize with us. He came around after I explained the Arab-Israel issue, and how this song specifically symbolized Israelis celebrating the occupation of Palestine. I did this all in our common language, which was French. I didn't know any Italian except a few words that I had learned traveling back and forth to Rome and Portofino and a number of common expressions that my uncle Faisal had taught me. He told me, "When you meet an Italian boy, you only need one or two expressions: '*Ti voglio bene*' and '*Ti amo tanto*'—I love you, and I love you so much!"

I ran into Dalida many times in the basement of the hotel, and I saw her on the beach one evening. She was wearing beach clothes, a green bikini, her thick blonde hair pulled up. Several golden bangles shone on her arm. She was lying on her belly on the sand, with no chair or umbrella, her kohl-rimmed eyes closed as if she were sleeping. I looked at her for a while and I loved her from that moment on. She was the epitome of beauty, of calm and simplicity. She looked very maternal with her impressively strong, taut body and her golden-hued skin. I still love her, I feel she is mine and a part of my world. When I heard the news of her suicide the following year I cried warm tears over her. At the time my cousin told me that I was crying for a slut, that God would let me burn in hell with her. The first time I cried over a death was that of the Qur'an reciter, Abdel Basit Abdel Samad, whose death no one else noticed. But I used to love him. I always turned on the television ahead of the 3 p.m. broadcast when he was reciting. "By the morning brightness and by the night when it covers with darkness." I wept when he said, "Therefore the orphan oppress not." But my cousin didn't know how much I loved him.

Despite Dalida's apparent strength and the wide world she created in nine languages, she was extremely delicate and had an attractive fragility about her. She loved like only a true Egyptian woman could, so it was no surprise that she ultimately met the same brave and tragic fate as Cleopatra.

Giorgio and I used to stare at the horizon from a wooden bench on the back of a boat in the little port. We listened to a local radio station called Nostalgie. Old French songs by Edith Piaf, Charles Aznavour, and Jacques Brel were playing when I said to Giorgio, "French has magical expressions like no other language, it is the most beautiful language!" He replied, with philosophical calm and closed eyes, crossing his right leg over his left knee, "You say that because you don't know Italian. I so wish that you knew my language! We Italians speak from here." He grabbed my right hand, put it on his liver, and repeated words while pressing my hand against his waist, "*Da qui, ici*, here." This was my first rhetoric lesson ever.

I also listened to conversations between a man and a woman, who were almost in their sixties, lying on their chairs looking out at the sea, a cloth umbrella above them.

It looked like intertwined trees, with tiny holes in the fabric that let the sun shine through. The saggy, freckled, sunburnt blonde woman, wearing a black bathing suit with white patterns on it, remarked, "Look how beautiful the sky is!" He peered at the bits peeping through the tiny holes above him. "Finality is more beautiful than the infinite. It's more familiar."

We skipped a few summers in Portofino and returned at the end of middle school, when Salma and Jude were in elementary school. By then, Giorgio had become a charming, muscular young man, bronzed by the sun and always bare-chested, with shiny black hair and white shorts. The most beautiful thick gold chain with the biggest cross I had ever seen hung around his neck. Rebuilding our memories was difficult since Baba didn't let me go out with Giorgio alone any more. I roamed the beach with my sisters—we swam, read, and listened to music. Portofino's houses were just as we had remembered them, as were the fishing boats and the bells of the ancient churches. Giorgio was always hanging out with the pretty girls, showing them around the alleys, taking them out at night to parties with amateur performers, singing rock and pop songs including "Hava Nagila". My family would always leave when that song began, and Giorgio would stay and dance with his pretty girls. That summer is when I first spotted Dr. Yaacoub, who was also staying at the Chateau Di Boticelli at the time. He was with a beautiful woman who looked like a little like my mother. They were together but each of them was alone. He followed the dancers from within his own bubble. I also chanced upon them walking through the village market and sitting on the beach. They didn't seem to be enjoying their time. In the square next to the town hall, there was a famous ice-cream shop called Paix that was mostly frequented by tourists. Yaacoub was in his twenties back then. Every evening, he bought a colorful ice-cream cone, sat on the bench across from the shop, and licked it like a tired child. His body was small and his long black hair hung down over his neck. He wore navy-blue shorts and a white cotton shirt that stuck to his bony chest. He also wore sandals with thick cotton sports socks. We thought it was strange that he wore socks with open-toed sandals. In any case, it's been a long time since then, and he looks much different now. But some faces impose themselves on your memory no matter the circumstances and history. Yaacoub's face is one of those.

Long ago, a small child with his parents hovered around Yaacoub and his ice-cream cone. His parents watched his friendly, affectionate movements encouragingly and didn't stop him. They were that breed of parents who believe that the world should happily accept whatever their child does. The child hovered around Yaacoub, who had made it clear he didn't want any company. The boy kept tugging at him. Yaacoub made sure that the parents were distracted and then he took the child's hand and bit it fiercely. Jude said, "Oops, he bites!" The screams of the two-year-old child filled the square and rang out all the way down to the nearby beach. That evening, Salma asked Mama, "Can you really wear socks with sandals?" Mama responded firmly, "No."

"But we saw a boy wearing socks with sandals!"

"Maybe he has some kind of fungus on his feet."

The next day, this small young man who seemed like a young boy was sitting alone on a rock on the beach, crying, his head in his hands. I went up to him. I knew he was an Arab and I tried to talk to him in Arabic, and asked "What's wrong? Are you tired?"

He lifted his head like Sisyphus and stared at my face, right into my eyes. I was unable to respond and he said to me, "Go." So I went. But I returned with two ice cream cones—one for him and one for me. This was my way of dealing with sad people. Baba would often reproach me for my empathic actions, "You aren't social services." I used to see this as a compensation for my family's feudal history, which, as I had seen in films, was said to have been cruel and unjust.

We licked our gelato on the beach. He was sitting, and I remained standing. I lifted my leg onto the rock he was sitting on, as proud of my initiative as an anonymous benefactor who makes a generous donation to an orphanage. We colluded in a silent friendship. We looked at each other and busily ate our ice cream. I searched for him after that incident but never found him.

When I told Salma on the phone that the boy with the gelato who wore socks with sandals was Dr. Yaacoub himself and that this was who would treat my cancer, she didn't believe it. She thought that I had been overwhelmed by the shock of trauma and disease. I assured her it was true and I could feel her anxiety. She said, "He's crazy." I responded, "Crazy people and eccentrics are the best ones to treat difficult diseases."

The day of my first chemotherapy session finally arrived. It was time to cross the threshold into a new world that I had started to yearn for, because it would truly be my own world, custom made to match my abilities. God had found me strong enough to undergo this trial, and I would never be the same again. From this day forward, my lump would burn away slowly. This would free up a place inside me, allowing me to breathe once more. The cells in my chest would open up. We often mindlessly tell people to "save their breath," without meaning it in the literal sense. But I came to learn the true meaning of that expression—surely as other people before me did as well. We have felt the agony of failed breathing, of the air that succeeds in reaching your heart, and the air that never makes its way there, slowly leading you down a path of destruction. It is in light of this that I spent more than a year, more than three hundred and sixty-five days, counting my breaths. When you breathe easily, you don't think about it, you don't think to thank the higher power above that you are able to do it.

My appointment was at eight thirty in the morning. Nasser slept over the night before without me having to ask him to. I put on my clothes. My jeans were loose and maybe two sizes too big for me now, but I wore them anyway—my narrow hipbones held them onto my body. I also put on a dark blue shirt. Nasser insisted that I bring a jacket even though it was the first of May. He also insisted we have cheese sandwiches and a cup of tea. How could he think about food when I was dying? Still we had a bite, then left.

The red liquid finally arrived after I'd received a number of injections of nutrients and medicines to prevent an allergic reaction. They came from a refrigerated dumbwaiter which everyone greeted with ceremony. They asked me my name about six times to be sure that they were giving the right chemo treatment to the right person. People around me were sitting in special chairs, some had friends or family with them and others were alone. There were also people lying down on beds in closed rooms. There were both Arabs and non-Arabs. A man brought food for his mother and sick wife, as if they were on a picnic. I slept for a little while on my chair, while Nasser watched the news on the screen in front of us. Jude's telephone call woke me. She wanted to check on me and tell me that they were all well. Who told her I was asking anyway? Or that I cared right now if anyone else in the world was well? I was not well. I felt very hot and then suddenly very cold. Nasser covered me, as I murmured apologies. He said, "Consider me a private nurse." I went back to sleep and woke when the technician came to change the solution. I found Nasser sleeping, holding the hand without the needle in it, his face covered by the book that he was reading, *The Geography of Diasporas*. I wished that I were fully healthy… I would have read that book in one evening. I could hear the voice of one man saying to another that Dr. Yaacoub was by far the best doctor and everyone who sees him will be cured. I felt hopeful again and went back to sleep for the remaining five hours of treatment.

A woman named Rania, also in her thirties, was lying on her treatment chair, which looked like the chairs at the dentist's office. She looked exhausted, but pretty nonetheless—tall and curvaceous, her jeans hugging her body tightly. She was wearing a gray Mickey Mouse sweatshirt and still had all her black hair; maybe the kind of chemo she was getting didn't make her hair fall out! Her cancer might be in her colon, for example. It did not appear to be her first session. The entire nursing staff here knew Rania.

The male technician bent over kindly and gently to insert the needle that would allow the medicine to flow into her body. At that moment, her husband entered in a fit of rage, shouting and disturbing our attempts to hold onto life in that room. "You love him! You love him! Ha! You come here to flirt…"

Rania shouted back, laughing, cursing, and crying as she said, "Get him out of here, I don't want to see him! He's crazy, he's an animal…"

They removed him while we all remained in a stupor. Rania stayed there all alone, sinking into her misery, not looking at anyone, not paying attention to anything. Her eyes remained glued to the television screen that was showing a documentary about polar bears. The young technician with the neatly trimmed black beard, dark eyes, and soft perfect haircut returned. He changed her IV bag. They didn't speak. He plumped her yellow hand with the needle in it. She didn't bat an eyelid as he stole a kiss from the palm of her hand. I felt for her completely. She was traveling through another universe that had nothing at all to do with this existence. Chemo is harsher than anything else; no human can bear it. It kills your heart before it kills your cells.

I returned home totally exhausted, waiting for my tumor to shrink. I could feel the air in my veins and my cells, but I knew it wasn't going to shrink today. I drank a lot of water as they'd told me to, and I saw my urine was red when I used the bathroom. I took the cortisone pills, but only time would make the metallic taste in my mouth disappear. I didn't fall apart as people said I would, in fact I sat up on the sofa in the living room. Nasser put a pillow under my feet and I picked up a book about Monet, Gauguin, and Van Gogh. Tammy, the maid, fed me a little chicken and rice. Nasser seemed optimistic. He said that some bodies are able to find a way to make peace with chemo and can withstand it without breaking down.

Later, I fell asleep, and woke up in the evening, nauseated. I needed to empty everything in my stomach. The location of the tumor started to prickle. I imagined that the red liquid had begun to burn the tumor and that I would mimic its movements as it started fighting with the malignant cells. I felt this burn. It was like my body was trying to escape through my skin—or maybe it was my soul that was escaping my body.

I slept for three days straight. Nasser kept giving me cortisone pills all the while, without me even noticing. I woke up hungry and weak. I didn't ask about anyone or even where Nasser was when he wasn't with me. I thought I saw rain but it wasn't the season for rain. I thought that seeing it was an effect of the chemo, but it turned out that it actually was raining in May. I spotted Nasser out on the balcony. He had put the two buckets from the bathroom outside and was watching raindrops collect inside them. He said, "Maybe we can use this water to clean with." I wanted to tell him he was crazy and should get out of my house! I'm dying and he's giving me advice about collecting buckets of water? But I didn't have the energy to argue with him. I wanted to be alone.

Two weeks later, my hair started falling out. I had been waiting for it to fall out since day one. From the day I was diagnosed, in fact. It was the definitive sign of my struggle with cancer. One big chunk after another fell into my hand. Whenever I pulled on my hair, it would fall out from the root. It took a long time to clear the front of my head. I put on a small, dark blue scarf, and whatever hair was left hung out of the back. I looked like a foreign tourist. This is how I went to Dr. Yaacoub so I could fix an appointment for my follow-up MRI. I sat in front of him as he looked impassively at my wrapped head and my face that had crossed over the threshold into misery. He indulged me with an incomprehensible laugh that stayed in my heart with the bitterness of a wound still gaping open to this day. Perhaps my scarf made him laugh, and he was mocking me. Gazing into his cowardly eyes that seemed to have no human feeling in them, I felt a sense of sorrow. I wanted to remind him of that day when those same two eyes of his were crying in Portofino. I wanted to remind him how he had brutally bitten a little child, and that I had bought him a gelato. But I left him, temporarily. Inside me all I could think about were Brian Mills's words in the film *Taken*: "I'll find you, and I'll kill you."

One more step toward God. Though I never was that far from Him, even when things in life tried to steer me away. He was always there, somewhere, deep inside me. My own private relationship with God made me ashamed of myself when I angered Him. But aren't real shame and silent anger enough? Why did He choose me for all this suffering? I know what people will tell me—they'll say that it's His punishment, a way to atone for sins, a random choice, or a test.

Every so often I would ask, "Why me? I'm not a prophet, or a holy person, or a Sufi. I am just a weak human being. I want to know why?"

"Why, Nasser, why me?"

Nasser replied, "The cloud doesn't ask why it's heavy and weighted down with water. It carries its burden voluntarily and travels with it gratefully. Isn't water an integral part of what it is? Human origins lie in pain, that's how God made us. The glorious green meadow doesn't resist the wind when it pulls at its grass, and perhaps even uproots its flowers. Instead it moves with it, in total submission. Birds don't curse the frosts, they simply leave for warmer climates—even if their journeys turn out to be adventures. We too are on a journey, *habibti*, my love, and I have total gratitude for that. Responses to your questions will come on their own, just like the meadows discover the mystery of the wind in the spring, and the clouds discover the secret of their extra load when it falls on the earth and returns to the sky, bright, light, and young again. Miracles can happen at any moment and we have to listen closely for traces of them. Your early diagnosis is a miracle. That you wake up every morning is a miracle. Your beautiful face is a miracle. Us meeting here in Amman and not Aleppo is a miracle. Miracles need time to take hold, and time demands our patience. I don't pray the required five times a day regularly, I drink a forbidden glass of wine from time to time, but I have a substantial relationship with God. No one can judge your relationship with God, except your own conscience. My daily miracle is waking up every morning, having a shower, and preparing to meet God. It doesn't matter which doctrine or path I follow. I talk to Him, explain things, complain, and I also thank Him. That is my sacred moment. I won't let anything in the world change this time or interfere with it. Afterwards I go back to my life, without caring about success or failure, meetings or awards, degrees or business cards that I have received. All those things are trivial so long as I've had my secret hour that day."

Nasser took me back in time to basic issues I thought I'd finished dealing with long ago, issues of building my relationship with God, the sacred, and existence. I've studied all the rituals of the world and their relationship with the sun, wind, stones, human beings, and magical powers. And here I was now, listening to him like a schoolgirl who doesn't know where her lesson is to begin. I needed to listen to my own words but I needed to hear them uttered by someone else. I needed to analyze all of the ideas that have molded me into the person that I am in this laboratory of bitter experiences. I need to regain my faith in the soul of the world so that I can truly resist this disease. Only then will I be able to make my existence about progress rather than retreat. But couldn't this have happened without so much pain and suffering? And what is the point of all this progress if it may just culminate in my death? I wished I were healthy enough to discuss all these ideas with him, to tell him about Buddha, Freud, Jung, and Levi-Strauss. I would teach him that geography is held captive to false expectations, that culture is an invention that rivals divine desires. But I am exhausted. How could I possibly find the strength to talk when just listening leaves me completely drained? He tells me to be patient, but to me patience is just selling time and getting pain in return without muttering any words of complaint.

Nasser talked, but I was on a different level of existence, a level of haggard breathing. I was jealous of him. He had plenty of space to breathe, to organize his life and his plans with God, while in my case, my suffering prevented me even from dreaming. I didn't have time to plan for tomorrows; I was closer to not having a tomorrow at all.

He listened to the news but only the summarized version. He then proceeded to give me a summary of the summary while handing me my daily glass of lemon juice—"Lemons bolster your immunity and fight the tumor."

He didn't want to burden me with news of the war but he also insisted that I stay connected to the world and to what was happening around me, so that I didn't see myself as joining the ranks of the missing. He wore his gray pajamas with a red striped robe settled in close to me on the left side of the bed. He then shifted a bit further away; I could barely take in any oxygen let alone handle any additional weight, even that of a lover. He talked to me about my country, about victories and betrayals, as if he were talking to someone who didn't have cancer. I wanted him to stop. His voice irritated me, and none of what he was saying was of any importance to me. The only thing I wanted to hear from him was that I would recover. I wanted him to tell me stories of sick people who had been cured and who had come back to life. Everything else that was happening in the world was utterly unimportant and was only happening because of arrogance and ignorance. Instead of making weapons, buying them, killing us with them, they should invent medicines that ease suffering and eradicate disease. I wanted to hear myself talk now—not sit there passively listening to Nasser. I wanted to hear my own words, depicting my own reality, not those of the international envoys to Syria. Talking during a countdown to delay the inevitable is a different kind of talking. The speaker knows the true weight of things and the difference between what is trivial and what is important and real. The final truth is that your body is your homeland and the greatest treason is for it to betray itself.

I begged Nasser to return to his own work and let me go to my chemotherapy sessions alone. He refused point blank. Eight sessions, three weeks apart and he did not miss one. He would spend the night at my house and we would set off for the hospital at eight thirty in the morning, coming back home around one. But I stuck to my demand that he not come with me to the biweekly MRIs that would show the shrinking of the tumor. After each one, I met with Dr. Yaacoub, who would read the results and revise the treatment plan in light of them. I told him that I wanted to be alone, to confront my new world, to learn its contours, to get to know other people who were a part of it. Nasser complied with this request. In fact, it was a false list of reasons. I really did want him to be with me every step of the way. But I didn't want to lose his patience or his love. I didn't want him to live a life that wasn't destined to be his. This suffering was my destiny, and it wasn't right to force him to participate in a life of full of mutilation, tears, and walking corpses.

I sat in the waiting room of the outpatient clinic, looking for some sign of hope in the faces that surrounded me. I rarely found it. Instead, all I found was pure gloom. I stared at the gray walls that were all alike, except the one with an electrical panel with black and red buttons behind the receptionist. I decided to make it a point of reference for my life. I told myself that when I come to the next visit, God willing, and look at this panel, I'll be feeling better, my tumors will be smaller, and my breathing will be deeper. A day will come when I'll look at it like lovers look back at a book filled with old memories, unable to come across it and not leaf through its pages nostalgically. I'll tell it that I have reached the finish line, and I am completely healed. The place has that ashy odor that sick people grow used to. It's a mixture of medicines and disinfectants, and hand-sanitizing gel, whose scent would soon become my favorite. Television screens hanging on the walls were all tuned to Qur'an channels, broadcasting the *"Anaam Sura"* supplications, and healing prayers. There were copies of the Qur'an on the table. We all need prayers, we all need to invoke God as some sort of reassurance. But the entire scene makes us feel like martyrs on the brink of death, attending our own funerals. The only things saving us are the occasional smiles of the nurses and attendants, who wear a little makeup on their fresh, youthful faces, and brightly colored scarves on their heads. They are the signs of life we are searching for while we are filled with such profound sorrow.

At first you feel like you are the only sick one. But you soon realize it isn't true. When you sit here, you see that the whole world has cancer. There is always someone worse off than you. Pallid, sickly faces, bald heads, no eyelashes or eyebrows—this is the world which Joumane

Badran now belongs to. It is a world called "Queues of Suffering." We all sit here waiting for the Savior.

When I have the time to pay more attention to him, I find that the Savior, our doctor, also needs a savior. He is hiding behind his masks, with the fragility of a Henry Miller hero. His skin is pale white, round eyeglasses circle his equally round eyes and he has a shaved head. When he first entered this line of work, he developed a certain sympathy with his patients and tried to be their equal. He still tries to maintain this. But we really dislike sympathy, even when it is genuine. He wears an untrimmed black beard a few centimeters long, from his neck to his up-turned mustache. Two small hands poke out of his wide sleeves—I only once spotted them outside of their thick plastic gloves. His wide fingers and neglected fingernails aren't elegant, but they signified a blessing to us because they could work miracles. His unconventional appearance makes him seem more like a spiritual healer than a doctor, as do the seriousness of the cases he treats. The secrets of the disease have brought him closer to the world of death than life. He finds his way into the minds of people in their final days: he discovers their bodies; he hears their last confessions; their final, most sincere words. He is the final threshold to cross before death, or he is the threshold leading toward life. This contradiction is what gives him his magic—black and white, life and death, hardness and fragility, childhood and old age, stability and instability, cowardice and courage.

Every time I see the Savior's face, it is worried and afraid for the patient whose suffering may hasten their demise. No one's strength rivals a cancer patient's. The

Savior cried a lot with his patients, cried until his heart broke and he had to accept the difference between his fate and the fate of others. Now, he doesn't leave room for the more difficult questions, maintaining his needed distance from his patients' hearts, avoiding making his way directly into the brutality of their final days. He isn't a god; he's not even a prophet. He isn't a leader of the people, with crowds deferring to his overwhelming paternalism. An aura of suspicion surrounds him, his cleverness is exaggerated, and his moods are terrible. But if you were forced to put your life in someone's hands, you'd place it in his without a second thought.

My hair kept falling out and in such annoying ways that Nasser proposed that we finish with it once and for all. I followed him to the bathroom as he'd told me to, like a child resigned to obeying a parent's orders. I stood facing the mirror in front of him. I was wearing only a cotton t-shirt that hung down over my suddenly very thin upper thighs. In the mirror I could see him busily plugging the electric clippers into the wall socket. The machine purred to life and he skillfully passed it over my head, front to back, side to side. He sheared my long, shiny black hair; clumps of it fell onto the pieces of newspaper he'd spread out on the floor and tiny bits of it scattered all around me like fragments of dreams that time had gotten the best of. As he relentlessly ploughed my head with the clippers, two hot tears remained suspended on my eyelashes. I took a moment to ponder: How did this strange man get into my bathroom? Why I am I standing in front of him half-naked? How is he the only one who has seen me in a way that even my mother didn't on the day I was born? He saw me completely bald, in a way I never expected to see myself. But this thought was quickly banished from my mind, along with many others that had been taboo not so long ago. I no longer cared about anything. Being freed from such ideas was the best thing about being sick. I was liberated from everything—from people and customs, time and place, right and wrong, even from nostalgia. If the experience goes well and you are cured, you will always feel less intense sadness, regret, guilt, repentance, desire, or joy.

I snapped out of it and realized that I was still with Nasser. I only had him, and I didn't want anyone else. I tried to recognize myself in the mirror. He was behind me looking at the new image of myself in the mirror. My features were all faded and white, like clouds covering a blue sky. Only Nasser's yellow shirt and my brown eyes glinted with a light that reached the mirror's glass, and then wilted, but resisted being totally extinguished. I rubbed my hand on my bald head and felt small bits of soft hair collect on my palm. Nasser did the same thing while staring into my eyes in the mirror. The palm of his hand was large enough that it encircled my head, making it seem even smaller. His hand slipped down to my chin and embraced my entire face. He pressed hard against my cheekbones and what was left of the flesh there reacted to the touch of his finger by twitching painfully.

"From the moment I saw this face, so violent in its innocence, I hoped I could hold it in my hands and it would be mine." He moved his hands gently around my waist and started kissing my neck passionately. Then he rested his forehead on my shoulders and kept kissing everything in the path of his lips. He was able to turn my moment of humiliation as a woman into a dramatic high. He whispered to me, "Joumane, Joumane, I can't stand your beauty, it's wounding me! I've finally found the meaning of carnal desires. You have something primal about you that has aroused my slumbering desires. It's the carnality of the Earth Mother, Gaia."

Nasser was talking about desires for the first time since I'd known him. I had thought a lot about him, in the way women often wonder about men. I wondered what desires lurked behind his serious appearance and his elegant prudishness. But such answers usually come at the wrong time. I didn't know if he was saying this now to be supportive and human, or as a disclosure that comes at a moment of truth. At this moment of intense struggle with my femininity, I felt his explosive masculinity. But despite all this, I gave him the little I had left of myself. I don't know myself if this was an automatic reaction, or one done out of habit, despair, or failure. But I needed his hands, his working glands, his normal breathing, his normal, agile limbs, his smooth, healthy, beautifully rosy skin. I needed his body's life. He gave it to me in special moments that knew no human misery. I stuck my exhausted, sick back onto his powerful, sound, healthy chest. His depths were shaken by a desire that most people will never know. Even in the flush of lust, we were driven by the fever of dedication, tenderness, and friendship.

The first chemo treatment sessions passed quickly. Then they started slowing down. It was as annoying as an out-dated train puttering through the impoverished country-side. The medicine was stronger, and my immunity had weakened to a minimum. I turned a wan yellow color and lost the rest of my hair—hair I wanted and didn't want. My mouth ulcers persisted, as did my dry throat. My hands turned blue as a result of the technicians trying to find veins that were too empty to give blood. It was like a scene in a movie. If my grandmother had seen me, she would have regretted the daily lectures she tortured me with: "Straighten your back, sit up straight, adjust your shoulders, cross your legs, pull your skirt down, stay out of the sun." Oh Nana, what good are corsets, high heels, and face creams, if I'm going to end up looking like I do now?

The doctor studied the lab reports in front of him, deciding the next dose. What, however, do the doctors, nurses, and orderlies care? They all go back home to their houses, their mothers, and their children after their shifts at the hospital are over. I, on the other hand, am going back to the bitter cortisone pills and water that the chemotherapy makes taste like metal. Chemo changes everything, the properties of everything in the world—not just how things taste. I sleep for days on end and urinate the R-CHOP chemotherapy cocktail I have been injected with. I have diarrhea, then I am constipated. My head feels like something even the devil wouldn't touch! Once, my eyes stopped seeing things clearly and Nasser came in only to find me trying to breathe like a half-slaughtered sheep waiting for the mercy of a sharper knife. I pleaded to be able to surrender to sleep. Surrender is not a negative word. It has positive connotations here since it means I will slip blissfully into a fourth dimension of existence. I can totally give up my body, dreams, and aspirations. Before this I would just keep suffering, suffering, and suffering… I suffered so much that the pain couldn't get any worse if it wanted to. It had reached its peak, and I thought, I will have freed myself from all this soon. My body will become a spirit separated from the world, time, and place, soaring in the skies of hope at a better time in the future. I didn't know if I was in bed or a coffin. I found myself at home, in Raqqa, in the Spanish-style bedroom with its two cherry-wood beds, made up with Cannon sheets from America, and woolen covers. Fadda, the maid, used to shake out those covers, along with the brown pashmina blankets embroidered with beige flowers. I could feel Mama's hands tucking me in.

Orange Dreams

She was perhaps the most stunning cancer patient you could ever meet. The bright smile on her tiny mouth could transform even the waiting room of a funeral home into a space of hope. She showed none of the signs of exhaustion or depression that cancer patients usually do. Her almond brown eyes seemed not to harbor that puzzling question you so often see reflected in the faces of cancer patients: "Why me?"

Hanoi was neither short nor tall, neither thin nor fat. She had a beautiful body. The disease seemed not to have physically affected her much. Her taut skin was tinged with gold, and her bald head glowed, practically emitting light. Her almond brown eyes looked typically Vietnamese. She wore a series of small, shiny earrings and a tattoo of a dragon slithered up to the middle of her neck, making its way from her collarbone to her left ear. She looked more like a hippie artist than a cancer patient. I wondered how this young woman had enough energy to look so beautiful while hovering over the edge of the abyss, while I was barely able to put on my clothes. Hers was the beauty of life surviving in a dramatic storm.

For the first time since I found out about my illness, I was curious about something—about Hanoi. Simply gazing at her gave me hope that there might be some light at the end of the tunnel. I really wanted to ask her about the minutiae of her life: Was she better? Totally recovered? How many doses of chemo did she take? How many radiation treatments did she undergo?

She got up to talk to the office coordinator working at the reception desk. She'd hiked up her white sports shirt, exposing a large swathe of skin between it and the waist of the loose-fitting gray trousers slung down around her hips. I noticed long lines around her belly button that resembled the traces of butterfly wings.

When she finished her inquiries, the only empty seat she found was the one directly across from me. She asked me if anyone was sitting there—unlike most patients here who just sit down in any open spot, dumbstruck with fear, indifferent to anything but the number of breaths they have left to take. I nodded at her to sit down. When I heard her speak Arabic with a foreign accent, I wanted to talk to her even more. So I blurted out, "That's a great tattoo!"

Her hand touched her neck.

"No, lower down… I meant the butterfly."

She raised her eyebrows as if angry. Then she paused, and unabashedly rolled her cotton trousers down a bit to reveal something incredible—a tattoo of a Kalashnikov! I put my hand over my mouth to stifle my surprised gasp.

She burst out laughing, contravening the conventions of the place. Everyone now looked over at us with misery and disapproval.

"Are you Arab?" I asked.

"American," she replied.

"So you should have an M-16, not a Kalashnikov." She raised her eyebrows again and we burst into loud laughter together.

"It's a Chinese-developed Kalashnikov called a Norinco. I'm half-Arab, half-American."

Hanoi, or Haniyah as everyone seemed to call her, was the only daughter of comrade Ayman Thabit, a Palestinian communist party cadre who supported the Palestine Liberation Organization from the time it was founded in the 1960s. In 1970, Thabit joined the party's military wing and was sent on a training mission to Vietnam, where the South was fighting a war of liberation against the Americans. At that time, Chinese-backed communist military cadres from all over the world had gathered in training camps there to witness live guerilla warfare in the mountains and jungles, equipped with Chinese-made Norinco-56 rifles, whose technology was developed from Russian Kalashnikovs.

Comrade Yan, her mother, drove a truck full of soldiers and loaded with blankets, rice, and strips of dried fish, delivering them to the revolutionaries in the south who were resisting the American puppet President Diem's regime. She had to stop north of the Ben Hai River, which separated the rival capitals of Hanoi in the north and Saigon in the south. Yan had to go off-road and hide in the jungle, protected by the abundance of green fig and cacao branches to shelter herself in the darkness. Bombs fell from the sky, releasing napalm onto Ho Chi Minh Road where Ayman Thabit was training along with his comrades for armed confrontations. After the raid eased up, Yan groped at her own tiny body. Her pale face was hidden by a straw hat and the corners of her black eyes were coated with dirt. Reassured that she was not wounded, she started evacuating those who were. She found Ayman hiding in a hollow tree trunk, with a shrapnel wound in his chest. She drove her truck to the revolutionary barracks all the while dodging American fire, as if she were moving a piece on a chessboard. Comrade Ayman was wailing in pain the whole way, his warm blood pouring out onto her shoulder.

Over a million people perished in that war, but Comrade Yan and Comrade Ayman survived and fell in love. They got married after the final battle to liberate Vietnam in 1973 and went back to live in the Gaza Strip.

Hanoi was born a year later. She was named after the victorious capital, and Ayman Thabit became known as Comrade Abu Haniyah. Abu Haniyah later became a renowned Palestinian name throughout the world's communist leadership. He would later be killed by friendly fire during the first Palestinian Intifada.

After the collapse of the Soviet Union, Yan and her daughter Hanoi returned to Vietnam, but the only place she felt truly welcomed her was San Francisco. So she decided to go there and open a little restaurant in the city's Chinatown.

As a result, Hanoi grew up in San Francisco. She enrolled in art school, specialized in ethnic dance, and got her
American citizenship. This freed her from the anxiety that
used to plague her whenever she thought about visiting
the Middle East to find her roots. She eventually decided
to settle in Amman and opened up a dance school to teach
salsa and hip-hop. The studio was located in the basement
of the Orchid Mall in the Sweifieh neighborhood. She
called it Norinco after the family weapon. When she was
diagnosed with lymphoma, the Palestinian Authority covered her expenses for treatment at the center, because she
was the daughter of a great fighter. Dr. Yaacoub supervised
her treatment and she later became his lover. She told me
confidently that she'd fallen ill because of her inter-gener-
ational exhaustion, having lived through so many painful
transformations. Her transformations were parallel to that
of the Kalashnikov—first a weapon of liberation, then a
logo on a vodka bottle, and finally a little tattoo under a
bellybutton.

The village of Lydda fell into the hands of Zionist para-
military gangs on Friday, July 9, 1948. Gunmen broke into
people's houses with the butts of their rifles and expelled the
occupants from them, later rounding them up in Nuwair
Square in the center of the town. The square was packed
with people from Lydda, along with refugees who'd fled
there from other regions in Palestine, searching for safety.
People thought that it was just another campaign to search
for weapons and fighters, for they'd grown used to them and
they all believed they'd be able go back home afterwards.

But this time it was different. The gunmen started pushing people out of the city. They expelled them rudely, hurling curses and swears every which way. Ramadan had started and people were fasting, so it was not long before they felt parched, the July sun beating down on their bodies, their hearts burning with desperation. The path they were made to follow was shaded by groves of orange trees that bade them farewell forever. Never again would they see these orange trees except in the pictures that revolution-aries, fighters, and activists would later hang on their walls. Never again would they taste their sweetness except when they were exported by Israel, to the places throughout the world where they were exiled. Then they'd have to buy each individual orange, with the blue "Jaffa" logos stuck on them, for as much as two dollars.

Yaacoub paused in one of the orchards where he'd spotted a well. He hastened to let his thirsty children drink from it. He opened the tap to fill a bucket sitting beside it. When he returned, overjoyed, he couldn't find his three-year-old son, Yusuf. He searched for him until evening fell, refusing to leave until the English mounted cavalry found him, threw him out, and his son Yusuf was lost forever.

Fatigue had exhausted the body of the small child; Yusuf had fallen asleep in the brush under a tree, and when he woke, he couldn't find his family. He cried for a long time. He was wracked by hunger, thirst, and exhaustion, so it was not long before he fell back asleep.

Another family, the Sharifs, had been recently forced out of their home in East Jerusalem and were fleeing to Ramallah. On the way, they stopped to break their Ramadan fast and found this little boy on the verge of perishing. Yusuf only knew his name and his father Yaacoub's name. They searched but couldn't find his family anywhere near where they'd found him, so they took him with them. From that moment on his name was Yusuf al-Sharif.

On April 28 of that same year, the family of Alif Alameddine had gathered around the lunch table at the house of his great-grandfather Alameddine Nashif, the owner of the most famous weapons repair shop in the old Yafa market. Because of his special relationship with the rebels, he stood in opposition to the British Mandate and was arrested over and over again by the authorities for his beliefs.

The doors of this house opened out onto ancient arched alleyways, and through its slatted shutters, you could see the windows open out onto the sea. Melancholy dominated the features of everyone in the family. None of the news from Palestine boded well. Zionist gangs were raiding towns and villages, uprooting people from their homes, and throwing them out onto the roads. Fishing was forbidden and Hajj Alif could barely manage to put food on the table. Once the British Mandate government established Tel Aviv as a major port, the sea in Yafa totally changed. The oldest ports in the Mediterranean were neglected, and vessels had to be anchored far from the pavement, waiting for ferries that would carry away boxes of oranges and return with all sorts of other goods.

The damp sea air, heavy with the scents of spring, wafted freely through the dining-room windows. Before the family had finished lunch, Uncle Samih burst into the room in total panic and told his brother Alif that Yafa was besieged from all sides. All the neighborhoods in the city were suffering from violence; Jewish sniper fire was raining down on its citizens. They had to flee right away.

When Hajj Alif Alameddine's family reached the coast by the port with the few belongings and life savings that they'd prepared ahead of time, they found thousands of other people from Yafa there as well, all waiting for boats that would take them away. From that moment on, they were considered refugees. It was their good fortune to be taken on one of the ferries to a Greek boat called the *Dolores*, which was anchored near the port and would take them to Beirut, along with the language of the sea and their memories of orange groves.

Had Hajj Alif thought about it for longer, he might have realized that the possibilities offered by leaving weren't much better than those he would have faced if he'd stayed put. His wife's health, worsening with his successive arrests, quickly deteriorated. Her heart weakened with the birth of the last of her children, Nabila, and she wasn't able to complete the journey. After arriving in the Port of Beirut, the Lebanese authorities wouldn't allow them to disembark for three days. That whole time the tiny infant Nabila was nestled in her dead mother's arms, sucking at her breast whose milk had dried up in her cold veins. She inhaled the scents, which she would be deprived of her entire life, just as she was deprived of her city and her house. Time did not allow her to keep any image of these things in her memory.

Yusuf was ultimately adopted by the Sharif family and they settled in Amman, where the Alameddine family also took up residence. Nabila was there too—her father's new wife raised her as her own—and everyone started a new life that was nothing at all like their lives in Palestine.

Yusuf always knew that the Sharif family had taken him in as a child, and the more he grew, the less important the "Where did I come from?" question became. It could have one day turned him into a great fighter, but it could have equally made him into a martyr or a criminal.

He joined the different resistance factions. He started missing school, being absent from home, he took up arms and joined the military wings of different parties. But his family stood up to his adolescent defiance and paid him a special kind of attention. They moved out of the camp. They changed houses, schools, and neighborhoods. They transformed him into someone else, someone who did nothing but devote himself to his studies. He finished secondary school with honors and won an UNRWA scholarship to study mechanical engineering at the University of Hanover in Germany.

Hajj Alif Alameddine died prematurely. After he passed away, his children lived in comfort because they'd gone back to their old business in the arms trade. Unlike their father, however, they used to sell weapons indiscriminately to everyone—rival Palestinian factions, Jews, and Zionists. This is how they built their own private empire and expanded outside the Jabal Amman area, westward.

Nabila started attending philosophy courses in the School of Arts at the University of Jordan. When Yusuf Sharif came home from Germany on one of his holidays, he met her at one of her girlfriend's weddings, and they fell in love. They married, and she accompanied him back to

Hanover. Nabila saw a safe and good future in Yusuf, far from the dirty business of arms trading that her brothers were drowning in, betraying the history of their grandfather and father, who had spent his final years crushed and defeated in order to maintain his image as a Palestinian freedom fighter who battled both the British and the Zionists. Encouraged by her husband, Nabila broke all ties with that reality, one she did not want her children to be associated with either directly or indirectly. Yusuf, however, discovered something there. It was the fragrance of a place he'd only ever had a whiff of but knew he could recreate with her. It was in her womb that this creation occurred, and they loved their child with all their hearts. It was thus that Yaacoub was born in 1970—the only name, and indeed only idea, that remained of his past.

Yusuf and his little family came back to Amman. He had an unusual specialty as a geothermal engineer, dealing with the energy generated deep inside the earth. But his short-lived and distant revolutionary past came back to haunt him. It deprived him of promotions he was entitled to, and prevented him from being able to lead projects that he himself had designed. When he decided to return to Germany he discovered he was subject to a travel ban. Yusuf's sedimented grief resulted in a heart attack that killed him.

Yusuf left Nabila and Yaacoub a project in his name that yielded a small financial remuneration, which he'd invested by buying a small apartment that was meant for Yaacoub in the future. Yaacoub was destined to be an only child because doctors had deemed another pregnancy too dangerous.

Nabila never rebuilt her relationship with her family, first and foremost out of loyalty to Yusuf. She decided to live her life on her own. She had earned a master's degree in philosophy and applied to work at the German embassy in Amman. She rented out the extra apartment, and the money she made all went to the College de la Salle Frères, where she insisted that Yaacoub study despite its expensive tuition fees. She constantly fought off the feelings of weakness that plagued her. She always had Yaacoub's future in her sights. He was the genius child who could triumph over his father's tragic death and reconcile her with the world again. When Nabila's difficulty making ends meet grew too stressful, she signed a contract with an emerging Gulf magazine to write a column offering to solve readers' emotional problems. When Yaacoub was growing up, Nabila believed he would never learn that she had written these articles. But the boy was sure that the letters filling his mother's mailbox weren't all from school friends in Germany, as she claimed. He knew that they were from those people she was selling illusions to, in order to make his dreams come true. So he never opened her letters, and he never asked her about anything that might have resulted in a burden he would ultimately have to carry.

Yaacoub inherited the very question his father used to ask, but to comply with his mother's wishes, he stopped searching for the answer. Nabila decided there would be no activities, no visits, no trips, and of course no political parties. His life revolved around his studies and his studies alone. This is how he learned French and German in addition to English. She used to take him to language centers in their little Volkswagen Beetle, waiting outside for his classes to end and then taking him back home. Before long Yaacoub was able to read Voltaire in French and Goethe in German, which practically became his mother tongue. He found himself between the lines of *The Sorrows of Young Werther* and wept bitter tears, climbed up to the roof and decided to walk just to the edge and drop. But when he saw people going about their lives in the street below, he took a step back. He knew from that moment onward that he was a cowardly child.

After the aborted suicide attempt, which he kept to himself, Yaacoub realized that he was happy with his superiority and genius, the admiring looks that he saw in his teachers' eyes, and the jealousy that he could sense in his classmates. He decided to emphasize this difference and thus devoted every bit of his youthful energy to becoming a cultured overachiever. As his difference became accentuated, his appearance started to change. His body became so thin and delicate it could be folded in half. The light in his eyes burned brighter, and he grew his thick black hair long, always gathering it up in a curled ponytail. The hair of his beard was long and soft. He looked like the colorful images of Jesus Christ in Western iconography. Despite his constant concern for his mother and their common aspirations, he knew there was a dark place within himself that light could never reach, an emptiness that could never be filled, an emptiness of terrifying origins. He felt different from his father's adoptive family, who were simple and uneducated people. He felt that he must be a descendent of geniuses. Perhaps his family was not even originally Arab, but British or Jewish—people who came from somewhere else. All these possibilities paved the path for his personal torment.

Yaacoub was able to rise above the torment, however, by studying medicine at the University of Jordan. He later won a scholarship to specialize at UCLA. Nabila had long been preparing herself for the day when her only son would leave her to start his own life. She knew she wouldn't have the same place in it that she previously had. But she would never let her own wishes, her loneliness, or her sadness stand in his way. She didn't prevent him from traveling abroad; she didn't beg him to stay with her. She didn't even ask him how he could leave for so long. He left her without a companion in this cruel world. How could she spend her evenings without the sound of his voice in the house, without drinking milk together in the morning and coffee in the evening? These moments constituted their ritual, whatever the circumstances, no matter what else was happening. Just as Yusuf had gotten used to not asking Nabila certain questions, it was also alone that he suffered through the sorrow of embarking on his journey. He was leaving the nest that had protected him through every hardship he'd ever faced. He felt that he was ungrateful and selfish, especially since he knew how broken up his mother was about his leaving, but he dared not even entertain the thought out loud. So instead, he bound himself to a vow that he would finish his specialization as quickly as possible, and then nothing would stand in his way to return.

After Yaacoub left, Nabila felt like an orphan, a widow, and a bereaved mother all at once for the first time in her life. She couldn't find any solace for her grief and loneliness;

even imagining the bright future awaiting her son would not do the trick. Her mornings felt very difficult and her evenings lonely and heavy. She had no desire to go to work and when she'd go, she'd lose the desire to come back home. She joined a reading group and started to attend their weekly meetings. This helped her manage her loneliness. One week, the group decided to host the Iraqi writer Karim Saad so he would talk to them about his latest novel, *The Amulets of Babel*, which had won a prize at the Amman Book Fair.

One calm, late summer evening—those evenings when you felt the need to wear a sweater or shawl because of the breeze coming over the al-Hummar hills facing Wadi al-Seer—Nabila went to a reading group meeting led by a Jordanian woman married to a famous plastic surgeon. She received everyone in a large glassed-in living room in her villa looking out over a tree-covered hill. Fulfilling her role as the protagonist in this story, Nabila met the handsome Iraqi surgeon Rashid Shihab from Tikrit there that evening.

Like many Iraqis, Rashid Shihab had chosen to live in Amman after the American occupation in 2003. In the years preceding the occupation, he'd moved around Europe as a military attaché in different Iraqi embassies. His position cast suspicion upon him, especially after he'd returned to Baghdad in the 1980s, because he'd worked for the previous regime. In that period, he had worked as a doctor in a military hospital. He had enjoyed many professional successes but he had never had the opportunity to start a family. He knew the horrors of the war his country was fighting better than anyone else, because he spent his days and nights treating soldiers' burns and disfigurements, mainly caused by deadly chemical and biological weapons. He also knew about other horrors, which had been locked away in secret files since the first Gulf War—the Iran-Iraq War—until he left Baghdad. He was well-regarded in Iraqi military and civilian circles alike and had become known as the man with the golden fingers. It was rumored that he performed a major surgery on Saddam Hussein's son Uday, after he'd been shot by one of his close friends because he'd stolen his girlfriend. The bullet had penetrated his cheek and disfigured his face, but no sign of it remained after this surgery. Many legends were spun around his professional career, the most famous of which was that his surgical scalpel was responsible for sculpting a number of copies of the late president. He never confirmed or denied this. An aura of mystery, strength, and success surrounded him and attracted women to him like a magnet: female doctors, nurses, and the wives of army officers, ministers, and political leaders. But he was always keen to stay away from anything or anyone that would cause him problems. Whatever temptations were there, he preferred a quiet relationship with a simple, beautiful, kept woman.

When Rashid Shihab moved to Amman, many hospitals opened their doors to him. He mainly performed plastic surgery on women, fixing their noses, lifting their bosoms, and tightening their stomachs. He was able to establish a stable income and life for himself in no time.

When Dr. Rashid attended a seminar given by his childhood friend, Karim Saad, he still looked like a Greek epic hero despite his sixty years of age, standing at the edge of a battle facing the wind, counting his losses and mourning his lost loved ones. The years of the war had not robbed him of his past glory. His wavy, gray hair was combed back along a part, exposing his features—the direct gaze of his lively dark eyes, his clear dark skin, his pointed nose betraying his sharp temperament, and his short beard that covered only a small space on his chin. His blue Levi's jeans showed off his solid military stature, which was reinforced by his short-heeled beige suede shoes. His carefully ironed white polo shirt outlined his little belly. He wore a thick golden ring with the crest of the University of Leeds, where he'd gotten his degree. All of this piqued Nabila's desire to discover the kind of pleasure that a man like Dr. Rashid harbored inside him—a pleasure derived from his unique experiences of success, fear, and pain, and the ruptures resulting from leaving his homeland in middle age. It was easy for Nabila to fall in love with Dr. Rashid Shihab the moment they were introduced. But what would make this esteemed man give his heart to a woman like her, especially now that she was in her fifties?

Nabila had lost her husband Yusuf at a terrible time in a woman's life. She was about forty years old, an age when every risk must be well calculated. This is not a time in life for a person to be scattered about in different relationships. They must store up spiritual strength and energy in order to survive.

She didn't make new friendships after Yusuf died, but rather went back to a few old ones with school friends. She stuck to her professional environment at the German embassy, which kept her busy with receptions, meetings, official national holidays, lectures, and a few vacations when she would travel to Germany with Yaacoub. They established a routine for their daily lives in order to try and move on again.

Despite the painful hole that Yusuf's absence left in both their lives, Nabila stayed strong. She raised Yusuf with great care. She knew that the boy needed a man to help raise him, to be a role model, and to help him unlock the secrets to coming into himself as a man as well. He would need someone to talk to him about puberty, how to wash himself properly, shave his beard, put on aftershave, reduce his armpit hair, and apply deodorant. He would need someone to take him to men's gatherings and to guide him in the way that men react to things, both firmly and gently. He needed someone to show him how men face up to success and failure, as men's logic when it comes to these things is totally different from women's. Yaacoub had lost all of this when Yusuf passed away and Nabila had to compensate for it, all the while trying not to break down. She didn't want him to be considered a "widow's son." As a result, she always surrounded him with memories of his father, most of them imaginary. She'd say, for example, "Your father did this, he said that, he asked to do it this way. If your father were here with us, you would have to do x, y, z." Nabila never tired of this kind of reasoning, assumptions, or justifications.

After all this, she found that there was still a lot of life left to live. It was too early still to know what would happen, but anyone observing her could see that she was a very capable woman. The depth of experience you could see in her eyes was the only thing that betrayed her age. Her well-preserved body, striking presence, and elegant originality gave her the appearance of a woman in her thirties.

Nabila was tall and had velvety-looking dark skin. She'd made exercise a lifelong habit, and thus was untouched by age and a single childbirth. She had sharp brown eyes, a small nose, and shapely breasts. Her short hair, dyed burgundy, was held back by a white gold chain decorated with a large black Tahitian pearl and small, shiny Tiffany diamond clips—she would wear these every day since Yusuf gave them to her on their first anniversary. She was always elegant, in jeans or cotton trousers and a chiffon shirt with a carefully chosen black, beige, gray, or navy-blue blazer to top off the outfit. She seemed always to be dressed to the nines, since work at the embassy required her to be on call and ready for a meeting, a mission, or even a short trip.

It seemed that Nabila's pituitary gland produced ample oxytocin, the hormone that bridges distances between people and helps incite intimate relationships. Yet her calm demeanor managed to make her come across as cold most of the time, as did her extreme caution in developing personal relationships with the people around her. People who got too close to her felt there was a boundary to respect; the glowing embers of her confidences lay hidden under false ashes that she had put there herself, in the guise of protection. And despite all that time, all those long, harsh, lonely days she'd endured, she had only allowed herself to share this fire with one man.

Vladimir Bericikć, or Didi, as she liked to call him, was a German violinist of Serbian origins, whom the German cultural center in Amman had sponsored for a one-year cultural exchange program. Bericikć fell in love with Nabila at first sight. At that time, she was existing in a strange state of wonder. She had just crossed the threshold of forty, feeling that the experiences she had lived through had indeed been beautiful, despite the fact that up until then, she had not realized their true essence. And now they were slipping through her fingers: youth, love, vitality, joy, and beauty...

She almost fell into the trap of a midlife crisis and lost everything—her luck, her marriage, her family, her nation, her decisions, and even Yaacoub who she found to be as much a reason for her misery as a solace to her. Bericikć extended his firm, loving arms to save her from all this and she allowed him to penetrate her defenses.

Vladimir Bericikć was three years younger than Nabila and the son of the Serbian politician Radovan Bericikć, a prominent member of the Czech movement that resisted the Nazis and supporters of Tito after the Second World War. His name became well known in the final battle for the liberation of Sarajevo in 1945 when he was only twenty years old.

Vladimir was born in 1951 and grew up supported by the state—something that was granted exceptionally to children of revolutionaries. He studied the history of music at the Fine Arts Academy, specializing in the violin, which he'd played since childhood.

When Serbian forces entered Bosnia and Herzegovina to annex Serbian territory and create what became known as Republika Serbska, Vladimir couldn't tolerate what his compatriots were doing to the Bosnian Muslims. Their abuse, massacres, and attacks were destroying his country. He was a Bosnian Serb and also feared reprisals by Muslims. So he packed his bags and fled to the Serbian capital Belgrade in 1992. He couldn't stand to settle there. He felt that he was surrounded by crimes he had no part in, that he was condemned for the murder of his countrymen because of a historical accident that made him an Orthodox Christian Serb. So he left Belgrade, the place where the Serb nation was supposed to be, for Germany, where he had a glorious family history of resistance. He found Berlin to be closer to and more compatible with his soul than his own country and thus decided to settle there. He joined the German Philharmonic Orchestra and became first violin. He was later granted German citizenship in an official ceremony.

With Didi, Nabila was like a woman of twenty again, but with the experience of a forty-year-old. She began rediscovering the secrets of her body that had long been ignored: hot spots, turn-ons, what she did and didn't like. She reached two or three orgasms every time they were together, often in the morning when they would make love in Vladimir's little apartment in Jabal Luwaybda. Afterwards, Nabila would rush off to work so that she could make it home to be with her son almost on time. She started going to beauty salons and lingerie shops, picking and choosing the newest and most attractive pieces to make up for her lost youth and pleasure. As soon as summer came, she went swimming and sunbathing so that her skin turned a beautiful mermaid's golden brown.

With his Aryan origins, Didi melted into her details, which embodied everything his grandmother from Sarajevo had told him in stories about the wives of the Sultans, who he was descended from. He spoiled Nabila like a princess. He would make her breakfast every time she came to visit him, feeding her with his hands, sitting at her small feet with his violin ready. He would play all the songs she liked: Strauss's *Blue Danube*, Beethoven's *Moonlight Sonata*, and Korsakov's *Scheherazade*. Whenever he was with her he suffered from what could be called a "dyslexia of the senses." He was lost in her dark skin, her tisane-scented hair, and the Eastern spices in her pores, all of which prompted him to compose a passionate serenade in her honor that he called, "Musk." He opened most of his concerts with it.

The only night that Nabila spent away from Yaacoub, she spent with Bericikć at the Dead Sea. The massage that Didi gave her was magical; it was enough to make her dispense with men for years to come. He kneaded her with his fingertips and his eyelashes awakened her nipples. She could hear the sad suffering of the Balkans in his moans. When her body's warm fluids gushed forth, the scent of Dinaric mountain forests spread through the room—ripe mulberries, pine trees, hot springs. The semen that poured out onto her body was thick and unfermented like cream made from mountain goat milk. In his arms, she returned to her land, which she only knew from maps. She wondered if he smelled the scent of the sea and orange groves in her body too. Did he sense that pain and anguish that had been left in her soul when she was torn from her roots?

Vladimir felt that they truly resembled each other. They had followed the same path of transformation, coming from an ancient Ottoman region led into diaspora and exile by European colonization. Just as Nabila lost her mother through immigration, Vladimir's mother was killed in a 1995 NATO raid on Sarajevo against the Bosnian Serb army. It is this kind of violence which often makes victims into lovers.

During the year that Bericikć spent in Amman, Yaacoub's relationship with his mother became strained. Before this, their quarrels were like those of any teenager and parent, arguments that quickly resolved themselves no matter the cause of the conflict. The reality was that they believed in each other and they both knew that the love they shared was unconditional. But Yaacoub was experiencing an Oedipal crisis; he knew what tied Bericikć and Nabila. He hated Bericikć the moment he laid eyes on him and, by extension, hated his mother for wanting to be with him. He always hinted that he knew exactly what she was hiding, and taunted her with cryptic gestures, questions, pursuits, even screams at times, always accompanied with words like humiliation, treachery, shame, betrayal, and deception. Then, suddenly he would stop, recoiling from the mere imagination of the moment when she would actually be frank about her relationship with Bericikć, avoiding that reality by slamming the door to his room. He hugged his little wooden dolls that his father had bought him in Baden-Baden when they used to go on holidays and stay in a mountain cabin in the Black Forest overlooking the source of the Danube. Morning would dawn, Yaacoub's eyes still glued to the wooden clock hanging on the wall that Yusuf had bought for him on his last trip there. Every sixty minutes a little bird would pop out of the clock, assuring him that the lovely days he'd had with his father were indeed real and not just in his mind. He would then explode into bitter sobs.

That one night that Nabila spent with Bericikć was a turning point in her life. When she came back to Amman, Yaacoub wasn't home. Night fell, and still no sign of him. Nabila broke down. She searched for him like a madwoman, looking everywhere that he could possibly go. But he rarely ever went out anywhere. He was in his third year of university, and he never stayed out late at a café or friends' houses, even with his father's family whom he loved very much. Nabila had thought that the worst punishment her son could inflict on her was when he refused to speak even one word to her for an entire month. But going missing was another thing. She cried like she never had before in her life. She felt the misery of the entire world festering within her. She had destroyed everything that she created in life for a fling, and her relationship with Vladimir Bericikć was a whim that deserved punishment. She swore that if her son came back in one piece she would throw herself on him, beg his forgiveness, and forget being with a man forever.

Yaacoub spent the night in the mosque across from the house and returned the next morning with a heavy heart. He found his mother had aged twenty years in one night, her face had hardened, her eyes were swollen and red from sobbing. When she saw him, she screamed like a wounded lioness, and she started furiously beating him. After a while, exhausted from their fight, they both collapsed into a long embrace.

Bericikć's year in Jordan came to an end. He tried unsuccessfully to extend it. Nabila prayed to God he would leave quickly and wanted to be done with him without having to break his heart. He offered to stay so they could be together, he offered to take her with him anywhere she wanted to go in the world. She refused. Deep inside, she had always known that the affair would ultimately come to an end, even in her moments of unbridled joy and extreme pleasure. So she decided in advance that she would only love within the limits she had set for herself, which would help protect her from growing too attached to anyone or giving too much of herself. Thus, Yaacoub managed to end her beautiful dream, forcing her body to return to its isolation—no one knows more than single women how long and hard Amman's nights can be.

Yaacoub's long absence in America liberated Nabila, no matter how much it pained her to see him go. She felt that life owed her a lot and that she could now start to recover some of that debt. Their weekly telephone calls only served to confirm that he was fine and building a secure future for himself. Yaacoub was starting to slip between her fingers into his own private world, further away from her than at any time before. He had his own worries and friendships, and soon he would have a wife and children of his own. No doubt she would be overjoyed, but none of this would be hers. Yaacoub would be with his wife, and his children would be in their parents' arms. If Nabila had died at that moment, no one would know about her death. Who would care about the loss of a single woman who'd decided to stay cut off from her family and sent her only son to America for four years, possibly longer?

In contrast to this melodramatic death, Nabila married Rashid Shihab officially only three weeks after they met. Neither of them thought about the results of this adventure. They took the decision with the same ease that two friends might decide to eat lunch in a seafood restaurant downtown. But she did experience a few moments of extreme anxiety before she called Yaacoub to tell him that she'd gotten married.

Yaacoub received this news with a satisfaction that could only result from psychological development. An image of his father flashed before his eyes and he cried a tiny bit. But then he wished her a happy life. When they hung up the phone he felt he'd been relieved of a heavy burden, and that the fate that had long threatened to plague him would no longer harm him. He sighed deeply and told himself, "Dr. Yaacoub has a stepfather now." He smiled, capable of discerning the irony in his words.

—

When Rashid Shihab lay down in bed to sleep after having performed a series of surgeries three days in a row, Nabila, naked, slipped in next to him, in a spontaneous celebration of her ageless body. She sat up and contemplated his jeans hanging on a peg, kneading the knuckles of his elegant brown fingers. She blamed herself for having so long been opposed to life's copious generosity, the kind of generosity that can be found almost anywhere, but that we unfortunately tend to take for granted. In reality, Nabila's house was less than one street away from Rashid's, in the Khalda neighborhood. She lived in a building across from the kindergarten of the Sands National Academy School, next to the Nazarene Evangelical Church. He lived on the hill across from the Sands National Academy itself, but in the main building just east of the Bashiti signs. This meant that it was the Khalda highway alone that had delayed their meeting more than seven years.

Now they were finally together. This meant more to her than simply having another child to take care of—as most people thought. Indeed it meant more than having a kindred soul to ease her loneliness, as most people believed. No, any pet can occupy that role. This was something altogether different. Life had begun again after fifty. Suddenly, she could wear a dress with a zipper down the back. She no longer needed a chair to reach her shawl on the top shelf of her cupboard. When she had a headache there was always someone to give her two Panadol pills and a glass of water, telling her to sleep it off, eagerly asking her when she woke up, "Feeling better?"

"Yes."

"Do you want to go out for a little walk?"

"Of course."

At first, Nabila did not have all of these scenarios in mind. She'd forgotten about them completely. But now they came back to her, with significant clarity, making her acutely aware of the new kind of freedom a woman gets once she marries a man, especially after middle age. She was now free to sleep at Rashid's house or hers, which she kept even after they married. She was free to indulge her carnal desires or be silent about them, free to pamper Rashid, free to let him pamper her. Indeed, Rashid was doing a lot more than that—he loved her truly, deeply, unconditionally. Their love did nothing to alter their lives except by bringing additional security and a calm, authentic happiness. He was also very generous in every aspect of their lives. Since she only trusted German cars, he bought her a new Volkswagen, upgrading her from a Golf to a Tuareg. He gifted her two elegant diamond rings even though she said it wasn't necessary. He told her, "Nabila my love, I must! It's the least I can do!"

In the evenings they went out on long walks together to get their blood pumping; it was one of the things they'd both agreed they loved doing. They walked up nearby Maarif Street from six to seven in the evening. Then they stopped and leaned against their car, parked on the side of the road, looking at the orange sun discreetly sinking behind the King Hussein mosque in the Dabouq orchards.

In the winter, Nabila loved spending nights at Rashid's house, though it was detached, located in a wide-open expanse that did not protect against the snow and wind. But it was still warmer than hers. She loved the marble fireplace into which Rashid threw chestnuts, picking them up with metal tongs after they'd opened. He peeled them with the very same fingers that renewed the beauty of Amman's women. Then he fed them to her one after another, her lips painted cherry red until she finally declined saying, "That's enough. They have so many calories…"

Rashid didn't care about any of that. He loved Nabila exactly the way she was. He loved the real woman in her, the woman who had been exiled from the sea as a baby, who had kept the power of the metaphorical oar for half a century. He held her in his still-strong arms, telling her, "Nabila, my love, you are everything to me!" She loved his thick Iraqi accent. "You are my life, you are Baghdad, Amman, and holy Jerusalem rolled into one!"

Nabila laughed, nuzzling her face in his soft neck and expressing her reservations about using the expression holy Jerusalem in this context.

The fire in the fireplace didn't go out until after midnight, when Rashid fell asleep and she was lying on the recliner in front of him reading a book by Osho, the bliss in her heart stirred by the snow falling against her window. She believed that she had finally made complete and eternal peace with life.

Yaacoub came back from America with a specialty in bloodborne diseases. He didn't stir up any trouble with his mother and Rashid, and each of them avoided confrontation with the other. Nabila split her time calmly between the two houses on the edges of the Khalda highway. After he got the equivalencies of his diplomas, Yaacoub found a job in the cancer center right away and entered its endless, work-filled corridors. These two men who shared Nabila, also shared a mutual respect for the other. This was fostered by their professionalism, and it came from a genuine understanding of manhood that was cultivated by their Arab upbringing. This could be described as a series of wars. Rashid spoke about Iraq and England; Yaacoub talked about Palestine and the States. Nabila listened to them, pleased with the harmony she had created.

Rashid Shihab fell in love with Yaacoub out of a paternal instinct he had up until then felt he'd missed out on. He hadn't thought about how lovely it would be to have a son until he saw Yaacoub, coming and going, and receiving them with kindness, the same way he received his patients with professionalism and dignity. He was successful in his work and accepted challenges with the courage seen in the sons of important men.

Yaacoub himself respected Dr. Rashid's experience and medical expertise, the harsh conditions he'd worked under, and his pride and courage in his work as a military doctor. But this did not mean that he would ever take his own father's place. Yusuf al-Sharif, who died at only twenty-five years of age, could never be replaced. But he had to admit that he couldn't have asked for a better husband for his own mother.

Dr. Rashid didn't know that God loved him so much as to put him in the care of Dr. Yaacoub. Only three years after he married Nabila, he was diagnosed with an aggressive pancreatic cancer that gave him less than a year to live. Nabila dealt with this unexpected blow with the spirit of a desperate fighter. She carried on only because she had no other choice, saying whatever occurred to her: "Enough is enough," "There are no compromises in life," "Only God knows why all this has happened to me!"

Yaacoub's care for Rashid allowed Nabila to reflect calmly on the beauty and happiness that she'd been granted during the three years she'd spent with Rashid. This time together allowed her to truly understand what it meant for a woman to have a wonderful man in her life. And no cancer patient could aspire to better quality medical care and familial love. As a patient, no one knew this better than Dr. Rashid. He was more aware than anyone else what the true outcome of his situation would be. He knew how fast and how irrevocably the stages of an aggressive cancer could progress. He also knew it was a miracle that he could be treated by the person who was closest to him in the world—Yaacoub. Their knowledge was terrible for both of them, especially when Rashid started feeling the end approaching and could no longer endure the pain. He called Yaacoub into his inner sanctum where there were no witnesses other than the earth and sky, and he said, "Yaacoub, my dear, I want you to take care of my last days, for your father's sake. God have mercy on your father's soul."

Yaacoub nodded his head deferentially and kissed the forehead of this sick man who refused to leave his own house. Yaacoub organized his hospice care at home, comparable to what you could find in the best medical center.

Like two knights out of a tale in the olden days, Dr. Yaacoub pledged to his mother's husband that he would prevent him from suffering in a humiliating way. He lived up to his promise. After he'd stabilized him in an irreversible coma, and using well-practiced techniques, he turned off the machines that made his vital organs work, reduced his oxygen pressure so his heart slowed, and euthanized him.

After Rashid's death, Nabila went mad. Not simply because of the tragic loss that she'd already tried to prepare for, but because of the cold crime committed by her only son. He astonished her by saying that there is only a fine line separating a doctor and a murderer, a line called science. Her wails turned into angry bellows of betrayal: "There is no greater sin you can commit in either our religion or our laws. You could have avenged me in a way that would have been more merciful for the two of us.

Killers kill, Yaacoub, and I simply cannot even think about losing you too."

She knew that Yaacoub wasn't really taking revenge, and that she was throwing words around like a crazy person. But she was afraid for her son, of God's punishment, and of the entire crime he had committed. After the ordeal, Yaacoub received condolences for Rashid's death for three days and then went silent. He couldn't explain what had happened, that he and his mother were of two different minds about managing the crisis. They believed two different things and couldn't negotiate a compromise. Nabila didn't know cancer like he did. She didn't know the havoc it wreaked on the human body and on a person's dignity. She didn't know that what Yaacoub did was the result of a pact between two courageous men—two exceptional doctors—and that it was a frequent occurrence in American hospitals.

Nabila lived through the ordeal, but the wound from this new loss would never heal. Rashid was more than a rock of stability to her. He was more than joy, more than comfort. She started to fear that this endlessly treacherous world wouldn't hesitate to take her son from her too. He begged her to forget the fears that existed in the deep recesses of her mind and to exchange them for what she'd learned from Hegel, Nietzsche, and Schopenhauer—otherwise her terror would see her confined to the madhouse. Their relationship cooled. Nabila hid behind a wall of despair and Yaacoub disappeared into a heavy silence. His gloom was ill-befitting a man in his forties. But he found it useless to make any effort to change. Only time could fill this totally unjustified chasm in his life.

Dr. Yaacoub was living through this terrible time right when Haniyah had reached the final stages of her treatment and life once again returned to her lovely body.

Russian Roulette

"My chemo treatments were exhausting and distressing, because the idea of cancer is so miserable. But I resisted and never gave up! Five difficult sessions and I didn't give up, not even once. The tumor was on my neck, here on the right side," Haniyah explained to me.

I looked at where she was pointing and saw no sign of it.

"My small mass disappeared after the first session. Honestly, it didn't hurt as much as people say cancer will. The chemo didn't affect me as much as it does other people I've heard talk about it. Perhaps it's because I took the decision to not be in pain. Pain is up here." She pointed at her head. "Here in your mind."

No man could resist Haniyah's magnetism. I was a woman, I was sick, and even I couldn't take my eyes off of her when she moved or talked. Her movements were as balanced, rhythmic, and graceful as those of a wild gazelle, whereas so much motion tends to make most people lurch about in chaos and confusion. Her features were strong and firm, enhanced by the severity of the disease. There were volcanoes erupting inside her eyes and the pores on her face. But her radiation-filled lips weren't burned by the chemo that had dried up the water in her veins until they atrophied.

"I got my health back quickly. Everything came back after the last treatment—the color in my skin, my periods, my hair even started to grow." She looked at me with reassuring sympathy. "Don't worry, everything will come back even better than it was." I nodded my head with a half-smile and asked her to keep talking. She was positive and I needed some positivity in my life.

"Did you always wear a hijab?"

"No."

"Did all your hair fall out?"

"I don't know. I shaved it off when it started to fall."

"Why do you cover it? Take off your scarf and face up to your circumstances. Enjoy the transformations. Let the sun and wind heal your illness and remind your body of life. Let them fix the troubles you've experienced."

I was quiet. She was right. Who was I covering my bald head for? No one knows me in this country. But it's a style I decided to adopt, for fear of the stares that would remind me of my illness on the off chance I managed to forget about it for a second. Women who wear the hijab can partially avoid the issue of their hair. I only care what Nasser thinks and he says that I look beautiful. He told me that hair distracts us from the beauty of the face, that someone who has a beautiful face should get rid of her hair even normally, so people can contemplate her innocent eyes, sharp nose, and enigmatic mouth. He says he can't tell if my mouth is actual living flesh or a jewel. Nasser's exaggerations can sometimes be annoying and now I can't listen to them without crying.

Hanan was another a patient I met on one of the long days we spent together in the waiting room. She wore the hijab and said that she couldn't even take off her head cover at home. She didn't want her husband or children to see her, so she managed to hide her bald head for a full year.

Haniyah said, "Dancing is what saved me, dance heals. Do you know Zorba?"

"Of course."

"Zorba said, 'When my youngest, Dimitri, died I stood like this and danced. People were shouting, "Zorba's gone mad!" But if I hadn't danced at that moment I would have gone insane from the suffering.' Martha Graham once said something that is included in the introduction to every book about modern dance: 'To me, the body says what words cannot.'

"When I came here for the first time, I met a young man who had completed his treatment and was at the hospital for a follow-up visit with the doctor. I asked him all the typical new patient questions. He seemed healthy as he told me that he had found illness to be simple, simpler than love. He found that his girlfriend leaving him hurt him much more than the disease did—God is merciful, people are not. From that day on I didn't ask any other questions. I decided to believe in healing. So what will you do?" She spoke succinctly and looked at me with a mirthless smile. "This illness chooses an elite. They say it's the evil eye bringing down those that luck had favored up until now."

I looked at another patient sitting across from us, speaking on the phone. She had her seven- or eight-year-old daughter with her. I heard her saying that her daughter didn't go to school today because she'd come to the hospital with her mother. And the woman was blind! My God, who would envy a blind person so much she would fall ill with cancer?

Haniyah was still new at navigating the theater of experience; she was taken by the artistry and rhetoric of life coaches and self-help books. Though my body was withering and dying, she wanted it to speak. She was too pedantic for a new cancer patient who had stumbled into this world that even the sun's rays can't brighten. Or perhaps I'm exaggerating my own suffering and misery. But the doctor always told me that each case is unique, no one is just like another, and so you can't learn anything from listening to someone else's experiences.

There are only two kinds of people in the world: the ill and the healthy. For me there are no other criteria for division: neither culture, nor wealth, nor gender. At first I envy people who are healthy, but then I take a mental step back and feel genuine happiness for them.

One of the early steps that I took to get to this stage was inventing my own lexicon of private *du'a* prayers. I collected them from the prayers of the prophets, the needy, the oppressed, and the beggars. I repeated them constantly, "Oh God, you are the only God, praise you. I was one of the wrongdoers. Now I praise your name, this great name you gave yourself, or that you taught someone in your creation, or that I kept in my knowledge of the unseen. Please heal me fully, quickly, and don't leave any disease behind." Nasser taught me to repeat, "You are capable of everything. You are worthy of the answer. I put my faith and trust in you. Oh God, help me conquer the scourge of patience. Oh God, I have been touched and you are the most merciful of the merciful."

This made me feel somewhat reassured. But I reviewed my life far away from Nasser, in complete secrecy. I was much too worried that if I talked about all my obsessions I would lose him. I ask myself every day why Nasser is with me. It would be better for him to be with a healthy, happy woman, full of joy and vigor, who would take him with her through a life filled with strength, energy, and love. They could travel together, stay up late, attend conferences and dance performances, go to art galleries and the cinema. Why is this exciting man in his fifties, who could now be reaping the fruits of a long, patient struggle after having left his past life, betting on a woman who is half-dead? She spends her days observing which of her cells are dying and which are being born, thinking about her tired cells and paying no attention to anyone except others undergoing chemotherapy.

Nasser's answers are bigger than my questions, he doesn't even know even the half of it. He once told me, "It's only by God's grace that you fell ill and not me." I winced in fear but then realized that there was a bigger story behind what he was saying.

"The British Mandate authority had banned the sale of tobacco at one point. Anyone caught with a pack of cigarettes was fined and imprisoned. My father was a serious smoker; one day he bought four cartons of cigarettes and put them in his car. His nephew, who was in his twenties, was with him. He was stopped by a patrol that searched the car. They found the contraband cigarettes and my father immediately claimed that they didn't belong to him but to the young man, who was stunned with surprise. Even though everyone considered his uncle to be a coward, liar, and meddler, he didn't expect his uncle to sell him out like that. The young man was held in the detention center, but as soon as evening came, his uncle had done everything he knew he could and gotten him out in time to be home for dinner with his family. The young man attacked his uncle angrily. But my father responded, "My boy, if you go to prison I know how to get you out. It's better than me going and you not knowing how to get me out!"

I wouldn't have been in the position to help Nasser… I wouldn't even have been able to provide him a fraction of the amount of help he was offering me. Everything he says is true, all of his examples are relevant and his wisdom sound. But the thrust of my questions remained the same: Why did I have to get sick for him to be with me? Why was one of us sick? Wasn't it possible for us both to be healthy? What would anyone in the world lose if I had not been afflicted with cancer?

At long last, the phone lines to Raqqa, which had been cut off for a month, were restored. Jude called me right away. "What would people lose if there was no war in Syria?" she said to me.

I can't think about war, I want to breathe. I want to get up from my seat like people normally do.

"We are being bombed right now."

"You all can breathe with enough strength that you are able to move from one place to another, from the living room to the basement where you are seeking refuge from the raid. But if I were there right now and they came to slaughter me I would be finished. I don't have enough energy even to get up from my seat. I would just succumb to the knife and that would be it."

Nasser came back home carrying shopping bags. He enthusiastically took things out and showed them to me. Adidas and Reebok sports clothes, cotton pants, t-shirts and sweatshirts in plain colors. There were two pairs of fancy sports shoes—one black and one white. These were things that anyone who was not in my position would be happy with. Nasser was like a father giving his children gifts, hoping to see joy and gratitude in their eyes.

"Joumane, I want our life to be calm, and I want your life to go back to the way it was—elegant, pleasant, comfortable. We won't neglect ourselves, we will preserve this beauty which we are going to need for a long, long time. It will help us recapture that very first moment I saw you and hold onto it forever."

I thought to myself, "Oh Nasser, you came into my life too late. I wish I had known you before these terrible times. Perhaps you would have been the happiest man in the world. Now you want me to confront my death elegantly, pleasantly, and comfortably."

I kissed his cheek gratefully and wiped away my tears, for I had promised myself after indulging in one long cry during the first days after my diagnosis that I would never cry again. I wouldn't mourn and I would stop lamenting my lost youth. Dr. Joumane Badran must now move on. She must stop complaining, be grateful, and face her destiny like a knight chosen by God faces his stubborn archrival. I was grateful that God had extended his hand to me through this darkness, and had sent Nasser to me, for it is a darkness that does not seem to want to dissipate soon.

Our Armenian neighbor, Umm Marie, whom we all used to call grandma, told us on the day her husband died, "God won't abandon me, He is always with me, just like He was with my mother. My mother lost her family in the genocide. She came to Raqqa with an Ottoman convoy that trafficked single women as captives and domestic laborers. She fled with some of her friends and they managed to reach a village. The people living there welcomed them, gave them food and drink. She prayed all night and said in confusion, 'You have forsaken me!'

"One of the pious people of the village overheard her prayer and told her the story of the woman who God had carried, the religious woman who used to pray continuously, who was so selfless she would feed birds with her only loaf of bread. When she would walk on the seashore, she'd look at the sand and see two sets of footprints. She wondered what they were, and it was not long before the answer came to her. God was walking with her; He was following her footsteps. When she fell very ill, she went back to the beach and prayed. She looked and saw only one set of footprints. She wailed, 'God, why did You abandon me to such injury, where are Your footsteps that never left me behind when I needed them the least?' 'I didn't leave you,' He replied. 'I am here. I am carrying you now. Those footprints on the sand... look at them well. They are My footsteps, not yours.'

"After a few days, my mother felt well again and my father asked her to marry him. He was a cobbler and quite poor, but he loved her and had also lost his family during the war. They were happy, content with their lives, but though the sun's rays helped them forget their tragic past, the dark brought it back in in nightmares. They battled those nightmares with their tenderness for each other. During holidays, their love was reflected through prayer and beautiful dances. I lived my life with Abu Marie and all of you here, but with memories of things far away too—like happiness, joy, and prosperity. No matter what, God doesn't abandon us; He never forsakes us."

As my treatment went on, Haniyah and I built a strong friendship. She took me on like an experienced sailor takes on an apprentice, never letting him stray too far from the shore, teaching him to read the moods of the waves, the maps of the stars, and the movements of the winds. Friendships between cancer patients are precious because they have no hidden interests or ulterior motives. Their goal is simply for those who have been through the disease to lessen the pain of those whose suffering comes later, to take them by the hand and look after them. Whenever I felt hopeless, I called Haniyah. Whenever there was a change in my situation, I asked her, "Did your eyesight ever change? Did you have double vision?"

"Of course... chemo affects everything, it impacts your vision, your hearing, and even your spirit. Don't listen to your body right now. All the signals it is sending you are wrong. Let your body deal with the medicine and soon you will find your own rhythm."

"When will I feel better?"

"When the treatment is finished."

"Will I reach the state you are in? Will I walk without getting dizzy, without demons pounding in my head? Will I be able to breathe without fatigue and exhaustion over every breath? And my lung will be done with this blight that afflicts it night and day?"

"All that and more!"

I just want to reach her state of health. I won't be greedy, I want nothing more, for she has reached the stage where everything is normal and working well.

"Did Dr. Yaacoub tell you anything about my condition?"

"Of course not. Yaacoub doesn't talk about his patients at all. He also doesn't hide anything from you. If he told you that you're on track, then he really means what he said."

Haniyah didn't resemble me at all; she was calm and collected. The doctor was with her, he cared about her, he slept next to her, he answered her questions, and he looked after her all the time with top-quality care. As for me, my obsessions were eating me alive and I couldn't find satisfactory answers. At our few, periodic appointments, the one question I'd ask would inevitably lead to one other: "Will I make a full recovery?"

"*Inshallah*. God willing."

"Will the cancer recur?"

"We hope not."

An answer gives life, and an answer takes it away. While Haniyah can get the answer she wants from him,

I must go home to Nasser and have speculative conversations on the legends of creation, the secret of the earth and the heavens, and then take from these conversations unsatisfactory answers that are closer to interpretations. I want him to tell me: *"You will make a full recovery. The cancer will never come back. You will be done with this nightmare and wake up to find it only a memory."* But it is only my housekeeper Tammy who tells me this.

Two weeks after my sixth treatment session, I had an MRI. I went to my usual appointment with the doctor. I walked into his office and sat on the black leather chair in front of his desk. Everything was small, even the doctor himself, but my hope was large. He always made me wait, coming in a little late with a celebratory air about him. It doesn't matter. Let him celebrate his bloated ego, he deserves it when he brings us good news. One day I'll celebrate it with him, in this place, which for me is like the solitary confinement cell of a person on death row. Its every corner gives off the scent of death and its gray curtains represent the torment of the grave. Haniyah, on the other hand, sees it as containing her love. It surrounds her with hungry kisses and passionate caresses. I want to ask her about the details, how the doctor distinguishes between the body he is healing and the one he is loving. If I asked her, she'd tell me everything, she is never secretive about her relationship. But I stop myself because once your idols have fallen, they can't rise again. I don't want the doctor to become a human being, so I can at least preserve my fantasy of being healed.

Cancer patients see everyone as more fortunate than them—the beggar who stands outside the coffee cart on the sidewalk next to the center, random people walking by, vagrants stumbling down the street. They say to themselves, "What have I done to deserve this affliction?" Answers come from those who haven't been through this hell: "It's a test; you'll be rewarded for your faith, your good deeds." Or, "It's atonement for evil. Any evil can become a deadly tumor."

After this we discover what we'd rushed to judge, since cancer patients see mercy anywhere they can: emanating from the earth, pouring down from the sky, surrounding us on every side. No one else can feel this mercy.

The doctor looked at the report of the image before him. I could tell he was perplexed, but happy, like someone who'd won on a gamble. He told me, "Your tumor is gone."

The way I received the news frustrated him. My joy was different because the disappearance of the tumor didn't mean the end of my suffering. This is only one step toward my goal; I have more cycles of treatment ahead of me. But I will follow this treatment confidently, so it can shed light on any mysteries and find any tricky cells still hiding somewhere in my chest. That is why we decided that I would take two additional doses of chemotherapy, forty-two more days of hell. They would be like the previous ones, but the final cycles reveal the true meaning of patience. Unexpected surprises at this point could be horrific.

Haniyah said, "I got cancer and fell in love." Then she laughed seductively…

I fell in love with her too. I missed her, I couldn't wait to see her; she was a remnant of a wonderful life that had given up on me. We sat in the spacious main hall of the building, the blue room with rows of black leather chairs crisscrossing it in length and width. We each had an IV cannula tube inserted in the back of our right hands. We sat and drank glasses of bitter-tasting water. We had to finish our glasses in fifteen minutes before we could go under the x-ray machine, which looked like a piece of playground equipment in a graveyard. "Take a deep breath... now, hold your breath... you can breathe freely now."

Then the technician would come and inject the colorful liquid into the needle, so that the fire water would burn our throats, the veins in our hands, and our reproductive organs.

Needles only hurt children. They scream and cry because they don't realize the enormity of what comes later. The idea of death is unclear in their minds. Knowledge is painful; parents are tormented by their children's inevitable suffering. I thanked God I didn't have children and that Mama died before my own illness could make her more miserable. Up until this moment, I hadn't dealt with the idea that I could be deprived of motherhood. I'll file that one away for later. For now my focus was on healing and recovering, being able to breathe normally again, and the non-recurrence of the disease. After this I would be able to think about repairing the rest of the damage. But there is no escaping the fact that the chemo has burned my ovaries, ended my periods, and could even prevent me from being able to ever have children. This would be an enormous loss and if it happens, I will surely lament it in the future.

I used to dream about having a daughter with two brown braids or an Oedipal son who was jealous of his father.

Lina is a lady in her forties whom I met one time when I was waiting for the doctor. She told me that the most difficult thing she had to deal with was the idea of leaving her ten-year-old daughter alone after she was gone. "A girl needs a mother to care for her, to help her understand how to live life. Who will remind her to study seriously and conscientiously to make up for our past failures? Who will tell her about puberty? How to wash and wear her clothes when she gets her period? How to deal with her breasts and hips filling out? What she should eat or avoid so she'll have enough iron in her body? Who will care about her disappointments, depressions, and mood swings? I thought about writing down detailed notes for her. But in the end I found a way to talk to her about everything in great depth. We talked about all the things I wanted to tell her in one long session that was completely open and transparent. I explained to her how to fight bullying and harassment, I told her she had to fill the world with noise if something like that happened and she had to denounce the perpetrator. Even before this, I had already told her not to trust anyone, to avoid abandoned places and revealing clothes, and to stay away from the corridors between the shelves in supermarket. I cautioned her against physical contact with girls as well as boys. I forbade her from sleeping over at anyone's house… But life was generous with me and my prayers were answered. I was able to be with her when she reached puberty. She matured early. It took me two full years but now I am better. I hope the disease won't recur and I'll be with her forever. I can see life in her eyes and I rely on that whenever I need it. Serious illness is so bitter and harsh when you have children."

Time passed as I watched people sitting. I could sense my face growing tense. If I'd looked in the mirror, I would have found my face to be absolutely miserable. Cancer is bound together with death; everyone affirms this constantly. I looked at the people sitting around me, and everyone was represented: believers and unbelievers, those who've surrendered and those who still complain, men and women. I started to play a little game I felt forced to play. Which of us will die first? Who is the closest to falling off the edge of the abyss? Who will escape? Each of us has a life, a family, loved ones. What will they do when they go home at night? I looked at their miserable clothes.

Everyone who comes here gets dressed in a rush. It's mostly *galabiyas*—in both summer and winter—or tracksuits. Women cover their heads. People look at any woman whose hair isn't covered and try to guess if her hair is real or if she's wearing a wig, if her eyebrows are drawn on or if the natural ones are still there. Not many people dare to inquire. Those with experience don't ask, only new people have questions. Questions mean hope, and there is an equal probability that the answers could mean suffering and disappointment. My place is here amongst these people who God has selected for suffering, who have been cleansed by their experience of the world's impurities, who love each other. They respect each other's torment. They believe that God selected them because they have a hidden secret and are not simply ordinary human beings.

The only people who laugh or raise their voices are the people accompanying the cancer patients. They are often rude and boorish. They look at us with pity and seek refuge in God, hoping to never suffer from what we are afflicted with. They do this right in front of us. They hope for us to heal, but in this rude way. They don't know the heartbreak that resides in every one of my cells, all of which are prepared to die. After two or three days they will die, but they will pass down the memory of the suffering to the fresh, newly born cells.

When someone's phone rang and the owner answered it, I heard their voice and I was surprised. Do dead people answer the phone? But they're not dead yet. I overheard a woman who had come to see the doctor, talking to her son about the feast that she had prepared for her relatives the day before. I was stunned, and when the woman went in to see the doctor I asked him, "Has your mother been cured?"

"Cancer free for three years now, thank God, *hamdillah*."

"*Hamdillah*."

"She only suffers from joint pain because of the chemo."

A strange elation overtook me—I had the same look on my face as a man who suddenly confesses to a woman that he loves her.

I found her in a miserable state. It was the first time I'd seen misery etched in her features. But Haniyah was beautiful even in her suffering.

"Why do you insist on keeping your hair so short?" I asked her. "You're getting better, you should get rid of everything that shows you've had cancer!"

"It's nicer, and it's more trendy. Even people who don't know I am sick are 'impressed by my courage' as they always say. When women lose their hair it's an issue. It means we need to believe more in the beauty of our faces, especially when we dance…"

"Are you afraid of getting your scan results? Worried?"

"Of course! I worry every time. I replay my whole experience from the beginning. Whenever I see their faces, I remember my face. When you're better you too will come to your routine follow-up exams and be overcome with worry. But it will slowly dissipate. Each time it will be a bit less. But let's be clear—the worry will always be there. We're afraid of going through the whole thing again. And it's not only worry… there are countless other things that assail us too. After cancer we're never the same again. But don't be afraid, it won't recur."

"I hope so, *inshallah*. I want to get better first and then think about the next step—not recurrence or getting rid of it for good."

I didn't ask her if we would be better or worse off for having had this experience. All I knew was that I was living through it now.

"My situation is different and exhausting," I said. "The tumor is bound to my lungs and therefore also my breathing. The treatment itself poses difficulties as well— the radiologist says I have small lungs. If they'd been bigger the battle would have taken place in a bigger arena. And you have Dr. Yaacoub with you at all times…"

"You have Dr. Nasser with you at all times. Dr. Yaacoub wasn't with me from the beginning. We only started to get closer just before my final chemo session, when I'd already shown signs of getting better. That's when I started living life again. My mother was with me at first, but afterwards I begged her to go back to San Francisco. She had her work there and I was doing much better. That's when Yaacoub entered my life." She sighed, "Yaacoub!" and her features shaped into a reassuring smile, like a bouquet of passionately interwoven flowers.

"Why did we get sick?"

"It was our bodies' response."

"I ate healthy food and exercised regularly."

Her lips twisted, as if puzzled. "Cancer is like your body giving you a final warning. It warned you many times before this in gentler ways. You worried about them, but you still neglected it carelessly, so it rebelled. We don't think about our bodies in themselves. We dedicate our bodies to other people—to their bodies, their desires."

"You're a dancer. You're graceful. Didn't you take care of your body?"

"But not for its own sake. For the sake of my dancing and other people's standards. I never thought about staying at home for my body, eating healthily for it, doing things for it so it could support me. I kept it beautiful for my partner, or to be more feminine, but not for its own sake. Don't you spend time in the camps for other people's bodies?"

I thought back to the many times I didn't sleep at night or didn't eat. The times I'd cried, worried, lost my temper, been afraid, the times my chest tightened in panic.

How can a person live in our oppressive world without falling ill?

—

The sixth and seventh treatments went well. One week after the eighth session, though, I was lying in bed and my temperature spiked. I couldn't hold on any more. I felt like the angel of death was swooping down upon me. Nasser took me to the emergency room that evening. I had tried for all these months to withstand the pain, debilitation, and battles. I tried to stay home and avoid going to the ER, but this time it was stronger than me. The emergency room was not as scary as I had imagined it would be. Most of the patients were looking for painkillers or other ways to counter the side effects of their chemotherapy. Those people who were worse off were lying in beds. The ER doctor said that lymphoma accompanied by a fever is worrying and ordered an x-ray. I worried, but Nasser assured me that my lymphoma had gone and that it was a chemo side effect, nothing more. I believed it not only because he was saying it, but also because that's exactly what Dr. Yaacoub had confirmed many times.

The ER was packed full of potential future residents of heaven. They put me in a chair instead of a bed because I was able to sit up. A few steps away from me there was a patient lying in a hospital bed; his gown was open, his body exposed. He was emaciated. The torment of the disease had diminished him to a skeleton.

At nightfall Nasser should have gone home to his daughter. I begged him to but he refused. He was living between two kinds of hell, this poor man. The preliminary report and x-ray reassured us—the fever was a breakdown of my body because of the build-up of the chemo, nothing more. They would give me some nutritional supplements in an IV and keep me at the hospital overnight. I implored Nasser to leave me in their care and finally he did.

The man by my side was getting more and more exhausted. There were two men in the room with him. One looked like he was in his twenties and was probably his son. The other was in his fifties, his brother perhaps. I dozed off for a moment and a faint noise woke me. A team of people had gathered around the man, and then slowly dispersed. I looked over at him, and he had faded away. His soul flooded all around me. I felt it leaving with a rush of heat and then cold air blew in as if someone had opened the door, even though it was early September and still warm outside. The young man wept quietly, and voices started murmuring condolences, "May he rest in peace." They covered him quickly and moved him from beside me onto a stretcher. Tears poured forth from a place deep inside me that I was discovering for the first time. I want this torment to stop now. I can't take any more, please God, please Lord spare me of any more of this.

I got ahold of myself and went to the dance studio. I had to celebrate my last chemo session somehow, even if I didn't feel completely healed yet. I could barely walk and was extremely fatigued; my body couldn't support my constrained breathing. The spot where my tumor had been hurt and my hormones were totally imbalanced, making me feel cranky. Nasser said that we had reason to celebrate, because there was only a little more treatment left—only the radiotherapy.

"I'm in pain and I'm tired, is this really the last of the suffering? Everything hurts, I don't know even how to describe the kind of pain or where it is."

"Healing pains, these are healing pains, my dear. Snow melts, and on the night it melts it is colder than it was on the night when the snow fell, since the molecules that stuck together on the ground are starting to detach. Then they have to leave and leaving is painful. After the snow, we need bright sunshine to get our lives back on track again, to cleanse our bodies and the corners of our houses of the humidity that has settled into them. We need the sun to drive out the mold from the rotting wooden window frames. Go toward the sun!"

"How?"

"Go see Haniyah, dance, enjoy!"

Nasser was getting on my nerves. His answers were colder than the snow that he was talking about. I knew that he was growing tired of me, of all the worry I had put him through, no doubt. He did everything he could to support me, but I couldn't do anything but go on needing him and being grateful. I listened to him talking to his daughter, who had moved to the States to be with her mother and continue her studies after having finished high school. She said she wasn't having fun. She was depressed, felt alienated there, and wasn't getting along with her mother. He replied to her, "Go out with your friends, have pizza, you'll feel better!"

I told myself that Nasser was strange, so strange that I can't decipher him, even now. It's also strange how many different kinds of relationships I've had with him. His way of being a father is lovely—I wished that I'd been his daughter. I compared him with Baba who was so absent from my life. He was living out his own epic story in the war.

I took the elevator down to the dance studio that was located in the basement of a big mall. Its glass door, covered with a life-sized black-and-white silhouette of two Latin dancers, opened into a small reception area. The studio's Ukrainian receptionist sat at a desk and registered new members for lessons in high-heel hip hop. That day, Haniyah was standing in front of a huge CD player through a door to the right. The room was spacious and had a shiny brown parquet floor. Its walls were all mirrored.

Haniyah repeated Zorba's words, "I'm a little tired, I confess, but what's the harm in that? We fought and we were victorious. So I'm happy!" She added, "Yaacoub says that this disease is a journey and this medicine is like any other medicine, we take it to get better."

"But Yaacoub isn't suffering through the hell of actually taking it."

"What do you know about him? He grew up a without a father!"

"We've all lost parents: you, me, and him. But I'm talking about experiencing the death of the self. Don't you think about your grave? What will happen the first night you are buried? Don't tell me, 'We're all going to die.' I know that. But some of us are more likely to die sooner than others, and that's us. Yaacoub is still a prisoner of life and only suffers from the weakness and pain of other people. He sees this every day, but he remains at a distance from it. He hovers over the threshold to hell, trying to help other people who are swaying at its precipice. He is safe, but at the same time, terrified of it. We burn, and we put a salve on our burns. Nasser is also an observer of our hell. In a way, cancer frees us, doesn't it? This disease is a part of death. That itself is liberating."

"A person can be cured of cancer, though, but an orphan can never heal," said Haniyah. "You don't know Yaacoub. You think he's like a machine, a man who studied hard and wears a white coat. It's difficult to read his facial expressions, but behind his thick glasses are two eyes that didn't inherit their beauty from anyone else. They are so beautiful because they've shed so many tears. You don't know him at all."

I wanted to tell her to shut up, and that I do know him. I knew him before she did. I saw his eyes before she did. I saw his tears many years ago; they were the tears of a defeated child and an adolescent instigator. I saw his real, innocent face before it became a wax mold. I bought him a gelato. You weren't with us in Portofino—you are Vietnamese.

I was jealous of Haniyah. She was stealing my acquaintances, things that were mine, and keeping them to herself. She couldn't admit this because she didn't feel things in this way. Yaacoub's gaze was so profound that his eyes could drown out some of chemo's torment. But because her pain was limited, she couldn't express this well either.

I was happy with my jealousy because it was a sign of life. I was still able to feel things—miraculously, the chemo hadn't burned up everything inside me. I always felt jealous of her when she took on the role of teacher or expert on life. This wasn't because she'd been diagnosed a few months before me, but because she was the doctor's lover. I escaped my own infirmities by thinking about their relationship. It made me feel more alive to imagine its contours. She told me that fear had forced her to pursue him, like a police dog hunts down the scent of drugs. This was after she'd been cured, and she was afraid to take even one step backwards toward death. The thing cancer patients are most afraid of is relapse: that life will slip through their fingers after they've tasted survival. Life after the end of treatment looks different—like a mother returning to her children after being away for a long time.

"I could tell he was making a huge effort to act neutral around me, like he did with other patients. But he started calling me into his office last, after all the other patients had gone, so that we could talk about the States—San Francisco and Los Angeles. He missed the good times he had experienced there in the language we both spoke, in the school we both had attended. This shared history is what helped me get through to him. Then he visited me at the studio. He loved the world of dance, it wasn't at all like his world, and he started coming more often, sometimes every day."

Haniyah's assessment was wrong. Yaacoub was using her as a way to connect to his longing for his own roots, whose tenuousness still hurt him. The history of her father—the Palestinian communist comrade Abu Haniyah—helped him search for the heroism he'd been deprived of and that his father had been deprived of before him. He was searching for the power of the resistance and the appeal of its political parties. Haniyah's parents' history in the struggle, enhanced by her tattoos, took him right into the thick of his own troubling questions. What was I doing with these two Palestinians who were so bound up in their history? I wondered what he did when he saw the tattoo of the Kalashnikov on her bellybutton. She replied, "He wiped it off and then pulled the trigger!"

Her peals of laughter echoed off the large dance studio's mirrored walls. I don't know how to describe my feelings—somewhere between jealousy, disdain, affection, and gratitude toward life—since I'd started paying attention to this paradox that had brought us all together: her, me, Yaacoub, and Nasser. I was glad I'd noticed this—it meant that I cared about something other than cancer. That itself was a good sign.

"Did I tell you that I can take apart a Russian Kalashnikov and put it back together piece by piece? I can also do it blindfolded, just a little more slowly."

"Ha, I don't believe you."

"All the children of my generation learned how to do it. It has eight pieces that are easy to take apart and put back together. I was trained on a hill outside the city. I also know how to shoot well; I often still train in my mind. My trainer used to say that mental practice can be as good as actually doing it. I aim between the head and the chest, where there is no helmet or shield. The lethal shot is one in the throat or the face. The traditional Kalashnikov swerves to the left when you shoot so I have to aim slightly to the right of the target and practice getting used to its resistance when it bounces on my shoulder. I hold it between my arms, balanced on my right shoulder. I release the lever from the safety position to the middle, then two more positions down, to continuous or semi-automatic fire: hold, prepare, release, fire, shoot…"

"Did you ever fight in a war?"

"No. But I used to dream about fighting against Israel. The first time I saw an Israeli face to face was in a hotel in Sharm al-Shaikh where we'd gone for the wedding of a family friend. He was sitting in the lobby, thin, with a mustache and a beard, wearing a hat. I shuddered at the sight of him and felt pale. I didn't have a Kalashnikov with me though—I was wearing a pink dress and carrying a little golden purse!"

"Ignore the war now and remember that you are in Norinco—a dance studio, not a battlefield."

I didn't want to have to wait so long for details about her relationship with Yaacoub. It was time for revelations. I wanted to know everything about the two of them. It had taken me a long time to heal enough to be ready to hear and be moved by love stories. I was like the children in an African river valley who are eager to hear a story before their afternoon nap. They have to wait for their mother to finish her work, evenly watering the soil to keep the dust down, before she can tell it to them. I want to be well, like Haniyah is now. When I am, I will decide if I will destroy this world or just let it be.

Haniyah said, "A woman will love a man who reminds her of all her loved ones—the man who has the tenderness of her mother, the strength of her father, the laugh of her sister, the kindness of her brother, the courage of her first lover, the self-control of the second, the cruelty of the third, the embraces of the fourth…"

I thought about Nasser. I unpacked the image I had of him in my mind: He had the same serious features of my aunt's neighbor who wouldn't notice me standing on the balcony for hours because he was so absorbed in reading Pesoa. He had the same warm smile of a distant friend who one day caught me when I was about to fall on the stairs of the anthropology department in front of a whole crowd of students. He really was a lot like the loved ones who were lost to me, or from whom I'd fled. We all have a map of love in our minds. It begins with the collection of images of the people you've loved since childhood. You continue on sorting through personal histories and at a certain moment you complete the collage and your lover appears.

Haniyah was seductive. She had well-articulated thighs and you could see the beginning and end of all of her muscles, pronounced like those on Greek statues. Her skin was slightly pale. I couldn't find any flaws in her body. She continued on talking, "I pushed him to be with me, because he really wanted to, but stopped at the moment of slipping into a relationship. He didn't want to be that doctor who was in love with his patient. But for me each step in that direction meant a step closer to survival. I wanted to finish with that stage and become a former patient, and after that strictly become his lover. He used to know when to stop, when to give, and when to withhold fairly. Giving and withholding have equal weight on a balance. This is what most men don't know. A woman doesn't just ask for love any which way. But when she is at the edge of an abyss of pain, fear, or weakness, she has to find him. She doesn't need anyone else, but she also should not have to wait for him for too long. After a certain amount of waiting, she will pass a point where even the strongest magic in all of history wouldn't be able to bring her back to him.

I couldn't be like Haniyah. She lives her life in practice whereas I stop at the limits of theory. I can only sum up her passionate pleasure with cold terminology, I haven't yet mastered any other language.

"He's like Pygmalion, he loves seeing himself and his power in you."

"I don't know who that is."

"It's a legend."

"I love legends."

"Google it."

She tapped on my lips, as if she were typing it on a keyboard and searching for it on Google.

"Pygmalion was a sculptor who hated women," I told her. "Once he sculpted a beautiful woman from ivory and fell in love with her, so he asked Venus to make her come alive. She did, and he took control over her body. His story has become a way for people to explain an emotional complex whereby someone molds another person to suit their own needs and desires. It's like the director who turns an ordinary girl into a movie star, then falls in love with her, and monopolizes his own sick image of her. In reality he is in love with his own power to create and looking for a way to satisfy his own over-inflated ego. Yaacoub is in love with the power of life that he was able to transmit through you. He is in love with himself."

"But he's cured dozens of other women, hundreds even. You aren't being logical!"

"They don't look like you. He just uses different ways to manifest the power of life."

"I do believe he has a real problem with women, though. When he saw me dance here in the studio for the first time, he pulled me to him. He did it calmly and mechanically. Afterwards he turned into a possessed maniac and I was afraid of him. Then I got used to it. When he pulls out of me, he weeps and calls out for his mother..."

It was hard to hear her say these things. I want a doctor to cure me, not a maniac who weeps when he sleeps with a woman and calls out for his mother! As I listened to her critical commentary, prompted by our discussion of mythology, unanswerable questions crept into my mind: What did Nabila do with the little jumpsuits that he sometimes vomited milk on? To whom did she give his little blue and white hats? Did she keep his baby shoes for his children like other mothers do? I also thought about how he took the news of his father's death. How did he return from his graveside, leaving him all alone under the soil? How did he pass his first fatherless night?

"In you, he is searching for a Virgin-Whore. You are the perfect representation of this—a mix of pure, virginal women and a group of whores at the same time."

"Ha ha, thank you, I really love that! But I am still out of danger, and my health is good. No man can love a woman about to die... he won't kiss a body he knows in a few days will be worm food."

"Have you ever seen a dead body?"

"No, I was very young when my father was assassinated. All I remember of his death is a box wrapped in a flag, bouquets of flowers, and massive crowds."

"They stuff the body's openings with cotton, tie a sash around the head so the loose jaws stay in place, then wrap the whole body in a white cloth."

"Why white when it will be covered in dirt almost immediately?"

"Hm. I don't have an answer for that. Perhaps to make the dead pure so they can confront their sins, or to declare peace here on earth…"

"In Vietnam they are Buddhists so they usually burn bodies. They gather the ashes in precious jars or fertilize the garden with them, or make them into glass crystals that they shape into a pendant. They might take them to a skillful craftsperson to fashion into a ring or even turn them into fireworks! My mother's people practice the ritual of heavenly burial. They put the bodies in a high-up place like a mountain peak so that predators will eat them. It is a practice of moral generosity to honor sharing between all creatures. In these places souls reincarnate and the soul of the dead being occupies another living creature. The donation of souls is the pinnacle of nobility, a bit like organ donation."

I kept trying to redirect the conversation back toward Yaacoub, and she complied. She responded to my persistence and kept feeding my curiosity, not in order to anger me—she was done with acting so trivially, like a cancer patient would—but she had that desire to listen to her own voice, even if only to be sure she was alive and had fully recovered.

She lifted her foot onto the plastic chair I sat on and fastened the buckle of her silver shoe, with its rounded toes and square high heel. She looked at the clock hanging on the wall. I still couldn't get up easily, the chemo deposits in my tissues were still making my muscles feel heavy. I had lost my former agility by spending so much time lying in bed.

She was wearing thick nylon stockings with a short, sporty black cotton skirt that covered only the top of her thighs, and a tight, long-sleeved black cotton blouse. A half circle was cut into the chest and back, so that her pale quince-colored skin showed through. Her short black wavy hair was stuck to her head, shining like the hair of a newborn baby. This revealed her taut, elegant tattooed neck, free of any other design or accessory, except the beauty of healing. Why do people decorate and exhaust themselves caring about colors, dyes, and adornments that weigh down their bodies? The most beautiful adornment is health. Haniyah shone through her healthy body as if she'd never been afflicted by cancer at all.

A twenty-something young man entered. He was medium height, with brown skin. His long, thick brown hair that covered his neck was held back by a little girl's plastic headband, revealing his powerful features. He was stuffed into a gray tracksuit, tighter fitting than usually seen on a man, accentuating his muscles. Haniyah said, "My friend, Akram. He's my partner in the studio, and the number one dance teacher in Amman."

He greeted me neutrally, noticing that I didn't belong to their world and perhaps guessing that I had recently risen from my grave, as I was pale, yellow, still wearing a turban, and my Levi-brand jeans felt loose on my body. Their world stopped at appearances.

She pushed the remote control to turn on the studio's sound system and the rhythms started expanding slowly. Suddenly, something that had been slumbering in my soul awoke. It was a tango practice and the music was La Cumparsita.

Haniyah assured me that life force is not imaginary. She is a straightforward and uninhibited woman who knows how to look after herself. She is her own first priority. The world comes next. That means she doesn't wait for anything or anyone. She gives as much as she takes. Anything beyond that is forced labor and, as she put it, the era of forced labor is long gone. I'll admit I admired her personality, but I couldn't be like her. I was more serious than her, and also more tragic.

Whenever I felt miserable and desperate, meeting up with her would help recharge my battery. She told me one evening, "If your man is over forty, dance the waltz with him. You will give him the time to discover you—your depths, your femininity, your elegance. That's all he needs. If he's under forty, dance the salsa with him. You'll show him your passion, your fire, you'll show him that you're alive. That will do it." I followed up, "How old should I be? I don't have a lot of time." She replied, "It doesn't matter. A woman who knows how to dance is ageless. This is what all women want. And you have plenty of time ahead of you!"

Haniyah always let her partner lead. Letting him lead was not obedience as I used to believe. I never gave in to weakness, failure, or domination, in the same way that I never gave in to love. I was always vigilant, measuring the distance to the edge of the abyss and stopping right there. This vigilance robbed me of pleasure, and prevented me from losing myself in something until the end. So everything I experienced was limited. Had I known earlier how short life really was, I would have chosen different ways to live my life. So what if a person tastes failure, subservience, or weakness? No one dies of experiencing a bitter or happy ending. Who would give you an hour of her life, if all her cards had been burned?

"Dancing is like building a shell around you and then emerging from it: it is both introversion and extroversion," Haniyah told me. "It is also like building shells for others so they move in and out of them as well.

"The Arabic word for shell, "*qawqaaʻa*," is so hard to say. So much effort to pronounce those letters! The English word *shell* is easier! Perhaps Yaacoub built a thick shell and I helped get him out of it, but I also know how to make him go back inside."

I thought about the snails at our house in Raqqa. They would disappear and we'd never know where to.

"He was very discreet. Even in our most intimate moments, he didn't stray too far from his shell. It was only afterwards that he changed. Then, his desires were set ablaze. He revealed them like a seasoned diplomat, he started to speak while we were having sex, he cursed, used vulgar Arabic street language… Once I asked him how he came to know all of those obscenities. He told me that when he went to visit his father's family in their old house, he would listen to the children cursing late at night when adults couldn't hear them. He loved all those vulgar words and committed them to memory!

"When I dance I can pick him up in my arms and throw him back into his shell, I can pull on his beard—ha ha—and it quivers like the threads of a spider's web. Have you ever touched a spider's web and had its delicate threads cling to your sticky fingers?"

I conjured up an image of Mama with Jude and Salma when they were little, playing on the beach in

Portofino, wearing their little colorful bathing suits. Jude's was blue with pink hearts and Salma's was brown with orange stripes. I asked her, "Hanoi, does he have fungus on his toenails?"

"Who? Yaacoub? Why?"

She thought a bit, smiling to herself, but her smile quickly changed into an uncomfortable stare—a reproach, an accusation maybe...

"I don't know about that, but the nails on his big toes are yellow and twisted."

My God, Mama, I thought, you really did know everything!

Radiation therapy is more like recovery than treatment compared to the torment of chemo, but it still wasn't as easy as I'd expected it to be. I'd almost lost all hope. I was so close to the finish line, I could see it clearly... I just had to break through the tape stretched across it with my body that has so far steadfastly endured this marathon.

It took the team a month to prepare the plan for precisely where to direct the radiation beams onto the site of the tumor, so as to hit it directly. The point of this was to kill any malignant cells that might have remained, without causing damage to any of my organs. It was my first chemotherapy and cortisone–free month since I'd begun my treatment journey, and my hair finally started growing back. The radiation process itself was painless. I took off my turban and the whiteness of my scalp accentuated by the prickly black dots sprouting atop it surprised me. They wouldn't fall out again. My upper body had to be naked, and looking at my nakedness in the mirror was painful. Why must I subject my body to all of these humiliating things? I lay down on the table, putting my head in a protective metal mask that they had custom-made for me ahead of time so it would fit me exactly. They closed it tightly and it gave a clank. I closed my eyes and the huge radiation room disappeared from view. I could breathe through the nose holes, still struggling with my heavy breathing, but I knew this weight would now start to slowly lift itself from my chest. I looked like a medieval knight ready for battle. Everyone left the room. They turned off the lights and left me free to pray, far from my body, trapped in profound darkness, like a fetus inside a strange womb, asking no questions. Or perhaps I was more like a seed planted deep in the earth, starting to germinate where no one could even see it. Ten minutes later the light came back on and I could hear the technicians' voices. I put on my clothes and left. The day of the final treatment came. I had done twenty daily sessions, with breaks on Friday and Saturday. Not so bad! A month would pass just like the one that came before. Radiation depletes what little energy the body has—it chips away at it like a hammer on a limestone wall. All my bones hurt. I was plagued with vertigo and near constant vomiting. Water couldn't quench the dryness that attacked my mouth and throat. From time to time, my cough came back. The pain in the location of the tumor bothered me so much that I was unable to bend over. The doctor supervising the treatment told me that this was from radiation burns, a common side effect, and that the pain would only last a bit longer. The light burned the living cells near my heart; the skin under my left breast was black and peeling off in flakes. She assured me this was normal, just like any burn caused by heat. She said that the important thing was that my lungs were strong and could withstand the impact of twenty sessions. She said that my life after having undergone radiation therapy would be better. I asked her about a complete recovery. She replied that according to the tests, I had already made a full recovery with the chemotherapy. This was an adjuvant therapy, which would reduce the possibility of the disease recurring.

"So there is a possibility it could recur?"

"Recurrence is always a possibility."

These answers frustrated me, like a gratuitous death right at the height of joy, like a person who was saved from drowning in a sinking boat only to slip on a banana peel and hit her head.

I filed what she was saying away in the back of my brain where I flung all the information I didn't want to deal with. Dr. Yaacoub had counseled me not to listen to anyone's words but his. I love his extreme monism... it offers me peace in the same way a loving Greek god offers an auspicious destiny to an epic hero.

I waited my turn at the pharmacy in the cancer center to get my prescription cough syrup and throat lozenges to offset the effects of the radiation therapy. I sat next to a man who looked like a shaykh in a mosque. He'd also taken a number in line and was waiting for his prescription. He seemed calm, his fifty-year-old face betraying no signs of the disease. I was in the mood to strike up a conversation with someone—it reassured me that I was slowly regaining my connections to life on more than one level. It was a wonderful coincidence, in this place where the competition is between equally depressing things, that he had undergone the exact same therapy I had. His tumor was also in the gland between his two lungs, but he had needed fewer sessions because his tumor was smaller. That was five years ago. He told me that he'd forgotten all about it and only came for regular check-ups or when something else non-cancer-related showed up, like a cold, because he had insurance at this center. He said God was good and would heal me like He had healed him, reassuring me that life would get better. He'd even gotten married again after he was cured and had more children!

I finished the radiotherapy sessions at the same time every day, left the center, and came face-to-face with a hearse at the main door of the center, near the island of bushes in the middle of the road. The driver always stood testily, leaning on the car door and waiting for a body that had been shrouded inside to be taken directly to the cemetery. The corpse doesn't get to go back home, it doesn't get to bid farewell to its bed or the recesses of memory. The family will all follow it to where it will disappear into the ground forever. They complete their duty, satisfying their consciences by exchanging condolences, "At least he (or she) isn't suffering anymore." Then they immerse themselves in their own lives again. The car is like an ambulance. The dead bodies enter and exit through the back door, which has a Qur'anic phrase stenciled in black on it: "Every soul shall taste of death." The name of the Islamic Sedrat al-Muntaha association is written in the same script on the side door. On my first days of treatment, I would be struck by these words from a distance and fall into an unmistakable depression. I would turn away from them but even if I walked down a different sidewalk, something in my mind would draw me back. I resisted this—Nasser would come pick me up in his gray Mitsubishi, and I would throw myself into the refuge of the passenger seat and escape.

The hearse is still standing there today but my feelings about it are less pronounced. There is more distance between the two of us now, and it seems my date with it has been postponed until further notice.

The day of the last session drew nearer, and I wanted it to be a normal day. Things were going well, soon it would be the end and my appointment diary would be empty—no more chemo treatments, no more radiation. The plan was that I'd have an MRI in one month, then another a month later, then again in three months. If everything went according to plan, I'd then only have to go in for regular checkups every three months. In the following year, only once every six months. I really hoped that my body had learned its lesson and was done betraying me. I'd go home after the appointment, lie down on my bed, and read *Meditations* by Marcus Aurelius, a book that emanates solace and comfort: "O my soul, the time I trust will be, when thou shalt be good, simple, single, more open and visible, than the body by which it is enclosed. Thou wilt one day be sensible of their happiness, whose end is love, and their affections dead to all worldly things." It was a bit easier for me to read now, and my relationship with books would improve further when my hormones started to balance themselves out. This relationship would be one of the few things that I'd keep from my old life.

I asked God to let this goodbye to the warrior's mask be final, and I saluted the crew of technicians who had helped me get better. Cancer patients also have their own little joys and festivities.

Haniyah met me at the gates to the radiation center. She came to pick me up so we could have lunch at the studio to celebrate my final session. We walked toward her car, pain gripping my chest, my body fatigued. I tried to convince myself that I was healed—that like Odysseus I was leaving the land of the dead behind. Now all that was left was rest, recovery, and prayers. I was surprised when Haniyah stripped my gray turban off my head. She unwound that long piece of cotton, tied it loosely to the antenna of a car on the side of the road and hurriedly walked away. The driver didn't notice it and took off, my turban flapping above the car like a banner. I found myself facing the world naked—with only the truth of my experience, like a sheep shorn of its wool in the spring. Haniyah said, "God, your hair is pretty… in a month you'll need to use a comb again!"

I was wracked with the anxiety of my cancer coming back. I would ask Nasser, "Why am I in pain? Why am I coughing? They said I was totally healed." And Nasser, blissful in the wake of our success, would say, "It doesn't matter, you're in a bit of pain—they're healing pains."

Baba called. I hadn't heard his voice in two months since the lines from Raqqa had been cut off. It was difficult to get to the Thuraya satellite phone stations because of the number of snipers that had multiplied lately. Everything was chaos; no one knew who was killing whom. We used code words on the phone, for fear of Daesh, al-Nusra, the Assad regime, the Free Army, the Righteous Guardians of God…

What matters is that my family is still alive.

"Hi Joumane, how are you, dear? Are you finished?"

"Baba, why did you give up on me?"

"What…? I can't hear you."

"I'm fine Baba, *hamdillah*, I've finished my treatments."

"Thank God, you've finished, *hamdillah*. God had mercy on us, now it's all in the past, forget it now."

"Baba, I'm exhausted."

"Don't worry, that's normal. Having your appendix cut out can leave you in pain for a year, so you must be reeling now from all the treatments you underwent. By God, you are going to come back from this strong as a horse, stronger than the strongest young woman."

"How are you all?"

"We're fine. Things are getting better, less tense, *inshallah*. What are they saying where you are?"

"They say the situation is getting better."

"Of course, of course… Tamerlane passed through, the Guru passed through…"

"*Inshallah*, Baba, *inshallah*. Do you have food?"

"Oh yes, we have everything. We could send you some if you wanted."

Jude grabbed the phone. "Joumane! How are you?"

"Exhausted."

"The important thing is that we're done. You will get your health back one step at a time."

"I'm afraid it's going to come back."

"It won't come back. Others have all been cured, everyone who's had a case similar to yours, Abu Farah, Rahaf, Claudia... Your cancer is over and the war isn't."

"Jude, come here."

"And the worry I carry with me everywhere, who will I leave that to? Women are about to be forbidden from traveling without a chaperone. God loves you, he took you far from here, and He loves Mama because He took her before she saw all this darkness. Planes are bombing us from above and gunmen are killing on the ground. Our father's sister—*Sans-Culottes*, Auntie Soueida—died."

"No..."

"Really."

"How?"

"She was tired. She had bladder cancer and underwent difficult treatments. Then she had a surgery in Damascus and died one month later." The word "cancer" shook me again, and Jude scolded me, "This isn't your case. You're better... enough. It's finished."

"Poor Auntie without her underpants!"

"Of course, poor Auntie, thank God that Mama died with dignity. They weren't able to properly bury Soueida because of the bombing. Instead, they buried her in her brother's back garden. A week later they came and moved her to the cemetery. The person who dies without finding a grave has a lingering bitterness about them. People search for a way to cover their family's dead bodies so that the street dogs won't eat them."

I hung up thanking God that, at least, they were safe. I stored her words in the back of my mind and devoted myself to my own suffering. It was as if I had never known my Auntie Soueida and had never eaten the sweets she made.

I waited for my regular check-ups with an anxiety that made time difficult to conquer. Every detail of Dr. Yaacoub's cell became familiar to me, and his waxen face finally softened into more normal expressions. He laughed, we spoke for a while, we looked at each other's faces and hid from a question dangling out there somewhere, waiting to be asked. We didn't speak about Haniyah; it was as if she didn't exist in our world. The first moments of the visit were by far the most intense. He would look at the MRI report on the computer screen in front of him, and he and I would enter into a round of Russian roulette. He would have the gun in his hand, a bullet loaded in one of the six chambers. He would spin the cylinder while I waited and hoped the bullet would not come out and kill me. He would tell me, "The tests are normal." I would win this round, but I've become a hostage to this gamble for life, whenever it's time for my next appointment—in one month, in three months, in six months. Each time, Yaacoub and I will play a new round of Russian roulette.

Ramadan came, and I fasted once again. I hadn't been able to fast during the previous Ramadan because I was undergoing treatment. Nasser's three children were coming from America to spend the month with him. He was totally engrossed in preparations to welcome them. I told him he could hire Tammy to help him put everything in order at his place. I no longer needed her to work in my house, and in fact I wished that I had been able to help him myself and participate in the celebrations with them. But I preferred to stay away—I already am away; they're his family, but who am I in that picture?

Nasser apologized for needing to be so busy with them. I asked him not to say sorry. I was the one who needed to apologize for every second I had kept him busy with my illness, my obsessions, and my pain. I couldn't possibly ask for anything more. He was a saint who had given me what my father, or anyone in my family, was unable to. I wanted him to be the happiest man in the world in whatever way he chose to be. I would content myself with my slowly recuperating body.

Despite my loneliness, I felt really good during Ramadan. After the evening prayer, I would log in to my Facebook account, which I hadn't done in four months. I'd had no interest in being in touch with anyone except my family, whose Internet service was cut off. Nasser used to also beg me not to listen to the news from my country or read childish political debates on Internet sites. I surfed the web for a while and came across something written by a young man from Raqqa. I left it for a second but then decided to read it. A familiar name stopped me in my tracks: "The engineer Suhayl Badran was kidnapped in front of his own house"! I knew this wasn't a joke. I knew it was something real, something we should have seen coming.

Salma later said to me, "They grabbed him in front of the house from a car with tinted windows. One of the neighbors saw it happen and Baba shouted to them that they inform us. It was about seven in the evening. The kidnappers called after midnight and asked for a ransom of fifty thousand dollars."

Before this happened, Salma and Jude had investigated similar kidnappings. They and other relatives had formed a kind of crisis center for people in this situation. They identified possible culprits and started family mediation. By the time I could finally speak to Salma, my mind had pictured all the possible scenarios. I surrendered to the cruelty of my family's tragic fate. My sisters were strong women. Jude asked me to hold on, the problem wouldn't take long to solve. I felt that she was unusually calm in dealing with calamities. Salma announced that she would gamble with Baba's life, by being slow in paying the ransom. She decided to negotiate with the extremist faction whose identity we'd verified.

I didn't contact Nasser. I let him enjoy being with his children. I threw my body onto the same chair in which I had received the news of my cancer diagnosis a year and a half ago. I put my hand on my screen where I kept Messenger open, waiting for news. Sadness also needs energy, and I didn't have enough to be in more pain. The cancer used up all of my energy. I stayed online until morning. I found a picture of Baba and bade him farewell. He was a great engineer—pure, elegant, noble—who stood alone like a willow tree, giving everyone shade while no one supported him in return. What is he doing now amongst those murderers and extremists—hateful people who have begun ruling a part of the country illegitimately, murdering people illegitimately, and completely destroying the state illegitimately? The flesh and blood of our best citizens is what makes up the state. We built it with our love and sweat, our deprivation and dreams, and it was destroyed in a matter of days. I harkened back to the days when he used to carry me as a little girl and we would sing together, "*Salima ya Salaama*" or "One Way Ticket," or "My beloved Syria, you are my dignity come back to me, come back to me, you are my identity. *Tam tatam, tata.*" After that he told me how Henry Ford had changed the face of the world by building things people needed. He said if you had asked people what they wanted then, they would have told you faster horses! Afterwards, he told me that the best things ever to result from war were Romanticism and the waltz. I watched him detailing his plans, and he told me about a tourist resort on the river, a small camp for oil workers, and healthy homes for people with low incomes, with a green belt that prevented dust storms. Everything he built was eco-friendly and clean, cleaner than the time he lived in.

I told Salma, "I am begging you to pay whatever they are asking. I'll send you anything you need. John will transfer me any amount we don't have." She asked me to calm down. She said that I was far away and I didn't know the customs there anymore—nothing in Raqqa right now is how it was when I left three years ago. She said that God has not forsaken us. I assured her that, no, He has not forsaken us.

The news that came three days later indicated that Baba was well. They had given him his daily medicines, especially those for his heart, and this gave him a better chance of survival. Two days later Salma heard his voice on the phone; at first he spoke steadily and then he burst into sobs. The man who took the phone from him spoke in what sounded like a Saudi dialect of Arabic, saying that if she didn't pay what they asked, they'd cut out his tongue. I imagined his torment, I imagined him speaking without a tongue. How would he say, "Joumane," "Syria," "chivalry," "*habibti*," "what is right shall eventually prevail"?

Salma assured me that it was just a war of nerves. People who are asking for money are keen to keep their victims alive and will in the end take whatever amount they can get. I had always known that Salma was tough, but I never imagined that she would be able to negotiate with the most dangerous terrorist group in the world so calmly! She brought the amount down to fifteen thousand, telling the negotiator on their side that we didn't have more than that, that we'd spent all our money on our mother's treatment before she died of cancer and now she was spending the rest of it on her sister's treatment for the same disease. He told her, you own many things. She told him, come and take them. Pick a time for delivery and how you want to take things. Two hours before the set time, Baba was back home. He looked bedraggled and thin, with a long beard, but he was fine and in good health. It was actually Jude who was the mastermind behind his return. She said that someone she worked with in the soup kitchen had helped her to free him, but we had to keep it under wraps.

The bombing of the Islamic State's main centers in Raqqa intensified. Schools, government buildings, and luxury villas in the new neighborhoods were all bombing targets. The fighters and their families started flowing into neighborhoods inside the old town. They broke into people's homes and settled in to live with them. The aerial bombings had shattered their homes. Salma told me how

one night there was a knock on the door. She opened
it and there was a tall woman wearing a black cover and
a niqab. She confronted Salma holding a machine gun.
Salma winced and shrank back, and the woman lifted
her niqab to show she was an Arab woman. There was a
ruddy-skinned man behind her who looked Chechnyan,
dressed like the Taliban, carrying a baby in his arms and
holding the hand of a toddler next to him. The woman
pushed Salma back with the barrel of her gun. She wanted to speak to her but couldn't find her voice. Baba was
behind Salma, asking her to let them come in. A bit later,
two more families followed them in the same way. My
family packed up some things and left the house.

Baba's office was in the Thakanah neighborhood on
the west side of the city, and it was not in much better
shape, but my family moved there. Jude assured me that
the terrorists would not prolong their stay in a place where,
although they had their relatives nearby, they were isolated
from their leaders. Jude was full of strange tactical information, but it was always correct. They left our house, but
only after causing tremendous destruction. Salma told me
this on the phone, laughing, as she sang the words of a
song about Palestine by Suleiman Issa, that we used to sing
in school: "Strange faces… on my stolen land, selling our
fruit and occupying our house."

They took everything that did not weigh a lot and
was worth something. The Louis XV chair was ruined
and smelled of excrement; they transformed the wardrobe
with the National Bloc manifesto on it into a pantry. It
was filled with oil and za'atar, jam, and bread crumbs.
But the worst destruction was of Uncle Yusuf's kids'

property—they occupied the hospital he'd given to his two sons who were doctors. They forced his staff to take care of their injuries. My cousin Ali, who was a neurosurgeon, shouted, "Anything that survived the socialist nationalization project has now been taken by the New Islam!"

The Salt of Pirates

My sister Salma didn't like to read novels, especially not Arabic novels. Her aversion to them was the result of an early emotional blow during the summer she turned twelve. She had picked up Naguib Mahfouz's *Khan al-Khalili*. It was probably the first novel that she had begun after reading only children's books. She finished it in one sitting and then cried nonstop for three days straight about the fate of Rushdi, the protagonist, who died of tuberculosis. She was a whimpering mess. Baba reacted harshly to her melodrama, which was not typical of him. He scolded her and told her she was mad, because when he found her shattered from weeping he thought that something terrible had happened to someone in our family. After this, Salma decided never to read a novel ever again. She started reading biographies of celebrities, success stories, and at one point became very interested in parapsychology. She grew into a beautiful young woman—she had a round face, brown hair, almond-shaped hazel eyes, and golden-brown skin. My friends used to say that she was a younger version of me, but they were exaggerating because she was much more beautiful than I was. Whether she was busily preparing food, leafing through the pages of a book, or watching a program on TV, I was always struck by how she looked when I took a moment to gaze at her. She was well proportioned, with her round nose, full lips, and a small stature appropriate for her elegant, soft features. She had a good sense of humor that always amused me. I was happy she was my sister.

She had a smooth life, with no major obstacles or problems, but no dazzling distinctions either. She used to try to maintain a strong, understated presence and aimed to succeed slowly, afraid of people being envious of her. She studied economics and majored in business administration at the American University of Beirut. She had ambitions to succeed in the field of business and looked for opportunities in the Gulf after she graduated. She got a quick answer from a British tourism investment company that had projects in Oman. She went there right away.

Salma didn't have passionate or emotional feelings for anyone. No one knew if she loved a particular man or even what connected her to people. She had points of view, rather than emotions. This meant she was able to succeed at her job as a liaison between the company she worked for and foreign embassies in Muscat.

The first deviation in life that Salma had ever confronted was falling in love with a pirate. It was exactly like the story of a princess in a fairy tale. I never would have thought that pirates were still around today until my sister told me her story.

At the time, the company Salma worked for sent her to the Musandam Peninsula, in the Sohar region. It was also called Foamy Island because of the way the waves crashed against the rocky shore on the steep coastline. It was the first Arab land the sun rose over each day. The island was still virgin territory, and their company had the privilege of claiming it for tourism. Until recently, it had been a closed military area because it was so close to the Iranian coastline, which was like a waistband with an Arab dagger cutting through the middle of it only forty kilometers away. Salma said that when she observed the scene, she realized how deceptive distances could be. She also said, "They didn't have any tourist facilities. We rented small white houses, like beach chalets, at the foot of tremendous mountains. They belonged to the local residents and were close to the primitive port, which was no more than a floating dock where steamboats belonging to smugglers between Musandam and the Iranian coast would anchor. The place was enchanting. You could just make out rows of majestic palm trees growing in the desert behind the extended, golden, virgin coastline."

She went on to tell her love story: "The ink-blue sea flows through narrow mountain passes and then expands toward a horizon concentrated toward the sea. It's a world not at all like the Mediterranean. From the coast, the water is so clear that you can see colorful red and gold fish swimming around cheerfully with other sea creatures—maybe crabs or sea lizards?—with pink and blue bellies, which leave the sea in small groups to scuttle onto the shore, which is green with thick seaweed. In that clean, odorless breeze, pregnant with a relaxing, heavenly floating steam, I craved the water. But it wasn't possible to swim—the beaches could not accommodate it. No one went swimming there. No women wore bathing suits. There were only a few young boys in white *dishdashas*, and little girls wearing embroidered dresses hiding behind the black *abayas* of their mothers, who carried straw baskets full of fish and vegetables.

"I decided to just wade in the water a little, not far from shore, and float on the raft belonging to one of the engineers who was with us. The raft was an orange inflatable mattress smaller than the one we used to have in our swimming pool back home. I stretched out on it in my cut-off jeans, a white t-shirt, and nothing else. I got into the water and lay down. I looked out over the endless blue before me. I spent some time absorbing the amazing silence and closed my eyes. I fell asleep for what I thought was a moment. When I closed my eyes, I was still rocking near the shore, but more time passed than I had expected because when I opened my eyes again I was at sea: I had passed through the narrow passageway, and was now surrounded by nearby mountains. I entered a state of anxiety that was really closer to fear and terror. The coastline had disappeared behind the strait, and there was no trace of any people or boats, not even a nearby island. There was no one who knew where I was, no one who would notice I was missing. I surrendered to my fate, which seemed close at hand—I would either fall prey to wild sea creatures, or I would drown. I began to pray, sailing through the heart of the mountains with their unique beauty surrounding me. There were no waves to push me and the sea was very calm. It wasn't the time for seasonal winds, but the birds were flying at a low altitude.

They were large, probably hawks, but they ignored me. No sooner had I breathed a sigh of relief than I felt the waters move near me and a dolphin—an animal I'd only seen previously in *National Geographic* magazines that Baba had received from America—jumped up out of the water. I knew from reading about them that they were friendly animals, but this one could easily flip over the float that I was lying on. Then I could end up like the prophet Jonah, who was swallowed by a whale. So I quickly started repeating the prayers my grandma always used to say: "There is no God but You, all glory is to You. I have been wrong and unjust!" It seemed the dolphin's movements were my salvation, since it jumped all around me and drew the attention of a little boat that was moving along the direction of the shore, from north to south. I heard the sound of a motor and rejoiced. I started waving my arms so that I almost toppled into the water. It was an old, traditional boat with triangular sails, but it had a steam engine. My distress became obvious. The engine turned off and the boat floated up to me. There were two men on board; they stretched out their hands to me but I was unable to climb into their boat. My body had weakened with fear after I realized I was saved. One of them threw me a rope ladder, I climbed onto it, and I found myself on the deck of their boat."

"Wow—thank God you survived this! How come you never told us? God granted you a new life!" I kept on scolding her, "How could you be so reckless? How did you let yourself get so close to dying?"

At the time, she smiled victoriously. She was proud of herself since she knew that no one else in our family would ever have an adventure like this one of hers.

She said, "Oh, but this is only where the fairytale begins, Ms. Joumane! I was trying to pull myself together as I first sat on the wooden deck, trying to breathe life in once again. But I soon burst into tears, when I realized that I was all alone with two strange men at sea.

"The younger one, who couldn't have been more than eighteen years old, was inside the cabin. He had taut muscles, dark skin, and fancy designs cut into his kinky hair like a soccer star. He was wearing cut-off jeans shorts, like I was, and a short green t-shirt torn off above his stomach with 'Peace!' written on it in yellow letters.

"The other man stood in front of me silently, puzzled by my weeping. He was about twenty-five—no more— and perhaps even a bit younger than me. Or at least, this is what I gathered from his eyes, because his body appeared to be much older. He looked like he could be mixed race. He had transparent gray eyes, like a wild cat. His muscles were practically popping out of his burnished skin. He was bare-chested except for a few sparse hairs, and his lower body was wrapped in a white *dishdasha*. He looked like an Arab corsair, his long black hair covered by a red Omani head wrap, embroidered with yellow Kashmiri patterns.

I tried to calm myself down but when I looked at him, I burst into a fit of sobbing once again. I was afraid of being raped, tortured, or contracting a disease. The boat's motor turned over and it crossed the water toward the strait. In mere moments, we'd turned around the moun-tain, and the coastline I had taken off from reappeared in front of us. He turned off the motor and said in English, 'Calm down, you're near home now. Nature just played a trick on you. The coast here is no more than a narrow strip of land, immersed in water, and after that you go straight into a deep abyss. The depths here aren't gradual like in the Mediterranean where you come from.'

"'How do you know that I am from the Mediterranean?' I asked.

"'Faces don't lie.'

The other young man, Jaafar, brought glasses of tea and I could smell the scent of cardamom and other exotic spices wafting from them. Ibrahimu handed me a glass, saying, 'You'll feel better after drinking this, it's Omani tea.'

The tea had a pungent taste. I gradually became more relaxed, especially when he asked in the Omani dialect, 'Should I take you on a little tour around or do you want to go back to shore right away?'

Rather than save myself, I decided to take a tour with this stranger!

"The oak-wood boat took off, plowing through the sea like a sword cutting through water—there was no foam, no surf, only the deep blue. It was as if I'd closed my eyes for a few minutes, taken a magic potion, and traveled three centuries back in time. Were it not for the motor that was hidden inside of the wooden box, there would have been no signs of the modern world at all. Only the three of us existed. Ibrahimu, who only knew a little bit of Arabic, said that his grandfather was Portuguese and was born on a ship that took off from Istanbul and raided the coast of Zanzibar in the nineteenth century. Arab pirates had stopped the ship but didn't kill the child. A poor woman from the Arab Mahra tribe there raised him like her own son. When he was a young man, the daughter of one of the ruling tribe's families fell in love with him. His blonde hair and blue eyes enchanted her. They got married and ran away to Mombasa together. They lived there off of trade from the sea and had his father, who was born a trader and later married a woman from Mombasa. She was a famous painter and would become Ibrahimu's mother. Ibrahimu studied in the ship-building academy. Jaafar had studied Spanish literature at the National University of Dar es Salaam in Tanzania.

"After he had told me all of this, I asked him bluntly and perhaps naively, 'Are you pirates?'

Ibrahimu laughed, and his pearly white teeth shone, highlighting his pink lips. 'That's what the people on the coast call us, and they frighten their children with stories of us!'

"I felt an inherited tremor of fear run through my body. But the Ford sunglasses he put on calmed me down and reassured me that I wasn't living in some kind of historical tale.

"We arrived at an interconnected chain of islands and anchored the boat on one of them. 'Is it inhabited?' I asked.

"'Of course, with fishermen and traders.' He pointed into the distance. 'Look at those mountains—they're in Iran. See how close they are?'

"The mountain peaks loomed ahead of us, impressive in their height and seeming to emerge from the bottom of the sea. He said, 'This is Maymzar Island. Its residents are Arab, with a lot of witches among them.'

"To me, the place looked like nothing but a massive pile of rocks. 'Where do the witches live?'

"'Their homes are in the mountains, they aren't exposed to the sea—the doors and windows face the interior.'

"'Wow. There is a seaside community that turns its back to the water?'

"'They wanted to protect themselves from pirates and invaders, so they built their windows to face the interior, so it would look to passersby like the mountains were uninhabited. The rumor then spread that the witches' magic hid the place and its inhabitants.'

We approached it to dock. Ibrahimu went into the cabin, and then came out looking totally different. He gave off a strong scent of amber, and he was wearing blue-flowered Hawaiian shorts and a bright white cotton t-shirt with long sleeves. His turban was wrapped on his head and his hair, which appeared to have been inherited from his Portuguese grandfather rather than his African grandmother, hung down over his shoulders.

As we disembarked, he said, 'Let's walk around the island a little.' I had an eerie feeling about this—bad thoughts and Hollywood movie plots rushed to my mind. But then the sounds of a live person calling out the *azaan* without a loudspeaker drowned out these thoughts. Calm, even joyful feelings washed over me, and I forgot that I came from a world of destruction, murder, and troubling news reports. I ran into a boy leading a black donkey with a pack saddle. That multiplied my joy. I thought of you!"

"Because of the donkey?"

"You used to talk about the differences between donkeys and horses, but not about their reputation for stubbornness, stupidity, or long memory. You used to say, 'Don't be like a donkey who's quick to comply. They don't hesitate to let anyone ride on their backs. People climb on them and they're set: the donkey will go with a tap on the neck and stop after another tap. Horses, on the other hand, only let their owners ride them. They'll only start after a great effort and they stop the same way. Getting them to move at all requires an authentic equestrian.'

"Jaafar told me that East African people who were sold as slaves were once gathered together here on these islands by traders, before they arrived at the Arabian Peninsula. The place where we stopped used to be a busy slave market. We passed by a big building, which looked like a traditional Omani fort, and he explained to me, 'They used to quarantine and burn the sick slaves in the cellars here.' His words echoed in the space around us. I felt a nasty chill and cringed. I saw before me Matisse paintings from that book you brought back from your first trip to Paris. I saw slave market rituals, humiliated souls, and captive bodies, ulcerated with disease and the scars of lashes from whips. I wanted to cross over to another road, but the two of them asked me to wait a moment so they could perform their noon prayer. Jaafar left me a papaya and a coconut he had freshly picked and peeled. Their prayers gave me a strange sense of calm amidst the weight of the heavy atmosphere that was thick with whisperings of the victims' tragic lives.

"We left soon after that. Jaafar had prepared lunch ingredients, and Ibrahimu began to cook. He said that I was about to taste the most delicious food I had ever had in my life. He really could destroy the myth of Mama's cooking. He made rice pudding with curry and coconut milk and poured a seafood sauce over it made of onions, tomatoes, and crushed corn. He served all of this on a blue-and-white melamine dish, topped with calamari, shrimp, mussels, and kingfish. Then he brought a small, square glass jar with pieces of blue, pink, and yellowish-colored transparent crystals in them. He took out a few crystals and sprinkled them over the fish, then invited us to eat. I took the jar and shook it, mesmerized by the crystals moving inside. I loved their undulating colors and couldn't get enough of the delicious fragrance of the food. 'Priceless salts from Hormuz,' said Ibrahimu. 'They give the fish a wonderful taste. Come on, try some…'

"Seriously, Joumane, I saw everything differently through Ibrahimu's calm and confidence. It was like he had been woven into my personal destiny. Even the salt—and what is salt? It's merely fine grains of white sodium chloride that stick together in the humidity, or coarse grains that Mama scooped up with a wooden spoon to make pickles! But with Ibrahimu these little molecules had other stories, different points of view.

"We sat and talked and opened our hearts to the wind and the sea. Being with this man is the closest I have come to knowing life's truths—no glamor, no disguises. He laughs with no artifice and frowns with no pretention. He has raw natural instincts and beauty. When I was with him I forgot everything that I'd learned about economic theory. When we were together we had no more human needs, and our resources were unlimited. Despite his power and strength, he had an intangible fragility as well. Perhaps he is in touch with his origins. I don't know how else to say it."

"Do you mean, because he has an African heritage, he understands things about nature?"

"Exactly. You always know how to say things better, Joumane."

"I don't know if he would see things this way... Maybe you create this fantasy because of the imperialist hyperbole they taught you at the American University in Beirut. It's your intellectual inheritance."

"Very funny."

"Ibrahimu said that he had to bring me back to Sohar for fear the tide would recede, we would get stuck in the sand, and it would be difficult to reach shore. Why did this wonderful time have to pass so quickly? Why do we start to lose things just when we begin to feel comfortable with them?

"Ibrahimu's stories didn't end when he announced we would return. When he got up to turn on the motor I got the urge to hug him. The motion of the waves encouraged me and I convinced myself that I needed to thank him for saving my life and showing me true beauty. I was also confused, lost in the Indian Ocean. Basically, I gave myself any and all justifications for why I should put my arms around him. So I embraced him from behind and pressed my face into his brown back. My nose filled with a sharp smell of incense and I almost lost my balance. Ibrahimu looked out toward the path of the boat and didn't budge. I thought that he wouldn't want to frighten me, and his stiffness pushed me even further. I wanted us to fold in on each other, so I nudged him to the edge of the boat to get him to respond to me. His body relaxed and he hugged me to his chest. I could feel myself give in to him.

"Oh, Joumane, I really hope that you are lucky enough to have what I had! His warm arms were unlike any others—bronzed by the sun, smoothed by breezes, and burnishing your sister's body."

"Your bum, of course!"

Salma laughed, and I was amazed at the depths of her feelings and courage. I wanted her to stop telling me this story and tried to stop my imagination from picturing her with a man—at the end of the day she was still my little sister, and in my mind still an innocent young girl!

"Jaafar appeared, carrying two colored bowls with a straw in each. He handed them to me. The bowl was made of half a gourd, with the flesh carved out and traditional African designs painted in green, black, and red. It was filled with cold mango juice.

"I didn't want to leave Ibrahimu. I wished I could stay in his strong arms and listen to more colorful stories about witches, fears, and desires. We spent the rest of the time in each other's arms, looking around at the sea, at the seagulls, with Jaafar in the background busily organizing the boat."

"Ibrahimu said that he had nothing to give me as a gift. My eyes inadvertently fell on the white pearl hanging around his neck on a black thread. It was magnificently large and pear shaped. He immediately grabbed it and said firmly, 'I can't give this to you. It was a gift from a mermaid and protects me from terrible things.'

"I had to believe this story just as I believed where that day had taken me. He told me how he and Jaafar used to go on deep dives in the ocean, fishing for oysters. On one of their dives, they found a clump of coral and swam over to it. He said to me, 'As soon as we got there, Jaafar just started swimming toward the surface without giving me any sign. I turned to my left and there was a woman kneeling down behind a branch of red coral. Her hair was also red. She was trying to free her baby's hands that were stuck between two intertwined pieces of coral. I collected myself, approached them, and saw that her lower half was a silvery fish tail. I cut the piece of coral with my knife and the *jinni* pulled her child out. I was avoiding looking at them. The whole affair did not take more than two or three minutes, after which I swam back up to the boat. Jaafar was petrified; his tongue was tied in terror. While I was catching my breath, trying to process what I had seen, a small white hand broke through the surface of the water and threw this rare pearl at me. It was so rare that one of the merchants on the coast told me there was none other like it in the sea. Please don't begrudge me this, I am afraid that if I gave it to you my mermaid would be jealous and might harm you.'

"I asked him if he really thought I'd believe his mermaid story.

"'You're free to do as you like,' he replied. He was completely certain of what had happened to him and I loved his absolute and honest certainty in stories about *jinnis*. What I loved even more is that I believed him. I gave him my golden pendant necklace with the Ayat al-Kursi from the Qur'an on it. The one Mama gave me when I graduated.'

"You told me that you had lost it! You made us all feel so bad over the loss of that hand-engraved masterpiece that Grandpa gave to Mama when you were born! And what you received in return was a jar of salt and a gourd to drink from. What an unfair trade!"

"If he had asked me to go back out to sea with him at that moment I would have," said Salma. "I wondered what would happen if Ibrahimu left the sea for dry land… would he have lost his magic and his power? Would he transform if he wore regular clothes, a suit and tie, or a winter jacket? I tried to imagine him as a child, a tiny baby in diapers and overalls, and then a boy in first grade, looking at his mother sitting and painting. I wished I had one of her brightly colored paintings, that I had known more about his amazing pirate grandfather!"

"Why didn't you ask him about all this? Weren't you close enough for that?"

"Because I made a grave error—I trusted in time! He asked me to come back and wait for him on the coast in two days. He said he'd bring me something I'd like, and that he'd take me to places no one else knew about. At the moment of farewell, he planted a lingering kiss on my neck, and followed it up with many short staccato kisses. His broad lips felt special, like they had an additional power. Their traces stayed on me. I felt my womb lowering, and liquid pouring between my thighs…"

I put my hand over my mouth and swallowed my own laugh. We grew silent—Salma and me.

"What happened next?"

"Nothing. You called me the next day and told me Mama had liver cancer and that she would die within a month. I packed my bags and returned to Aleppo to be with all of you."

We were quiet for a moment, each of us recalling those wild times in her own way.

"Isn't there a way to get in touch?"

"Pirates don't have addresses!"

I was completely certain that the time she'd spent with the pirate Ibrahimu were the best moments of Salma's life. After she'd told me her story, I started calling her Salma-the-Lady-Pirate. In reality, Baba and I had met Ibrahimu in person but we hid this from her because we didn't want to break her heart.

He had visited us in Aleppo after he inquired about Salma at the company she worked for in Muscat. He sat at our table and we told him that Salma had gotten married after Mama died. At that time, even after everything she'd told me about him, I imagined Ibrahimu to be a large man, with a thick red beard and a black leather patch over one eye. But he was even sweeter than she'd described him, and extremely polite. His eyes had the patience of sails in the wind. I would have sworn his blue slim-fit suit was Armani. He looked more like Spanish royalty than a pirate. I believed that it was only God's mercy that prevented her from meeting him, after she'd taken her path and he'd left sea for dry land, as she'd said. We asked him to stay a little while in Aleppo, to fulfill our duties as hosts. But he preferred to complete his journey to Istanbul. He asked me to give her two gifts. The first was a painting signed by his mother, Mulha Mahmoud. It was of little houses one atop the other, each painted in a bright, basic color—red, green, blue, black, purple, and yellow—on a dark blue coast. Their images were reflected on the surface of the water. It looked as if it had been painted twice—once standing, once lying on the page. The second gift was a blue alabaster candlestick that held one candle, mounted on a bronze base and decorated with small Latin faces. He said that it was part of what a group of pirates had taken after attacking a ship in Christopher Columbus's fleet back in the fifteenth century, when he was returning from America to Spain.

When Salma returned to Raqqa after Mama died, the private banks were allowed to open branches in our far-flung city for the first time. They were looking for employees with decent qualifications. Of course, in this place that was branded as rural with a touch of the Bedouin, they couldn't find anyone more qualified than Salma—in her education, her presence, and her intelligence. They chose her to be the director of the Lebanese Syrian Bank. We used to consider this a stroke of luck for our family because it meant she could then stay with Baba and relieve some of the heavy misery of Mama's passing. At the same time, I could take advantage of her presence to commute between Aleppo and Raqqa and do academic work and teaching at the University of Aleppo on Wednesdays. Then I could spend the rest of the week with them. Less than a year after Mama's death, I learned that Salma was thinking of getting married. She had developed a relationship with a man named Nasib who came frequently to the bank. He was an agricultural engineer from the University of Damascus, and despite how young he was—less than twenty-six years old—he had made a fortune working in Dubai. He bought land on the Euphrates and filled it with fruit trees—apples, plums, and peaches. He built a small villa, and around the time he met Salma he had applied for an industrial loan to build a dairy farm in the region, which was rich in developmental possibilities that had remained untapped thanks to the government's neglect. Dairy products, which all come from Aleppo and Homs, are often spoiled due to poor transport and storage conditions.

Nasib was the son of a former political prisoner, one of the socialists jailed for their party's refusal to join the nationalist front from the seventies onward. So when he came to propose to Salma, Baba hesitated before giving the marriage his blessing. Baba hated ideology, particularly its Arab version. He told Salma, "His social situation will be difficult because of his father's political legacy. All the branches of the security services will stand in the way of him making progress." She insisted that his security profile was excellent. He had been able to obtain industrial and commercial licenses, which no one else could obtain, and he would pay a lot for them if need be. I trusted Salma's decisions and her clear thinking, and so did Baba. The marriage took place shortly after.

She lived a good life with Nasib, and they had two girls within the span of three years, before Raqqa started to be destroyed. The army withdrew, as did all semblance of the previous government. Armed groups that later became known as Daesh and terrorized the world, entered and took our city and the capital of the region—Raqqa—as their capital. A soldier from the Shariah branch seized Salma's village and her farm. They took it as a residence. So she brought her little family to live with Baba. She comforted herself by saying, "At the end of the day they will leave. No one can take our walls with them: we will get our recompense from God."

The regime's army threw barrel bombs at the places where the Islamic State was gathered, at their headquarters. Most of these strikes missed their targets and killed civilians. But one time they hit the headquarters of the Shariah Committee—Salma's house—the legal center for the Islamic State, and pulverized it completely. My sister bore this with strength. I don't know what her real reaction was or what she looked like, because I was far away. I used to tell her on the phone whenever it was possible to communicate, "Your health is the most important thing!" I know that she used to think about my illness and thank God I was going to recover, with venom trickling into her heart for the people who destroyed her house and family.

Nasib calculated his losses, transforming suddenly from a young man who had many things, more than his peers, and who the world had smiled upon every day, into the father of two daughters and the head of a household with hardly anything to his name. He bore this silently for a long time and then decided to become a refugee. Another war broke out, but this time it was between him and her—"I will die here but I won't become a refugee," she said. "I know the consequences of claiming refugee status. The regime will return and will forbid refugees from coming back to their country. They will forbid them from regaining their former status."

"Sweden is granting refugees official residency papers. Each person gets ten thousand euros. I would be able to start again with security and dignity. Here in Raqqa no one cares about us, they didn't before and they won't even after the war is over. They've left us to a gang of criminals playing with our souls as if we were nothing more than ground lice. Then they bomb us from the sky. I'll go and sort everything out for us and then you will follow with the girls."

Salma's condition was that he register everything he owned, which was now actually trapped in the limbo of the new legal system, in his daughters' names. This is how

Salma operated. Her mind was always working even as she marched toward the abyss.

Nasib flew to Egypt and traveled by sea from Alexandria to Libya. He called her before leaving there. Four days later the Italian navy recovered his documents with those of the drowned refugees off the coast of Lampedusa.

The Knight of Yorkshire Castle

My sister Jude was the opposite of Salma. No one in the family trusted her opinion. My aunt Layla, who lived with us, spoiled her by indulging her too much. Whenever Mama would spank her, or she would fight with one of us, she would go to Auntie Layla's room and climb into her bed. Our aunt's room was like a magical cave. It had everything—precious jewels, mirrors from distant lands, sumptuous perfumes, Arabic kohl jars, local creams made of glycerin and lemons, and pictures of her sitting at the King David Hotel, from the time she went on a pilgrimage to Jerusalem to pray at the al-Aqsa mosque with her parents in 1960.

Because of all of this pampering and being spoiled, Jude was behind in her studies. She used to like to watch TV on winter evenings, holding two knitting needles, with colorful balls of woolen yarn, imitating our aunt who bought thick red plastic needles especially for her. When she was seven years old, Jude started knitting a green wool-en sweater for Rabih El Khawli, a Lebanese singer she had a crush on. She kept up-to-date with all of his songs and new releases and was fascinated by his long eyelashes and his green eyes. They were the reason she chose green as the color for his sweater. She kept working on that sweater for three or four winters, to no use—it kept morphing into an ever-stranger, ever more unidentifiably shaped piece of wool. Rabih El Khawli's sweater was a joke circulating around the neighborhood, and it was all because of Auntie Layla who spread the news about it amongst our neighbors and relatives. When the piece of wool got too long, my aunt started saying that it was like a slip for under a dress. Jude cried at the insult and she cried even more when she learned that her beloved Rabih El Khawli was retiring from music to enter a monastery and become a monk. But she recovered quickly as she realized that now he would need more woolen sweaters, because monasteries are usually very cold. She vowed to continue to listen to his old songs. Mama showed her how to make the sweater smaller because monks don't eat much and he would soon lose weight. We all waited for someone we knew to go to Beirut and take Rabih El Khawli's sweater, which in the end was more of a scarf because that was the best that Jude could do.

She had extreme views about things. She refused to drink milk because she claimed it was the urine of cows and she couldn't wrap her mind around people drinking urine. When a farmer who worked on our land took her to show her how the milk came from udders far from where the cow urinated, she sat down under the cow which then knelt down on top of her and almost killed her. She decided that cattle were predatory animals and boycotted their products forever. She used to believe that if she swallowed an orange, apple, or grape seed, a tree would grow in her belly and come out of her mouth. When she swallowed one by accident she would wail and sob all night long.

Jude also loved music, but there wasn't a teacher in Raqqa who could teach her to play even one note. But because she was the apple of his eye, Baba hired a music teacher for her who came all the way from Tartous. He went into business with this teacher, setting up a little center for music lessons. Baba gave him a small apartment to live in in a building he owned. Jude studied with him for about three hours a day, every day, until she mastered the solfège method. She went on to play the accordion really well. From that moment on our house was like a music box. People passing by on the street would stop in front of our windows listening to Jude playing Arabic scales, the long introductions to Umm Kulthum's songs, Abdel Wahab's waltzes, and Farid al-Atrash's tangos. Her personality matured and she became more responsible and honest. She read all about the careers of great musicians. She wanted to travel to the great musical capitals of the world to see what she had read about up close.

Jude grew up and, according to traditional standards and tastes, was the most beautiful of all of us. She was tall, full-bodied, with clear white skin and thick black hair that tumbled over her shoulders and halfway down her back. She had seductively thick eyebrows and black eyes that had a sureness about them that was both provocative and innocent—an angelic certainty. From the time of her post–adolescence she had the features of a married woman, but she was lazy, submissive, and cowardly. Calling her a hot mess would be an understatement. Hani's presence as her music teacher soon reassured her, and she became addicted to playing with him in lavish musical performances. We started to fear that she would grow too attached to him with the ardor expected of a teenage girl. Until one day he left. He went on a holiday to his family's house in Tartous and we learned that while there he had killed his brother's wife and had been sentenced to death. Jude couldn't believe it and had a breakdown. She turned to Auntie Layla's embrace, but my fifty-something auntie ignored her and ran away with Dr. Sadiq, who wasn't really a doctor. We only called him doctor because we couldn't find another nickname that suited him. He was actually a massage therapist.

My aunt Layla had suffered from pains in her neck, back, and joints. The doctors diagnosed these pains as cervicalgia and gave her a neck brace. She started going for daily massages. Sadiq was the only massage therapist in the area. We didn't know if he had actually studied physiotherapy somewhere, or if he had any training or expertise at all. But everyone who experienced his massages swore that they came out the other end relaxed and able to sleep better at night. When my aunt's neck pains proved so unbearable that she couldn't take it any longer, she inevitably turned to Sadiq. He prepared his own massage oils, and their smells made people with allergies or breathing problems—people like Baba—dizzy. Baba used to leave the house when Sadiq came around, his green metal box in tow, his big square body topped by his smaller square head. Meanwhile, my auntie would be lying on her stomach in bed, her body covered by a large blanket. She would submit to his hands and flat fingers with their bright white fingernails. She would start off groaning and screaming. Jude, Salma, and I would rush to her side like a battalion on guard duty against her nakedness.

Baba was surprised when my aunt and Sadiq eloped. He told her that he wouldn't have objected at all if she had informed him of her desire to marry Sadiq or anyone else. She was a mature and rational woman who had received a good inheritance from her parents, which made her financially independent. He would bless her marriage and give her a proper gift. But Layla didn't renounce her typical penchant for drama. She wanted to play the role of someone who was forced to endure her aristocratic background, loving a man her family would never accept. She couldn't admit that times had changed, so instead of running away with her driver, servant, or butler, she ran away with her massage therapist.

After all of this, Jude found herself with no permanent source of flattery, no one to put up with her spoiledness and laziness. We tried to surround her with love and attention, but she sank into a state of exaggerated selfishness. She passed secondary school with a higher average than we expected and got accepted into the dentistry school at the University of Aleppo, where they make all of the special supplies for dentists. After she started university, Jude became a different person—beloved by everyone, playful and hardworking. But we were always afraid of her reactions: when Mama got sick we didn't tell her the truth about the illness, because we feared she would go into shock. We let her keep working in Raqqa. Little Salma—who had come from Oman—and I took care of Mama at the treatment center in Aleppo. We told Jude, "Don't close your lab and delay your work. Mama will get well soon, and we'll come back home." Jude knew that Mama was going to die, but she deceived herself into thinking she was OK. This is how she always was—she would escape reality by just sleeping, by ignoring, by avoiding confrontation. She liked to remain ignorant and not confront anything. When Mama died, we all thought of Jude first. We hugged her and looked after her so that she wouldn't collapse from the shock. Baba succeeded in preventing her from marrying a young man from the university who she had fallen in love with. He had a wealthy father who worked as the director of one of the state associations belonging to the Ministry of Social Affairs. It was devoted to community programs and care for the elderly. Jude told us, "Had he not been noble he would not have run this humanitarian organization, and they would not have appointed him president to begin with."

Baba told her in return, "Recompense in this country does not take the form of work. When you are rewarded, your reward is the opposite of work." Baba's face swelled up when he spoke to Jude about this. He didn't like to reopen old wounds, and soon retreated into silence. He observed the destruction of the world around him like a Buddhist monk awaiting long-promised peace. He shook his head, knowing he was correct in his systemic analyses and his judgments about humanity. Baba remained silent and neutral as the world fell to pieces in the distance. But when destruction inched closer, Baba always transformed into a violent and victorious combatant. He told Jude that the man whose nobility she was praising, who would become her father-in-law and the grandfather of her children, had boycotted his own father who'd later survived by begging for charity from good people. How could someone who found his own father a burden, someone who threw his own father out into the street, how could this person suddenly take it upon himself to care for all the weakest people in society, ensuring they lived in peace and harmony? All the same, the position was open and the comrades in the party elected him to fill it. He got the position like any person in a country filled with contradictions. In this moment, Jude crossed the boundaries that we were used to stopping at in our conversations with Baba. She wanted to defend her love. She asked Baba if he had a monopoly over chivalry, was he robbing others of this, by disdaining them and thinking of them as mere rabble—this one a traitor, that one a turncoat, this one stingy, that one slimy...

When Baba realized that she was suddenly in a revolt against him, he raised his voice. He began intervening, his eyes bulging out of their sockets up toward the middle of his forehead. He looked terrifying. Jude pushed the door of the house open, and he told her, "Go on, go to him, go to them. Live in the shadow of social solidarity and perhaps he will take you to a shelter or an orphanage."

Jude could do nothing but move in the opposite direction, toward her room, and collapse into sobs. She soon left her boyfriend, and we didn't know if it was because she was convinced by her father's assessment, or to comply with his decision.

A lot of old and new water passed under the Euphrates Bridges as the revolution continued, along with continual bombardments of the places where multiplying numbers of factions had gathered. You could no longer distinguish the inside of buildings from outside because everything was being destroyed. Jude closed down her lab because, under the new government's laws, women couldn't work or even leave the house unless accompanied by a male guardian. She was alone one day, preparing dinner, when she heard the gradual whistle of a rising rocket. The sound grew nearer and her fear of what would inevitably come prevented her from going down into the shelter. She crouched into the corner in the kitchen between the sink and the dishwasher. If she had been able to dig a hole in the wall and hide in it, she would have. She didn't know if she screamed or not, she only heard the sounds of silence and a person walking by shouting, "Cousin… are you alive or dead?" That's when she knew she was alive and started laughing and crying.

Baba came home from his doctor's appointment with Salma and her daughters in state of stupor because they'd told him on the road that a rocket had fallen near his house. The glass of the windows was shattered and the short walls around the house were crushed. The rocket had fallen on the little shop next door, only ten meters away. There were only ten meters between Jude's life and death. She didn't tell anyone that she had sent Mahmoud the neighbor's son to the shop next door to bring her a can of tuna for dinner. Mahmoud was a round, redheaded boy of about ten. He was blown to pieces, and they didn't find any of his remains. Sometime later someone said that they had found his leg about fifty meters away, atop the town's clock tower which—before the arrival of armed groups—had a man holding up a torch symbolizing the 1960s revolution. Mahmoud's father didn't know why his son was in the shop. He hadn't received his salary in three months, and the boy didn't have a penny to spend on anything. He shouted mournfully, "My God! We don't kill, we don't steal, and we don't take anyone else's livelihood. What have we done? We drank a glass, we sang, and we had fun with a few women. That's all!"

We used to love Mahmoud. He loved all of us too. I always used to ask him, "Mahmoud, what do you wish for most?" He would answer, "An endless sandwich and a bottomless soda!"

After the rocket strike, Jude started wearing the hijab and decided to work in a soup kitchen. She found it a place where she could create something useful, feel helpful, and make a difference. She helped prepare food for needy families who often had one or more of their members engaged in factions fighting the regime forces. They were no longer necessarily people who had come from outside the region, but from the place itself. People were going hungry as a result of the chaos, the siege, and the constant bombings. Baba refused to let her leave home at this difficult time and work with these people from different walks of life, most of whom weren't local. There were extremists, members of the armed organizations—Chechens, Afghans, Tunisians, and Saudis, people Jude should not have been with. There were kidnappings, people held in captivity, stonings, and other inventions alien to our peaceful, civilized life. She became completely estranged from us, as if she hadn't been born from the same belly that carried us. Every time Jude went out, we worried that she wouldn't return for some reason, even though she was there with many other young women from Raqqa, including cousins of ours. But they weren't as beautiful or as elegant as she was. She used to go to the soup kitchen in a Range Rover that donors had allocated to her to transport volunteers in. Of course, she wore all black, including an *abaya*, head cover, and a niqab that covered her face. They gathered in the women's kitchen to prepare food for the needy and homeless—rice, chicken and vegetable curry, carrots and potatoes cooked in tomato sauce, meatballs, stews made of white beans, fava beans, or okra—anything that would provide filling meals for the fighters and their families. Baba and Salma lived another war through Jude, a war that prevented her from leaving this squalid archipelago of factions, made up of military men, converted Muslims, thieves, losers, the mentally ill, all of them carrying weapons. They were targets of the regime's bombing campaigns that didn't care that there were many civilians among them. This was a war where no one had rights. There were no treaties, no conventions concerning prisoners, women, and children. All values were suspended.

When Osama bin Laden established al-Qaeda in 1988, Ruh al-Amin was not yet born. He was born one year later in a tiny brick house that had a little garden with a plum tree and a lemon tree in it in Northallerton, the capital of North Yorkshire in the northeast of England. He was an only child, with no friends, since the families didn't like him mixing with their children, especially when they saw his father's beard, and his mother's *abaya* and hijab, utterly unlike their own mothers, even though she was English and called Kathy. She was his only friend. She had changed her name to Ayeesha after she married his father, Sharif Khan, who was an emergency physician in a clinic in a relatively isolated neighborhood at the outskirts of the city. Ruh al-Amin loved going hiking with her, and their favorite place to do so was an ancient Norman castle on a hill near their house. He always used to dream of becoming a prince and living there. When he turned sixteen, his father took him to London where rows of hundreds of Muslims prayed together, overflowing out of the Finsbury Park mosque, listening to Abu Hamza al-Masri's sermons while sur-rounded by British police. This man who came to Britain in the seventies surprised him. He had become an eloquent orator. He was missing his hands and one eye, having lost them clearing mines left by the Russians in Afghanistan. His father, Sharif Khan, had left Afghanistan—the country he should have been raised in—and escaped here, to the country of the infidels.

Sharif Khan originally traced his origins to the city of Faryab in the north of Afghanistan, where the Pashtuns were a minority compared to the Tajiks and Kazakhs, so his ancestors had left the north for the southeast and lived in vicinity of Kandahar, following their people. This was especially important because the Tajiks had informed the British that Ruh al-Amin's grandfather of his same name had joined the fighters in the mountains—who had taken on the soldiers of the great empire when they crossed the mountain chains between India and Afghanistan.

Sharif Khan studied medicine at Kabul University, and fought against the Soviets as a field doctor-turned-gunman.

After surviving certain death more than once, he left for Britain. It was there that he was sponsored to go to the Hudaibiyah training camp in the Philippines, with the help of the Pakistani secret service and Saudi funding. He returned to London, and he and his wife Ayeesha then attended two seminary sessions in modern jihad. He joined a Guidance Office, with the goal of unifying gangs of Muslim youth in a jihad outside the United Kingdom. Ruh al-Amin loved playing with the toy trains his father gave him when he finished memorizing the first part of the Qur'an. This was the only gift he ever got, because he failed to memorize the rest of the holy book. He would dismantle and reassemble the track many times a day, then make the lone car take off at a green light and stop at the crossroads, staring into the windows behind which the travelers' cardboard heads were visible. He waved at them, smiling and dreaming of extending the track further than these small bars enclosed in a circle.

Despite her poor English, Jude was taken by Ruh al-Amin's words about the resilience of Pashtun men, comparable to the harshness of their mountainous terrain, as well as their passion about the passing of time and their ingenuity in the use of weapons. This was the only resource they had to drive the English, Russians, and Americans out of their country and into the embrace of Islam. He danced the Attan for her, a dance of liberated Pashtun men, and said that he had left his affluent life in Europe and came here to meet her. This was God's plan for him, one of the secrets of the galaxies written on the great tablet in heaven. It was not up to any human to stop him in words or deeds.

When Ruh al-Amin came to our house, he didn't

look like the foreign fighters that we had seen on TV in Kabul and Peshawar. He was of medium height and was rugged, with light skin, narrow green eyes, and blondish hair hanging to his shoulders, tied back in a ponytail. His thick beard was only a few centimeters long.

He didn't look like the face of evil. He didn't show any signs of violence except for the Kalashnikov that never left his shoulder. Despite the cold weather, he wore black cotton trousers and a shirt that hung over them, with an Iranian-style collar. His khaki-colored military boots were a sober knockoff of Karl Lagerfeld—the inspirational leader of the Chanel House of Fashion in Paris.

When Baba saw he wasn't wearing Taliban-style clothes he calmed down a little, though Salma was still shivering in fear. She asked, "How did all these foreigners get to Syria? Why did they come from such faraway countries? Why did they leave Damascus, Latakia, and Aleppo and come to Raqqa?"

Baba liked having a man whose first language was English in the house. It filled him with nostalgia for Boston where he'd spent the best years of his life; he never lost his passion for thinking about those days. But he never thought this would be the scenario. He wanted the two of them to sit together and discuss politics and culture, over a glass of whiskey—or at the very least a bottle of beer. Then this native English speaker came along in the form of a jihadi!

He asked him only one question: "Why did you come here?"

Ruh al-Amin was sitting on the Louis XV chair, upholstered in blue satin, looking at a framed family photograph on the marble side table. It was a picture taken at one of our cousin's weddings—Baba, Mama, and the three of us, wearing our décolleté off-the-shoulder dresses. He carefully picked up the picture and placed it face down on the white marble. He averted his eyes and said extremely politely, "The place where I came from has straight, wide streets. Nowhere in either Yorkshire or London is there a place like the alleys of the seven lanes, which wind around back behind the castle. Do you know, Sir? Your castle here in Raqqa looks just like the one I used to play in every day as a child. I took my mother Ayeesha's hand and we would climb the huge staircase inside. My mother died of cancer, because she was barred from entering the United States to get treatment. They said she was a terrorist. Imagine, Ayeesha who taught little orphaned girls how to pray, knit, and embroider... a terrorist?

"Your country reminds me of my homeland. It looks like Kandahar, where trains are not bound to the constraints of English time. They are either late, or they don't come at all!"

Baba did not sleep all night and neither did Salma. He stayed up reading the Qur'an, something he only did when things were grave.

After I heard about Ruh al-Amin's pursuit of Jude, I asked Salma, "How is this possible? Why doesn't Baba lock her up, or tie her down?"

"Because death is so easy for us now. He didn't exchange one word with her. Even if she had gone back on her position, the Afghani would have taken her by force with his weapon. Getting into that mess is not at all like getting out of it. You're far away. You don't know the war. No one owns anyone else's destiny in the war."

Salma said that Baba cried even more after Ruh al-Amin's visit than on the day Mama died, or the day he found out about my diagnosis, and more than the day Nasib drowned. He knew that he would never see his little girl Jude again. He pleaded with God, "Lord lead us not into temptation but deliver us from evil."

Kamikaze

Now that I have declared that I have come back to life, I will resist thinking about recurrence. I will be happy for every moment in the present—for every breath I take and the hormones that have come back a year and a half after my radiation therapy, thanks to the passing of time and the huge effort I made to exercise, eat right, and be optimistic.

One Friday evening, Haniyah invited me to a dance performance by her students at Trader Vic's, a club attached to the Regency Hotel in the center of Amman. I wore a short, sleeveless, open-necked black muslin dress, so that my new tattoos showed. They were three dots in a straight line that went from my arm to the middle of my chest all the way to my other arm. The radiation technician drew them to indicate precisely where the beams should be aimed during my treatment. My hair didn't need combing—cancer taught me to leave it short, like a child's. It was like Haniyah's hair, and even more beautiful because my tighter curls were a darker shade of black. I wore square-heeled beige shoes that I had bought specifically to banish the very thought of high heels. I wanted a life without any kind of suffering. The only real adornment I put on was my pearl necklace, highlighting the natural color that had finally returned to my skin.

I walked a few steps down into the club and heard the sound of generic pop music, so I knew that the evening's entertainment had not yet started. In the middle of the dark lounge, I was greeted by the sight of Dr. Yaacoub's face. I felt confused. It was the first time in the three years since I'd started treatment that I had seen him outside the torture chamber. He looked exactly like the young boy I'd seen in Portofino, sitting alone at a small square table lit by a tiny lamp, staring out at the white porcelain salt shaker in front of him. He looked like he was plotting something. I hesitated to approach him, flooded by the memory of my childhood and his post-adolescence; there was no gelato shop here to buy him a cone. We finally stopped our game of hide and seek. He raised his head and found me close by. He waved at me and invited me over. I went over like a child making up with his father after being given a spanking. He stood at his table, getting up to hug me. He left his chair on the other side and invited me to sit down with him on the red sofa, facing the dance floor. He was a totally different person, neat and elegant, in a gray linen safari suit and a blue shirt. His dark shoes were almost sporty. After the usual polite chitchat, a silence fell over us. Each of us was stealing glances at the other, and then he smiled—he knew that I knew about their relationship. I felt that he was very close to me, the brother I never had, or an old friend coming back after having been away for a long time. But it was more than that. He knew my history, my weak spots, my tears, my pains, my body's phases that ranged from hideousness to blossoming health. I felt he was drawn to me as one of the many examples of his life's victories.

A crowd of men and women bustled in one after the other, among them young and middle-aged people, with some older folks. They caused a racket and sat down at tables that they pushed close together. All of them seemed to be in a party mood, judging by their clothes; they were dressed nicely but comfortably, with lots of bright colors, and they all looked somewhat alike. Most of the young men had on jeans and button-down shirts, while the women were in Latin dancing shoes with thick heels and small rounded tips, and short, tight-fitting dresses with doubled pleats or layered skirts, open backs, and accentuated busts. Haniyah stood out amongst them in her white satin gown that hugged her upper body in a corset, cinched at the waist with two layers of muslin that hung down to her mid-thigh. Her neckline was cut around the shape of her bust and was edged with rhinestones. It had strips of silver along the shoulders, one of which was intertwined with the dragon lying on her neck, and the other seemingly running away from it. Her silver shoes confirmed her creativity, and her skin-colored tights hugged her full legs, accentuating her muscles, which would expand and tighten as she moved. She came over and hugged us, lingering a while on Yaacoub who seemed a little reserved. Perhaps it was because I was there. But they looked very happy.

This was the first show Haniyah had put on in public since completing her treatment. She had rehearsed it in closed sessions at the studio. It wasn't so much an official performance as it was an interactive show with the students and teachers from the club, most of whom had taught dance, or had danced professionally somewhere in the world. Yaacoub looked at her passionately, cradling her bare shoulders in his arms. His fingernails still looked neglected. She shot me conspiratorial glances and I met them with a smile. I was really jealous of her because I felt that she had beaten me, that she'd taken a secret page out of my child-hood memories. I felt this made me like the mermaid who saved the prince from drowning, but another girl found him on the beach and claimed she'd saved him, so he fell in love with her instead. But Haniyah really had saved him. She was able to reach the dark, humid cellars he'd dug for himself in his own mind, and she brightened them up with a life-giving candle she possessed. She helped him navigate his way out of these passages and into the world. This man who had helped hundreds of patients through their suffering deserved to be happy. Haniyah was unaware that her helping him find happiness was a holy mission. I stole a few glances at him, I pitied him in his loneliness and imagined his happy childhood that had passed so quickly in his parents' care. No doubt he was a well-behaved child—he never once tried to climb up the slide in the opposite direction. But he never had the pleasure of taking care of a younger sibling, of feel-ing the affection of an older one. He didn't know how long to soak a hard cookie in milk in order to soften it and then eat it before it crumbled. Nabila wouldn't have been able to give him these experiences. He wasn't exposed to other naughty young boys; he was a quiet, submissive only child who was always alone. If Yaacoub were mine, I would have

taught him to slide down the handrail on the staircase, how
to put his feet on the wooden door beam, and climb up,
and how to stand under the water fountain and not get wet
from its spray. I would have told him tales of faraway lands,
tales that Nabila and Haniyah didn't know, like "Ghida's Sad
Camel," "Maree the Horseman," and "Alia's Tower."

The group made up of five men and two women
began playing guitars, a saxophone, maracas, and small
drums. The music they played for the dancers was a hybrid
of energetic diasporic African and Latin rhythms. It opened
with a classic salsa, a few couples swaying around the dance
floor in sedate, clear patterns. The male and female singers
exchanged roles seamlessly; one of them started when
the other stopped, with enthusiastic shouts. The dancers'
bodies communicated harmoniously and there was joy on
their faces. Two senior citizens were enjoying the dips and
turns of the melody. I, instead, was longing for Nasser,
who was absent right now and enjoying his time with his
children that he surely deserved. Meanwhile, the Cuban
music swept me away to the straw houses that line the
Caribbean shoreline where the descendants of Africans
enslaved by the Spanish live, returning exhausted every
night from the nearby farms where they care for crops of
coffee beans and spices. Instead of sleeping, they fill the
shore with songs of nostalgia for the homeland and freedom, their bodies knit together in passionate desire. The
rhythms sizzle transcendentally, making them feel alive and
connected to their ancestral lands so far away.

Haniyah's dance partner Akram came in, Yaacoub let
her go to him, and Haniyah surrendered to the music in a
solo sung a by a man whose voice held the smell of burnt

tobacco. Her upper body faced her dance partner. They approached each other with one footstep, and then retreated by two steps with swaying hips. Their bodies were in a state of total surrender to the music, ecstasy poured from their eyes and lips whenever the rhythm became more frenzied. Their movements intensified and became circular and rhythmic. Haniyah's upper body was no longer fixed in one place and moved with Bobby Cruz's rapturous music. Her shoulders appeared detached from her body, moving on their own but also as a part of Akram's body. She slid down between his legs, then he pulled her back up again. Blue veins stuck out of her neck and beads of sweat shone on her skin. I love looking at that vein on the left side of her neck, which could tempt a butcher, when she raises her head or laughs.

Haniyah had forgotten us and moved freely through the space like a mustang, difficult to tame. Akram surrounded her with his body and she was stuck to him. Then she pulled away in a violent motion, spurning him again. The beams of light between the darkness and shadows confused the scene, bringing it closer to uncertainty. With the final chord, the dancers' shouts, and the applause of the crowd, Akram covered Haniyah's body with his chest. She was lying beneath him, almost touching the ground, and he gave her a feverish kiss on her neck as thanks for sharing in this pleasure together. I stole a quick look at Yaacoub. His face looked gloomy, his right eyelid twitching as he observed these professional dancers caught up in the heat of the moment.

Later, Haniyah told me that he'd gone back with her to the studio. He was calm but he twisted her arms painfully, and told her that she should gain some weight, because she'd looked gaunt while dancing.

"Hmmm, what else did he say?"

"He said that he loves things he can hold in his hand."

"While he is wearing his scary medical gloves?"

"Without any restrictive barriers."

Her resonant laugh stood out, separating herself from him emotionally like a deserting soldier fleeing a battlefield. Haniyah didn't give me the answers I was expecting and so alerted me that I should listen to her without daring to cut her off.

"Men and horses have many qualities in common. They both have an instinct for war, and the thrill of the chase. A horse protects his rider, like a man does a woman. Both of them exult in their authority. The horse maneuvers its rider away from danger on the battlefield and the man leads his woman to somewhere he thinks is safe. Despite this, you can bet on a horse but you can't bet on a man. Horses will give their riders signs they are tired, playful, or injured. But men can go wild with no prior warning."

"Do you think he'll leave?"

"Perhaps."

She worried me. How could he go and leave me? How could he abandon all those poor, miserable patients! I might die if I couldn't find him in the hospital.

"Don't worry, he will leave me, not you! And maybe I will leave as well."

"And where are you going to go, then?"

She raised her eyebrows like a child trying to tease her friend because she got something the other one didn't. "I agreed to meet my mom in Kuala Lumpur. I'm exhausted, and I haven't left the country in two years. The next season of dance rehearsals begins in April and the first show at Trader Vic's will be the first Friday in May. Perhaps I should also take a little distance from Yaacoub. I don't want our relationship to become one simply of habit. You'll come to the show, of course. I'll call you when I'm back."

"*Inshallah.*"

She stretched her bare foot out on the table in front of us, pushing back her gray sports skirt. It seemed as if she'd regained her natural color very quickly. She slapped her thighs and the sound resonated. A red mark quickly formed on her satiny skin. She folded her leg behind her so that her heel came parallel to my face. "Look at the dry skin on my heel—it's so thick. Chemo burned it badly. Have you ever gone to a fish spa before?"

"Oh yes, I've heard about them but never been to one. The fish eat the fungus and dead skin off your feet."

"Exactly. They are *garra rufa* fish, also called doctor fish. Come on, let's go together."

"When my health is a bit better, I will. I want to go and see my family too."

"Your health is excellent. Come on! I'll introduce you to my mom. We'll have a great time. It will be a magical journey. First we'll set off to Kuala Lumpur, and then Beijing."

"Beijing… I don't know anyone who has gone there."

"What should I bring you back?"

"A bikini, of course!"

"Ha ha! Then we might go to Vietnam, we haven't decided yet. But I miss my grandfather; I miss him a lot.

He owns a restaurant in Hoàn Kiém, overlooking the lake, near the opera house."

"Is it also called Norinco?"

"You're funny... No, it is called Kamikaze, honoring the Japanese soldiers who committed suicide while confronting the allied forces."

Our wild laughs echoed throughout the studio. How is it that the paradoxes of endless wars can make us laugh? And then we hold onto their painful memories in every part of the world through names, clothing, music, spirits. Even this eighty-year-old man stuck in Vietnam couldn't escape the nostalgia for pain.

Haniyah's grandfather was sitting alone at his usual table, on a sidewalk next to the street that circled around the lake. His ancient ears couldn't make out the tunes coming from the opera house, which was welcoming a Chinese group for a performance of Carl Orff's famous opera *Carmina Burana*, in which no one is willing to confront the Goddess of Destiny, O Fortuna, the denier of pleasure:

> O Fortune,
> like the moon
> you are changeable,
> ever waxing
> and waning
> hateful life
> first oppresses
> and then soothes
> ...

Fate—monstrous
and empty
you whirling wheel,
you are malevolent,
well-being is vain

In the middle of the night, the musicians came out and took up their places between the big building and the neighboring market, men in tuxedos and women in black evening gowns, carrying their instruments and cases filled with the other things they needed. There was a conductor and three singers: the tenor, the baritone, and the soprano all carrying sumptuous bouquets of blue flowers, followed by fans stopping them to pose for photos. They arrived at the grandfather's nearby restaurant and filled both the inner room and the sidewalk outside. Some of them sat at the bar and asked for a Blue Kamikaze, the place's official drink, with seafood and rice.

At this very same moment, Yan was holding her daughter Haniyah's hand. Haniyah had just responded aloud to the co-pilot's announcement on the plane as he spoke to the passengers from the cockpit: "Thank you and good night!"

Less than an hour later, the Malaysian 777 plane, flight MH370 from Kuala Lumpur to Beijing disappeared from the radar screen in the Southern Indian Ocean, near the Vietnamese coast.

I met Dr. Yaacoub at Trader's on the day of the performance. To all of us at the time, Haniyah still existed. However, there was no sign of Salsa Night at the club.

The DJ was sampling old rhythms to create new ones. I sat down next to him. He wrote something on a paper napkin and gave it to the waiter, who then sent it to the DJ. Haniyah never appeared. I had tried to call her many times but her phone was always switched off. The next song that played was "I Found My Love in Portofino."

Yaacoub looked at me through his round eyeglasses, and asked me neutrally, "Do you know this song?" I answered him firmly, "No."

I apologized for needing to leave. My excuse was Haniyah not being there. He asked me if I wanted a ride home. I thanked him and got into my car. I asked myself what had actually brought me there. I had recently been reborn, and newborns are very fragile, they have to be protected from extreme changes. I looked out over the bridge to the sports stadium, but instead of going down under it, I turned in the direction of Rabieh and went up toward Tla al-Ali.

Amman is asleep. There's hardly any movement on the big streets. Spaces are wide open; the breezes that follow evening rain showers are still cold, though summer is starting. Nasser is still in California. He went there for his son's wedding and he promised to come back in a few days.

I find myself alone in an unfamiliar place. The only place I belong to is this building on my left. Some of the rooms are lit by white light and others are dark. No one is standing on the sidewalk in front of the little garden, the man who sells coffee has closed his stall, and the hearse has left. I sit down on a bench, facing the main gate. Cancer patients are leaving the emergency room, leaning on their

companions. Their suffering from chemotherapy has prevented them from sleeping through the night. They come
here looking for a way to stop the pain. Most of them are
wearing pajamas, some are wearing tracksuits. Their feet
have fallen into the first pair of shoes they could find, or
for some just sandals or slippers. In overcrowded rooms
bodies writhe in pain, in others there are bodies whose
souls have left them. There are also refrigerated bodies
waiting for the morning, so they can find their eternal
resting place inside the earth.

A few months ago, I was one of those people. Now I
am sitting on the sidewalk across the street. I might have to
come back, sooner or later. But even if I am able to go far
away from here, I will still carry with me in my very cells
the possibility that I may have to return. I am escaping to
Nasser, Yaacoub, Haniyah, or Baba like a fish that crosses
the entire ocean, fleeing from its own tail.

When I learn of it, the news of Haniyah's death will
bring me profound peace. I will finally feel that I have
been liberated from her power. It's better to know that she
died in a sudden accident, and not of cancer. The branches
of the willow tree sway in the powerful breeze, bend to
touch my head, and then sweep back upward. The dome
of the sky surprises me and slowly disappears before my
eyes. When the lights are turned off on one entire floor
of the cancer center, the stars shine brighter. Everything
seems certain—suffering, death, healing. The sky here is
close, so close. You can reach it with no rope, and no
ladder.

Translator's Acknowledgements

Many people deserve thanks in bringing the translation of this complex and rich novel to fruition, first and foremost its author, Shahla Ujayli. The ongoing support of the wonderful team at Interlink in promoting and translating Arabic fiction deserves my appreciation, Michel Moushabeck and Whitney Sanderson in particular.

Thanks also to friends and colleagues who worked with me on decoding and transforming this novel's language, imagery, and difficult passages to make it make sense in English. My sincere acknowledgements are owed to Rula Jurdi, Ralph Haddad, Bader Takriti, and Yasmine Nachabe Taan. Caline Nasrallah deserves special thanks here for working with me on the translation in two phases and offering so much technical and creative skill, talent, and energy to this book.

Much of the bulk of this translation was finished in a small Lebanese mountain village overlooking the mountains of Syria, while that country's devastation was being carried on just out of our sight but never out of our minds. I extend my appreciation to everyone who makes Ayroun a magical summer workplace and one in which so much productive translation takes place, especially the Nachabe, Taan, Fakih, Merhej clan.

Thanks to the people in Montreal who stood with me at work when the translation was being finished in challenging times: Adelle Blackett, Rula Jurdi, Malek Abisaab, Pasha Khan, and Aziz Choudry.

As always, my biggest debt of gratitude is to the people closest by who make it possible to engage in such a sustained and time-consuming project. I thank Yasmine Nachabe Taan, Amanda Hartman, Tameem Hartman, and rosalind hampton for being there.

This translation is dedicated to everyone working for a better, more just future for Syria.

Translator's Note

Aleppo, Damascus, Raqqa, Gabès, Amman, Santa Barbara, Dubai, Moscow, Baghdad, Haifa, Boston, Portofino, the Zaatari refugee camp, San Francisco, Hanoi, Saigon, Lydda, Jerusalem, Yafa, Belgrade, Sarajevo, Northallerton, Muscat, Musandem, Dar es Salam, Zanzibar, Beijing, Kuala Lumpur.

These locations and so many others between and beyond are the landscape of Shahla Ujayli's expansive novel, *A Sky So Close to Us*. The dizzying movements of the novel depict people displaced, people out of place, people trying to find themselves in their own places, and people trying to make new places their own. Thus, the Raqqan protagonist who spent childhood summers in Portofino meets a long-lost Iraqi-born cousin who is an Alitalia pilot, and later befriends a Gaza-born Vietnamese-Palestinian woman, the daughter of a Palestinian *fedayee* fighting US imperialism in Vietnam, who herself is suspended between San Francisco, Amman, and Kuala Lumpur. These and many other examples demonstrate how Ujayli plays with the reader's expectations in order to destabilize them and create the unexpected in her novel. Often she places her characters in the midst of historical moments and events to inject possibilities for reflection and introspection as they confront them.

In approaching my translation of this complex and detailed work of fiction from its Arabic original, *Samaa qariban min baytina* (A Sky Close to Our House), which became *A Sky so Close to Us* in English, I contemplated a great deal how to treat these multiple settings, diverse and cosmopolitan cast of characters, and detailed descriptions of so many different places, events, and contexts. There is an unspoken assumption in translation that it is easier to express cosmopolitanism in English, as the language is meant to be the universal language *par excellence* today. It is thus tempting for a translator to feel that a certain homogenization of language and expression is less problematic in such circumstances. As the translator of this novel, I attempted to balance my desire to create a readable text with the creation of a certain resistance to this underlying translational assumption in order to keep the Arabic language present in the English.

The global migration of people and the worldwide events depicted in the novel, however, do not make it merely international, global, or world literature. *A Sky So Close to Us* is also a very local novel—not only is it Syrian, but it also delves deeply into the history and culture of Aleppo and even more importantly, Raqqa. Ujayli's tender portrayal of a city much maligned internationally as well as locally in Syria harkens back to a time before it knew the ravages of the most recent war and occupation by the so-called Islamic

State. The novel is not therefore just about immigration, migration, refugees, and global movements of people—issues that because the book is so large it treats at an often brisk pace. My translation tries to capture this by shortening the length of many Arabic sentences and making them conform more closely to the shorter and more declarative style preferred in English. *A Sky So Close to Us* is also about the Aleppo of the 1940s, the history of Raqqa, and intergenerational trauma—especially of the Syrian and Palestinian people. Those detailed stories need a somewhat different translational approach. I have tried to respect them by not crafting them into the quick-paced movement of shorter sentences, but the opposite. In long narrative passages about the events of the Nakba, Palestinian refugee stories, people fleeing and surviving the war in Syria, as well as many sections about Syrian culture, history, and politics, I have tried to maintain the original's more discursive narration. It is here that my English attempts to capture the rich lushness of Ujayli's Arabic prose style.

As a translator, I have always thought that long, detailed narrative passages are easier to move from Arabic into English than other kinds of writing. The presence of more detail provides cushioning that allows for different translation choices, especially when Arabic and English words, expressions, and concepts are not identical and are difficult to express. Aside from the ever-present challenge of how to render tenses, which work differently in Arabic and English, long narrative passages seem to be more straightforward to translate in many ways than poetic, shorter, more elliptical or experimental expression.

This text's expansive prose narration did present

unique challenges, however. One of these is the translation of words and concepts that do not exist in English. How should one best render Arabic musical meters that do not have conceptual or linguistic English equivalents? The passage about Abdul Wahab's visit to Aleppo and creating a *muwashshah* as a pure *sikah* with no *huzam* is meant to be hilarious and make the reader gasp at its audacity. In English, the text now has a number of foreign words and concepts, which for most readers will remain opaque and understandable only through context. I opted to rather closely follow the Arabic words in order to try to suggest the humor of the original without over-explaining it, leaving it to the English-language reader's imagination.

Another type of translational challenge is how best to provide the cushioning and context for concepts that are very clear in Arabic but less so in English. In *A Sky So Close to Us*, local knowledge is contrasted with regional knowledge, including the use of insider humor and jokes. This means that the author discusses the view of Raqqans as backwards and rural to other Arabs, but also that she gently pokes fun at other Arabs who do not understand things about Syria. For example, when Joumane mocks her new lover Nasser's tendency to refer to all Syrians as being from "al-Sham," it is obvious to an Arab reader, but not necessarily an English-language readership, that because "Sham" means Damascus in Syria, people from al-Sham are Damascenes. Joumane would never refer to herself in this way, though others might see her as such.

In this text, we chose in consultation with the editor to leave the relatively large number of Arabic words in italics, at least the first time they are used. In a text like this, there are many words, especially those referring to local, usually Syrian, food, music, and other specific cultural items. This is a choice that I have not always made in my translations, but in this long narration full of details and so evocative of a number of different places, times, and contexts, it felt like a decision that would add to the translational feel of the English novel.

A Sky So Close to Us moves all around the world, tracing the lives of its characters, especially Joumane, Nasser, Haniyah, and their families. But it is rooted very much in the daily life of Aleppo and Raqqa, before the events that began in the winter and spring of 2011. As such, it is an evocation of better days and a real and vivid imagining of those days, but also an expression of a way that we can live in the world now.

Michelle Hartman